Obsession

Library of Congress Catalog Card Number: 94–74874

A catalogue record for this book can be obtained from the British Library on request.

First published 1995 by
Serpent's Tail, 4 Blackstock Mews, London N4
and 180 Varick Street, New York, NY 10014

Typeset in 10 pt Times by CentraCet Ltd, Cambridge

Printed in Great Britain by Cox & Wyman Ltd,
Reading, Berkshire

Obsession

EDITED BY SARAH LEFANU AND STEPHEN HAYWARD

To the memory of
Luis Buñuel,
obsessive freethinker

Contents

Introduction

Obsession has become pathologized. The word has become associated with the monstrous bogeymen of late twentieth-century life: serial killers, random mass murderers, child abusers and drug-dependent urban gangsters. We regularly read and hear about these modern monsters being obsessed with pornography and with weaponry. They themselves and their obsessions with violence, and in particular sexual violence, have become our own cultural obsessions, descriptions and images of which appear day after day, month after month, in newspaper headlines, television programmes and films.

But this is a view of obsession that is both narrow and doom-laden. And odd for a post-religious age: obsession as evil or obsession as sin. There are other kinds of obsession and the stories in this anthology explore some of them.

The word obsession comes from the Latin verb *obsidere*, to besiege or to haunt. In our post-Freudian world obsession has come to be associated with emotional instability or ill-health. Obsessive behaviour is seen as a symptom of a hidden trauma, one that has been hidden in the unconscious and that appears, displaced and transformed, made over into metaphor. The obsession is both the trauma and its representation. It is indeed a haunting, a ghost that will not be put to rest but stubbornly appears and reappears, not night after night but in each manifestation of what we call obsessive behaviour. But in what way is it a sign of instability or illness? Have we not become, perhaps, obsessed with ideas of disease and ill-health?

Writing is surely the prime example of obsessive behaviour: the working and reworking of lived or imagined experience and the displacement of that experience into metaphor. A writer is a person haunted by the desire to recreate in language. 'Writer's block', the inability to work through the experience with which the writer wants to come to terms through the act of writing, is, notoriously, the author's greatest fear and, when it takes hold, can itself become an obsession: an inability to express the obsession in the written word. It was, therefore, hardly a surprise to us that about half the contributors to this anthology, when asked to write a few lines about themselves mentioning their own obsessions, should have included the art and process of writing.

Do not fear. These stories are not self-regarding musings about the process of writing. They are fictions: the obsessions they explore may, of course, be metaphors for the authors' own obsessions, but that is not for us to say, and indeed it is not for us to speculate . . . Of course some of them are about forms of creativity: musical composition in James Hamilton-Paterson's 'The Anxieties of Desire' or model shipbuilding in Adam Thorpe's 'Rigging'. While writing features as an activity in Michèle Roberts' 'Lists', and reading and writing as a rather different kind of activity in Ivan Vladislavić's 'The Book Lover', in neither of those stories are the protagonists writers. In fact there is not a writer to be found in these stories. Instead we have Jeff Torrington's production-line worker, Jane Rogers' housewife daughter, Cherry Wilder's retired couple on holiday, mothers, lovers, wives, husbands, sons, friends. Ordinary people, not monsters. Their obsessions include, of course, sexual love and some of its many manifestations: longing for, looking at and lusting after; they include books, bodies, bric-à-brac, boys, boats and balloons; they include obsessions of the body and of the soul.

If an obsession is the focus of an attempt to recapture or recreate something that has been lost, then although that attempt is doomed to failure, the obsessive act itself acquires

....

its own meanings and its own part in the scheme of a life. Obsessions work in different ways, as is shown, we believe, in the stories published here. We see obsession as a rage for order and control over the external world and the difficult other people in it, and we see obsession as a flight from the external world, an escape from those wayward others. Obsession as tragedy, not only for the person obsessed but also for the object of the obsession. And, as importantly, obsession as comedy, the comedy of the inappropriate, of the hopeless.

These are not stories about cutting up women's bodies or the sexual abuse of small children, inner-city cannibalism or self-destruction through narcotic abuse. They are not stories in which obsessions are used as an excuse for alienation, for a fashionably decadent post-modernist loss of identity and, worse, loss of responsibility. These are stories in which obsessions are normalized rather than pathologized, which explore the tensions between will and contingency, between desire and fate, between self-control and the lack of it. They explore obsession as a mode of thought and behaviour into which we are all liable to fall. They deal in different ways with the obsession that is fed by the knowledge at the heart of human consciousness: the inevitability of death. And just as writing itself is no protection against the imminent decayingness of human flesh, so there is no achievement in these stories of obsessions: obsessions are endless, hopeless, part of us. There are no monsters here, but human characters haunted by ghosts that won't go away.

Sarah LeFanu
Stephen Hayward
1 May 1994

The Fade

JEFF TORRINGTON

McQuirr, scarcely half-awake, trudged to the clocking-on point. Once there a yawn froze in his mouth. The 'Tardis' had vanished! The chunky oak and brass machine had been ousted by a newcomer, a computerized whippet with a nasty slit of a mouth and luminous red numerals dancing like madness on its brow.

'Stick it in there,' Fawcett, the seats section greyback, ordered.

McQuirr stared at him.

'Your card.' Fawcett was pointing to the machine's slot.

McQuirr searched the rackful of unfamiliar cards. The greyback frowned. 'Forgotten our number, have we?'

'Two thousand and one!'

'You were issued with a new one – remember?'

McQuirr shook his head.

'In your pay-packet, last week.'

Fawcett's forefinger riffled down the shiny tabs. An irate queue of ops had formed behind McQuirr.

'Does it dish out fivers?' one of them asked.

'Be "late-warnings" unless that dozy bastard gets a jildy on,' shouted another.

The greyback located McQuirr's card. He handed it to'm. 'Get on with it!' McQuirr fumbled the operation and the machine began immediately to bristle with warning lights before finally playing its 'VOID!' card.

Fawcett groaned. 'Yo've got it arse-for-elb – That's better!'

The new time-machine gave an electronic burp then the card popped up.

Tommy Farr, the section shoppy, stopped McQuirr as he trudged towards the seats-hoist. 'Don't forget, there'll be an IE in your section today, John,' Farr warned. 'So, no buckshee breaks, no getting ahead of the game. You know the score. Anyway, Glover'll keep you right.'

'These clock numbers,' McQuirr said.

'What about'm?'

Fawcett had made McQuirr take note of his new number.

'Look at it,' he grumbled, waving a scrap of paper. 'Like a machine-part number. How'd the union let'm away with it? Shower of diddies. Organizers? They couldn't organize a piss-up'n a brothel.'

'Brewery, John.'

'What?'

'It's a piss-up'n – never mind. Just remember, soon as you drop that bit of plastic your name lights up'n five places. Don't be on the "late" print-out, that's all.'

The industrial engineer, Austin Seymour, had settled himself near a stack of seat-frames. Equipped with stop-watch, a selection of coloured pens, clipboard, and timing sheets, he beadily observed the operations taking place in the seats-build area. McQuirr glowered at'm. A locust, that's what he was, sitting there on a twig munching minutes.

'Wish I'd stuck in at borstal,' McQuirr said.

'So's you could be a wank wi a watch, eh?'

'As long as my bloody arm.'

'Eh?'

'New clock number.'

Glover shook his head. 'You still bitching about that – ?'

'Diabolical, so it is.'

'Slow down a bit,' Glover cautioned, 'that bugger's getting excited.'

McQuirr stacked polythene-wrapped seats alongside others on the floor. He hauled a Sultan rear seat from the unwrapped pile.

'Years, I had that number. Years. That's how I got my nickname.'

'Nickname?'

'Sputnik.'

'What-nik?'

McQuirr cut open a bag and tipped a slithering mass of polythene covers on to the bench. 'After yon Arthur C. Clarke movie: "2001" – remember?'

Glover checked off a sequence number on the telex print-out sheet. 'Never heard anybody call you "Sputnik" before.'

'It sort of faded away.' McQuirr took an armful of covers and folded them neatly over the stretched rope. 'It was when I worked on the wet deck. The lads got to hear my clock number, and – bingo, I'd a nickname!'

'They called you "Bingo", did they?'

'No, I told you – "Sputnik".'

'"Bingo" suits you better,' said the grinning Glover. 'Seeing's you haven't got a full house upstairs.'

'Bugger off!' McQuirr grunted.

During the break McQuirr waylaid 'Gentleman' Jim Corbett as he was passing the snack area. With his neatly clipped moustache and his impeccably groomed grey hair he looked like a debonair con man.

'Thought you'd be redundant,' McQuirr said.

Corbett removed his blue-tinted glasses. (For some reason he couldn't speak with them on.) 'Never been busier,' he said. 'Haven't a minute.'

A time-keeper without a minute! Corbett began to edge around McQuirr. 'Well, must press on.'

'Listen, Jim, do's a favour.'

Alarm spread in Corbett's grey eyes. When a punter wanted a favour it usually involved time or money. The glasses, already halfway to his nose, paused. 'A favour?'

McQuirr nodded, then dropping his gaze, mumbled something.

'What's that?' Corbett bent closer to catch the words.

McQuirr cleared his throat. 'I was, well, you know, kinda wondering who'd got two thousand and one . . .'

'Two thousand and one what?'

....

3

'It's my old clock number. I was just curious who had it.'

'Why?'

'Daft, I know, but – ' McQuirr drew Corbett to one side as a forky laden with seat-springs honked past.

'Nobody has it,' Corbett told'm. 'It's gone to that Big Time-Office in the Sky.'

'You sure about that?'

Corbett nodded. 'New system: Plant's been zoned off so that each zone has a max of 300 ops.' He began to explain the ramifications of the introduced system but McQuirr had stopped listening. The time-keeper's glasses slipped over his eyes. Then he was off. McQuirr watched him disappearing into the murk of Zombieland where a welding operation was lobbing lucid blue sparks into the air.

Like a probe, Seymour's penpoint sank into each squandered minute, extracted its essence, then wrote its epitaph in brisk fashion on the time-sheets. The industrial engineer seldom smiled, nor did he allow his scrutiny to wander far from its given task – to locate parasitic growths in the human energy fields: the wasted moment; the extra step; the blight of bad co-ordination; every input of misused muscle power, anything at all which checked or baulked the surging gallop of the Centaur Car Company.

McQuirr sheathed seats, stacked them, marked them off on the sequence sheet, barrowed them across to the hoist. The IE, he suspected, was paying particular attention to him; he could feel his gaze following his every movement as he juggled the three essential elements of his exercise – time, motion and rest. Seymour seemed to be relishing the complexity of the equation he was so precisely developing so that the consequences of McQuirr's removal could be gauged. McQuirr sped another surly glance towards the IE. There was no doubting what the twat in the tweed sports jacket was there for – quite simply it was to figure the means of his elimination. This wasn't the first time the Company'd tried to get shot of him. There'd been other 'hangman's rehearsals' as McQuirr called them – a description which

....

4

brought to mind a movie he'd once seen in which the public hangman had peered through the Judas of the condemned man's cell to determine the prisoner's 'dropistics' – a term the urbane executioner had used accompanied by a gallows grin. Although less covert about it, the IE was similarly assessing McQuirr's 'dropistics'.

A trapdoor, its bolts well oiled with use, dropped open in McQuirr's mind, plunging him once more into the void of 'that bitch of a morning' as he'd tagged it, the one when he'd returned home to find a letter awaiting him. It'd been sent to'm by the Company.

In a few terse lines it thanked him for his job application but regretted its inability at this time to grant him employment at Centaur . . . For McQuirr, who'd been working at the Plant for over a decade, this was mind-bending news. His wife had chosen to see the comical side of the screw-up. 'My, my,' she'd laughed. 'You must be really important down there – ten years, and they don't even know you're around!' McQuirr had found nothing laughworthy in the event. In fact, he'd taken it to be not only an insult but also a warning. Just like the movie's public executioner going through the grisly preliminaries of his profession, using a sandbag as a substitute for the real thing, so the Centaur (the farcical letter'd been but one of its ploys) measured McQuirr for the drop.

He'd never forget the hour he'd endured trawling the wet streets in search of an unvandalized phone-box. Even yet he remembered the odd sensation he'd had of being adrift from his body, of having to break into a run to catch up with it, for the further he'd got separated from it, the more he'd seemed to vaporize, to become nothing but a trick of light. People – how enviably solid they'd looked! – had seemed to pass through the evaporating cloud-man he'd become. Panic, like pronged lightning, had speared him to the core as his body had given its harried phantom the slip at a pedestrian crossing. Luckily he'd seen his flesh'n bone twin go into a launderette where he'd managed to pounce on the wayward

. . . .

body and inveigle himself back into it. A bizarre experience it'd been, one he'd divulged to no one, not even his wife. It was the stuff madness was made from. There was a public phone in the launderette. While he'd watched a grey shirt having soapy convulsions behind a machine's glass porthole, his identity had been restored. An administrative cock-up, that's all it'd been. He'd accepted the apology but, nevertheless, the obsession had continued to haunt him, that the Centaur Car Company was still intent on striking him from its payroll.

Glover nudged McQuirr. 'C'mon for chrissake, John – you're miles away!'

Snapped from his reverie McQuirr realized that he'd been staring into space, his hands idle. For how long he'd been in this trance he wasn't sure. But Seymour would know; that voracious locust feasted on every unproductive moment, gleaned it bare.

McQuirr's hands writhed in the slippery polythene, sought to grapple with its slick nothingness. He drew envelope after transparent envelope over velour-trimmed seats, and the more he dealt with, piling them up to his left, the more seats streamed off the carousel. His movements were jerky, uncoordinated. Quite often the polythene wrapper split and he'd to rip it off, junk it. From the corner of his eye he caught Glover's puzzled-looking glances. He was probably trying to work out whether he was putting on an act for the IE or was genuinely uptight about something. Was he ever anything else but uptight these days? The other night, for instance, while watching TV, the image of a fissuring iceberg had sent him panicking from his armchair. His alarmed wife reckoned it was high time he visited a head-doctor.

But the Centaur Car Company didn't employ an industrial psychologist. When faced with the mental casualties that came off-track with their cars, the Company tended to rely upon the 'it-never-happened' strategy. So, should a disturbed operator sit down one day by the edge of the flowing track in an unrestrainable fit of sobbing, or if a cackling

....

greyback in the canteen took the notion to fill his shoes with custard, the remedy was to deny it'd ever occurred. With a blanket of secrecy thrown over him, the unfortunate 'breakdown' would be taken to the edge of some administrative ravine and hurled over. Now and again the wan phantom of a victim might be seen wandering in its old working area but inevitably it would fade away.

McQuirr, Glover and a chaser called Troy, usually did the crossword during the lunchbreak. But not today, it seemed. Rising suddenly to his feet, as if reacting to the clue Troy'd just read out: 'Has this Wellsian character been overdoing the vanishing cream? (3, 9, 3)', McQuirr jettisoned the remaining tea from his mug, making a black star on the concrete floor.

'Where're you off to?' asked Glover.

'Breath of air.'

'It's pissing out there, man!'

McQuirr shrugged his shoulders. As he walked away he overheard Glover say: 'If you ask me – the bugger's cracking up!'

As if the rain wasn't flooding the yard fast enough, the wind was cuffing water over the storage tank's rim. McQuirr stood near the half-shut doors of the loading bay. He watched the water's white leaping, saw it cascading down the sides of the tank.

McQuirr went into the body'n white section and paused between lines of raw, unpainted Sultan saloons, the metal blemishes of which had been blue-circled for the discers. A roof leak tapped out a tattoo on an empty paint drum. From the snack areas came the low rumble of men's voices and the occasional yelps of triumph from card winners. Some of these ops turned in their seats to rake McQuirr with suspicious stares. Aware of their scrutiny, he felt a bit foolish as he pawed his way down a rackful of glossily new timecards. It seemed that Corbett hadn't been having him on, after all: there was no card to be found with a higher numerical value than 300.

....

'You there! Where's your permit?'

The question was volleyed from behind a group of Sultan estate shells. Stricken motionless by it, McQuirr suddenly relaxed. 'Jeez, Danny, you scared me shitless there!'

Danny Sutton emerged from the shells. A spry-looking man who was always on the go, he approached McQuirr with fists raised and did a bit of mock sparring. 'How goes it, Sputnik, me old son?' He dropped his hands. 'What're you arsing around here for?' He mimed a casting motion with an invisible fishing rod. 'You still drowning worms?'

'Had to get shot of my gear,' McQuirr told'm. 'Rheumatics.'

Sutton's grin widened. 'Don't come the fanny. You've already used that one to work your ticket from the wet-deck.' They walked on together. 'You should see the rod I'm packing now,' Sutton said. 'A right cracker. Telling you, take out a pike like it was a sardine.' This was the prelude to a fishy story that kept Sutton's mouth busy until they'd reached the main door of the stores area. They looked out at the rain. Sutton nodded in the direction of the nearby 'Broadmoor' (so-called because of its highly sensitive and militant workforce).

'Fancy a squint at your redundancy?'

McQuirr frowned. 'Redundancy?'

'Yeah. Them Daleks. Bastards'll weld anything that moves. C'mon, let's have a shufty.'

Battered by the rain, they skirted around puddles and dripping pallet stacks and went into 'Broadmoor'. A group of ops stood in the area where the unimates had been installed. In all there were twenty-two of these robot weld-ers, eleven to each side of the track. McQuirr eyed one. It looked more like a praying mantis than a Dalek, standing there with beaky head poised, awaiting the power that would have it pecking out welds at a rate no human could hope to match. An engineer who'd apparently elected himself as tour-guide was rapping out impressive stats: 'They can handle over one hundred car shells an hour.' He reached to

. . . .

finger the skeletal neck of the unimate nearest to'm. 'For that level of output you'd require over two hundred operatives . . .'

A grey-haired op who stood near McQuirr, said: 'You should see'm when they get going: like hens in a byre midden!'

McQuirr and Sutton walked around the machines, squinting at them from different angles. 'Soon won't need us, eh,' said Sutton. He shrugged. 'I guess we're for the broth pot.'

Maybe it was this remark or the sight of those brutish muzzles poised, waiting, that'd sent the pellets of dread skittering down the slope of McQuirr's mind. There was no restraining them as they gathered velocity, prising loose old fears as well as an avalanche of new anxieties.

'Give you the creeps, eh?' Sutton went on, completely unaware that he was speaking to a phantom which despite its desperate resistance was being slowly ejected from its body. 'A lick of oil'n a tap'n the arse with a spanner, that's all they need. Never strike, never shit and never get hangovers.'

Back'n the body'n white, they passed swiftly amongst the crates and pallets of metal stampings and skirted puddles in which dull rainbows glimmered. McQuirr's runaway body was now well clear of its former occupant. It capered around, waving its arms and looking slyly about itself; clearly, it was plotting mischief. Sutton, still oblivious of the bewildered spook at his elbow, dropped out when a punter from the Plant's angling club stopped him for a bit crack.

Meanwhile, McQuirr's body had brought a painter's ladder crashing to the concrete floor then began to hurl door hinges up at the complaining tradesman, who quickly ducked for cover amongst the roof girders. McQuirr's body now sent a forky driver tumbling from his seat and commandeered the vehicle itself. With its rightful driver shouting in pursuit it charged the rubber doors that led to the paintshop, where it was afforded not only the props to make mischief on an unprecedented scale but also to make it in glorious colour!

....

McQuirr, who'd given up all hope of reconnection with his body, wandered around the Plant. He felt himself fading, becoming progressively drained of energy, so much so that soon he was looking for a corner to hide himself in. But everywhere he turned he found a clone of Austin Seymour, complete with stopwatch, pens, clipboard and timesheets, waiting for him. Such obscenities plagued the place, breeding, hatching out. Those things in 'Broadmoor' with their fiery beaks and their staunchless energies would multiply too. Able to outweld two hundred men, from them would come a flux of inhuman power which, like a bore tide, would surge up the metal rivers that ran throughout the Plant, and all the hourly-paid minnows who swam in those streams would be swept away.

Officially, the incident in which McQuirr was involved that afternoon never happened. The personnel records might show 'Dismissed due to industrial misconduct' or, more accurately, 'Discharged for medical reasons', but the details of what actually 'never happened' remain oral. Since Glover was McQuirr's working partner, his version of what really took place was judged to be nearest the mark:

'Well, as I said, he'd been jumpy all morning. It was obvious after chuck time that he'd been out'n the rain. I mean any daft bugger who'd go out in the piss when he didn't have to, well, he's got t'be one short of the full deck – right? So, he starts going on about them auto-welders they've stuck'n "Broadmoor", only he calls 'em "Daleks". They were going to take over, that's all he kept saying. Nothing the unions could do 'bout stopping 'em – that kinda shit. To listen to'm you would've thought they was out t'have *his* job in particular.

'Any roads, he clams up for a bit. Done that a lot, McQuirr. One minute it's gab-gab, the next it's the "broodies". Y'know, go into trances, stare into space. Gave me the creeps it did. Well, it happened this way, Seymour, who's doing the watch number on us, slopes off for a riddlemeree or something. Leaves his clipboard'n timesheets on a crate,

....

10

don't he. And that's when it happened. It was like something went *twang* inside McQuirr's noggin. Next I knows, don't he go rushing across to where Seymour's sheets are, lifts the whole batch and, before you could blink, he's made confetti of it! But he's not finished. He grabs a can from the glue table and scampers with it towards the new time-puncher. But the loopy bugger'd gone'nd lumbered himself with a duff can that should've been binned on account of its glue having hardened off. He could've stood there till kingdom come waiting for a pour.

'Clueless, as well as glueless now, he takes to bashing the time-puncher with the can. Brained the bloody thing. Put its lights out. By then, of course, the Bull comes charging from his office and sticks an arm-lock on McQuirr. What's that? Took a swing at the Bull? No way. That's crap! I'll tell you what the poor sap did – began to blub. That's what. Pathetic.

'They took'm into the office but couldn't get tuppence worth of sense out of'm. All the time he keeps parroting his clock number, his old one, that is – two thousand and one. Eh? Come back here? No chance! By the time he gets out of the booby-hatch he'll be on two wheels and zombie's zube-zubes. Come again? Miss'm? I suppose so. He could be a bit of diddy at times but he was quite good at crosswords . . .'

Life After High School

∙∙∙

JOYCE CAROL OATES

'Sunny? Sun-ny?'

On that last night of March 1959, in soiled sheepskin parka, unbuckled overshoes, but bare-headed in the lightly falling snow, Zachary Graff, eighteen years old, six feet one and a half inches tall, weight 203 pounds, IQ 160, stood beneath Sunny Burhman's second-storey bedroom window, calling her name softly, urgently, as if his very life depended upon it. It was nearly midnight: Sunny had been in bed for a half-hour, and woke from a thin dissolving sleep to hear her name rising mysteriously out of the dark: low, gravelly, repetitive as the surf. '*Sun*-ny – ?' She had not spoken with Zachary Graff since the previous week, when she'd told him, quietly, tears shining in her eyes, that she did not love him; she could not accept his engagement ring, still less marry him. This was the first time in the twelve weeks of Zachary's pursuit of her that he'd dared to come to the rear of the Burhmans' house, by day or night; the first time, as Sunny would say afterward, he'd ever appealed to her in such a way.

They would ask, In what way?

Sunny would hesitate, and say, So – emotionally. In a way that scared me.

So you sent him away?

She did. She'd sent him away.

It was much talked-of, at South Lebanon High School, how, in this spring of their senior year, Zachary Graff, who had never to anyone's recollection asked a girl out before, let

∙∙∙∙∙∙∙∙∙

12

alone pursued her so publicly and with such clumsy devotion, seemed to have fallen in love with Sunny Burhman.

Of all people – Sunny Burhman.

Odd too that Zachary should seem to have discovered Sunny, when the two had been classmates in the South Lebanon, New York public schools since first grade, back in 1947.

Zachary, whose father was Homer Graff, the town's preeminent physician, had, since ninth grade, cultivated a clipped, mock-gallant manner when speaking with female classmates; his Clifton Webb style. He was unfailingly courteous, but unfailingly cool; measured; formal. He seemed impervious to the giddy rise and ebb of adolescent emotion, moving, clumsy but determined, like a grizzly bear on its hind legs, through the school corridors, rarely glancing to left or right: *his* gaze, its myopia corrected by lenses encased in chunky black plastic frames, was firmly fixed on the horizon. Dr Graff's son was not unpopular so much as feared, thus disliked.

If Zachary's excellent academic record continued uninterrupted through final papers, final exams, and there was no reason to suspect it would not, Zachary would be valedictorian of the Class of 1959. Barbara ('Sunny') Burhman, later to distinguish herself at Cornell, would graduate only ninth, in a class of eighty-two.

Zachary's attentiveness to Sunny had begun, with no warning, immediately after Christmas recess, when classes resumed in January. Suddenly, a half-dozen times a day, in Sunny's vicinity, looming large, eyeglasses glittering, there Zachary *was*. His Clifton Webb pose had dissolved, he was shy, stammering, yet forceful, even bold, waiting for the advantageous moment (for Sunny was always surrounded by friends) to push forward and say, 'Hi Sunny!' The greeting, utterly commonplace in content, sounded, in Zachary's mouth, like a Latin phrase tortuously translated.

Sunny, so-named for her really quite astonishing smile, that dazzling white Sunny-smile that transformed a girl of

....

13

conventional freckled snub-nosed prettiness to true beauty, might have been surprised, initially, but gave no sign, saying, 'Hi Zach!'

In those years, the corridors of South Lebanon High School were lyric crossfires of *Hi!* and *H'lo!* and *Good to see ya!* uttered hundreds of times daily by the golden girls, the popular, confident, good-looking girls, club officers, prom queens, cheerleaders like Sunny Burhman and her friends, tossed out indiscriminately, for that was the style.

Most of the students were in fact practicing Christians, of Lutheran, Presbyterian, Methodist stock.

Like Sunny Burhman, who was, or seemed, even at the time of this story, too good to be true.

That's to say – *good.*

So, though Sunny soon wondered why on earth Zachary Graff was hanging around her, why, again, at her elbow, or lying in wait for her at the foot of a stairs, why, for the n-th time that week, *him*, she was too *good* to indicate impatience, or exasperation; too *good* to tell him, as her friends advised, to get lost.

He telephoned her too. Poor Zachary. Stammering over the phone, his voice lowered as if he were in terror of being overheard, 'Is S-Sunny there, Mrs B-Burhman? May I speak with her, please?' And Mrs Burhman, who knew Dr Graff and his wife, of course, since everyone in South Lebanon, population 3800, knew everyone else or knew of them, including frequently their family histories and facts about them of which their children were entirely unaware, hesitated, and said, 'Yes, I'll put her on, but I hope you won't talk long – Sunny has homework tonight.' Or, apologetically but firmly: 'No, I'm afraid she isn't here. May I take a message?'

'N-no message,' Zachary would murmur, and hurriedly hang up.

Sunny, standing close by, thumbnail between her just perceptibly gap-toothed front teeth, expression crinkled in dismay, would whisper, 'Oh Mom. I feel so *bad*. I just feel so – *bad*.'

....

Mrs Burhman said briskly, 'You don't have time for all of them, honey.'

Still, Zachary was not discouraged, and with the swift passage of time it began to be observed that Sunny engaged in conversations with him – the two of them sitting, alone, in a corner of the cafeteria, or walking together after a meeting of the Debate Club, of which Zachary was president, and Sunny a member. They were both on the staff of The South Lebanon High Beacon, and the South Lebanon High Yearbook 1959, and the South Lebanon Torch (the literary magazine). They were both members of the National Honor Society and the Quill & Scroll Society. Though Zachary Graff in his aloofness and impatience with most of his peers would be remembered as anti-social, a 'loner,' in fact, as his record of activities suggested, printed beneath his photograph in the yearbook, he had time, or made time, for things that mattered to him.

He shunned sports, however. High school sports, at least.

His life's game, he informed Sunny Burhman, unaware of the solemn pomposity with which he spoke, would be *golf*. His father had been instructing him, informally, since his twelfth birthday.

Said Zachary, 'I have no natural talent for it, and I find it profoundly boring, but golf will be my game.' And he pushed his chunky black glasses roughly against the bridge of his nose, as he did countless times a day, as if they were in danger of sliding off.

Zachary Graff had such a physical presence, few of his contemporaries would have described him as unattractive, still less homely, ugly. His head appeared oversized, even for his massive body; his eyes were deep-set, with a look of watchfulness and secrecy; his skin was tallow-colored, and blemished, in wavering patches like topographical maps. His big teeth glinted with filaments of silver, and his breath, oddly for one whose father was a doctor, was stale, musty, cobwebby – not that Sunny Burhman ever alluded to this fact, to others.

....

Her friends began to ask of her, a bit jealously, reproachfully, 'What do you two talk about so much? – you and *him*?' and Sunny replied, taking care not to hint, with the slightest movement of her eyebrows, or rolling of her eyes, that, yes, she found the situation peculiar too, 'Oh – Zachary and I talk about all kinds of things. *He* talks, mainly. He's brilliant. He's – ' pausing, her forehead delicately crinkling in thought, her lovely brown eyes for a moment clouded, ' – well, *brilliant*.'

In fact, at first, Zachary spoke, in his intense, obsessive way, of impersonal subjects: the meaning of life, the future of Earth, whether science or art best satisfies the human hunger for self-expression. He said, laughing nervously, fixing Sunny with his shyly bold stare, 'Just to pose certain questions is, I guess, to show your hope they can be answered.'

Early on, Zachary seemed to have understood that, if he expressed doubt, for instance about 'whether God exists' and so forth, Sunny Burhman would listen seriously; and would talk with him earnestly, with the air of a nurse giving a transfusion to a patient in danger of expiring for loss of blood. She was not a religious fanatic, but she *was* a devout Christian – the Burhmans were members of the First Presbyterian Church of South Lebanon, and Sunny was president of her youth group, and, among other good deeds, did YWCA volunteer work on Saturday afternoons; she had not the slightest doubt that Jesus Christ, that's to say His spirit, dwelled in her heart, and that, simply by speaking the truth of what she believed, she could convince others.

Though one day, and soon, Sunny would examine her beliefs, and question the faith into which she'd been born, she had not done so by the age of seventeen and a half. She was a virgin, and virginal in all, or most, of her thoughts.

Sometimes, behind her back, even by friends, Sunny was laughed at, gently – never ridiculed, for no one would ridicule Sunny.

Once, when Sunny Burhman and her date and another

. . . .

couple were gazing up into the night sky, standing in the parking lot of the high school, following a prom, Sunny had said in a quavering voice, 'It's so big it would be terrifying, wouldn't it? – except for Jesus, who makes us feel at home.'

When popular Chuck Crueller, a quarterback for the South Lebanon varsity football team, was injured during a game, and carried off by ambulance to undergo emergency surgery, Sunny mobilized the other cheerleaders, tears fierce in her eyes, 'We can do it for Chuck – we can *pray*.' And so the eight girls in their short-skirted crimson jumpers and starched white cotton blouses had gripped one another's hands tight, weeping, on the verge of hysteria, had prayed, prayed, *prayed* – hidden away in the depths of the girls' locker room for hours. Sunny had led the prayers, and Chuck Crueller recovered.

So you wouldn't ridicule Sunny Burhman, somehow it wouldn't have been appropriate.

As her classmate Tobias Shanks wrote of her, as one of his duties as literary editor of the 1959 South Lebanon yearbook: *'Sunny' Burhman! – an all-American girl too good to be true who is nonetheless TRUE!*

If there was a slyly mocking tone to Tobias Shanks' praise, a hint that such goodness was predictable, and superficial, and of no genuine merit, the caption, mere print, beneath Sunny's dazzlingly beautiful photograph, conveyed nothing of this.

Surprisingly, for all his pose of skepticism and superiority, Zachary Graff too was a Christian. He'd been baptized Lutheran, and never failed to attend Sunday services with his parents at the First Lutheran Church. Amid the congregation of somber, somnambulant worshipers, Zachary Graff's frowning young face, the very set of his beefy shoulders, drew the minister's uneasy eye; it would be murmured of Dr Graff's precocious son, in retrospect, that he'd been perhaps too *serious*.

Before falling in love with Sunny Burhman, and discussing

....

17

his religious doubts with her, Zachary had often discussed them with Tobias Shanks, who'd been his friend, you might say his only friend, since seventh grade. (But only sporadically since seventh grade, since the boys, each highly intelligent, inclined to impatience and sarcasm, got on each other's nerves.) Once, Zachary confided in Tobias that he prayed every morning of his life – immediately upon waking he scrambled out of bed, knelt, hid his face in his hands, and prayed. For his sinful soul, for his sinful thoughts, deeds, desires. He lacerated his soul the way he'd been taught by his mother to tug a fine-toothed steel comb through his coarse, oily hair, never less than once a day.

Tobias Shanks, a self-professed agnostic since the age of fourteen, laughed, and asked derisively, 'Yes, but what do you pray *for*, exactly?' and Zachary had thought a bit, and said, not ironically, but altogether seriously, 'To get through the day. Doesn't everyone?'

Tobias was never to reveal this melancholy reply.

Zachary's parents were urging him to go to Muhlenberg College, which was church-affiliated; Zachary hoped to go elsewhere. He said, humbly, to Sunny Burhman, 'If you go to Cornell, Sunny, I – maybe I'll go there too?'

Sunny hesitated, then smiled. 'Oh. That would be nice.'

'You wouldn't mind, Sunny?'

'Why should I *mind*, Zachary?' Sunny laughed, to hide her impatience. They were headed for Zachary's car, parked just up the hill from the YM-YWCA building. It was a gusty Saturday afternoon in early March. Leaving the YWCA, Sunny had seen Zachary Graff standing at the curb, hands in the pockets of his sheepskin parka, head lowered, but eyes nervously alert. Standing there, as if accidentally.

It was impossible to avoid him, she had to allow him to drive her home. Though she was beginning to feel panic, like darting tongues of flame, at the prospect of Zachary Graff always *there*.

Tell the creep to get lost, her friends counseled. Even

....

her nice friends were without sentiment regarding Zachary Graff.

Until sixth grade, Sunny had been plain little Barbara Burhman. Then, one day, her teacher had said to all the class, in one of those moments of inspiration that can alter, by whim, the course of an entire life, 'Tell you what, boys and girls – let's call Barbara "Sunny" from now on – that's what she *is*.'

Ever afterward, in South Lebanon, she was 'Sunny' Burhman. Plain little Barbara had been left behind, seemingly forever.

So, of course, Sunny could not tell Zachary Graff to get lost. Such words were not part of her vocabulary.

Zachary owned a plum-colored 1956 Plymouth which other boys envied – it seemed to them distinctly unfair that Zachary, of all people, had his own car, when so few of them, who loved cars, did. But Zachary was oblivious of their envy, as, in a way, he seemed oblivious of his own good fortune. He drove the car as if it were an adult duty, with middle-aged fussiness and worry. He drove the car as if he were its chauffeur. Yet, driving Sunny home, he talked – chattered – continuously. Speaking of college, and of religious 'obligations,' and of his parents' expectations of him; speaking of medical school; the future; the life – 'beyond South Lebanon.'

He asked again, in that gravelly, irksomely humble voice, if Sunny would mind if he went to Cornell. And Sunny said, trying to sound merely reasonable, 'Zachary, it's a *free world*.'

Zachary said, 'Oh no it isn't, Sunny. For some of us, it isn't.'

Sunny was determined not to follow up this enigmatic remark.

Braking to a careful stop in front of the Burhmans' house, Zachary said, with an almost boyish enthusiasm, 'So – Cornell? In the fall? We'll both go to Cornell?'

Sunny was quickly out of the car before Zachary could put on the emergency brake and come around, ceremoniously,

....

to open her door. Gaily, recklessly, infinitely relieved to be out of his company, she called back over her shoulder, 'Why not?'

Sunny's secret vanity must have been what linked them.

For several times, gravely, Zachary had said to her, 'When I'm with you, Sunny, it's possible for me to believe.'

He meant, she thought, in God. In Jesus. In the life hereafter.

The next time Zachary maneuvered Sunny into his car, under the pretext of driving her home, it was to present the startled girl with an engagement ring.

He'd bought the ring at Stern's Jewelers, South Lebanon's single good jewelry store, with money secretly withdrawn from his saving account; that account to which, over a period of more than a decade, he'd deposited modest sums with a painstaking devotion. This was his 'college fund,' or had been – out of the $3,245 saved, only $1,090 remained. How astonished, upset, furious his parents would be when they learned – Zachary hadn't allowed himself to contemplate.

The Graffs knew nothing about Sunny Burhman. So far as they might have surmised, their son's frequent absences from home were nothing out of the ordinary – he'd always spent time at the public library, where his preferred reading was reference books. He'd begin with Volume One of an encyclopedia, and make his diligent way through each successive volume, like a horse grazing a field, rarely glancing up, uninterested in his surroundings.

'Please – will you accept it?'

Sunny was staring incredulously at the diamond ring, which was presented to her, not in Zachary's big clumsy fingers, with the dirt-edged nails, but in the plush-lined little box, as if it might be more attractive that way, more like a gift. The ring was 24-carat gold and the diamond was small but distinctive, and coldly glittering. A beautiful ring, but Sunny did not see it that way.

....

She whispered, 'Oh. Zachary. Oh *no* – there must be some misunderstanding.'

Zachary seemed prepared for her reaction, for he said, quickly, 'Will you just try it on? – see if it fits?'

Sunny shook her head. No she couldn't.

'They'll take it back to adjust it, if it's too big,' Zachary said. 'They promised.'

'Zachary, no,' Sunny said gently. 'I'm so sorry.'

Tears flooded her eyes and spilled over onto her cheeks.

Zachary was saying, eagerly, his lips flecked with spittle, 'I realize you don't l-love me, Sunny, at least not yet, but – you could wear the ring, couldn't you? Just – wear it?' He continued to hold the little box out to her, his hand visibly shaking. 'On your right hand, if you don't want to wear it on your left? Please?'

'Zachary, no. That's impossible.'

'Just, you know, as a, a gift – ? Oh Sunny – '

They were sitting in the plum-colored Plymouth, parked, in an awkwardly public place, on Upchurch Avenue three blocks from Sunny's house. It was 4:25 p.m., March 26, a Thursday: Zachary had lingered after school in order to drive Sunny home after choir practice. Sunny would afterward recall, with an odd haltingness, as if her memory of the episode were blurred with tears, that, as usual, Zachary had done most of the talking. He had not argued with her, nor exactly begged, but spoke almost formally, as if setting out the basic points of his debating strategy: if Sunny did not love him, he could love enough for both; and, if Sunny did not want to be 'officially' engaged, she could wear his ring anyway, couldn't she?

It would mean so much to him, Zachary said.

Life or death, Zachary said.

Sunny closed the lid of the little box, and pushed it from her, gently. She was crying, and her smooth pageboy was now disheveled. 'Oh Zachary, I'm *sorry*. I *can't*.'

*

....

21

Sunny knelt by her bed, hid her face in her hands, prayed.

Please help Zachary not to be in love with me. Please help me not to be cruel. Have mercy on us both O God.

O God help him to realize he doesn't love me – doesn't know *me*.

Days passed, and Zachary did not call. If he was absent from school, Sunny did not seem to notice.

Sunny Burhman and Zachary Graff had two classes together, English and physics; but, in the busyness of Sunny's high school life, surrounded by friends, mesmerized by her own rapid motion as if she were lashed to the prow of a boat bearing swiftly through the water, she did not seem to notice.

She was not a girl of secrets. She was not a girl of stealth. Still, though she had confided in her mother all her life, she did not tell her mother about Zachary's desperate proposal; perhaps, so flattered, she did not acknowledge it as desperate. She reasoned that if she told either of her parents they would have telephoned Zachary's parents immediately. I can't betray him, she thought.

Nor did she tell her closest girl friends, or the boy she was seeing most frequently at the time, knowing that the account would turn comical in the telling, that she and her listeners would collapse into laughter, and this too would be a betrayal of Zachary.

She happened to see Tobias Shanks, one day, looking oddly at *her*. That boy who might have been twelve years old, seen from a short distance. Sunny knew that he was, or had been, a friend of Zachary Graff's; she wondered if Zachary confided in him; yet made no effort to speak with him. He didn't like her, she sensed.

No, Sunny didn't tell anyone about Zachary and the engagement ring. Of all sins, she thought, betrayal is surely the worst.

'Sunny? Sun-ny?'

She did not believe she had been sleeping but the low,

....

persistent, gravelly sound of Zachary's voice penetrated her consciousness like a dream-voice – felt, not heard.

Quickly, she got out of bed. Crouched at her window without turning on the light. Saw, to her horror, Zachary down below, standing in the shrubbery, his large head uplifted, face round like the moon, and shadowed like the moon's face. There was a light, damp snowfall; blossom-like clumps fell on the boy's broad shoulders, in his matted hair. Sighting her, he began to wave excitedly, like an impatient child.

'Oh. Zachary. My God.'

In haste, fumbling, she put on a bulky-knit ski sweater over her flannel nightgown, kicked on bedroom slippers, hurried downstairs. The house was already darkened; the Burhmans were in the habit of going to bed early. Sunny's only concern was that she could send Zachary away without her parents knowing he was there. Even in her distress she was not thinking of the trouble Zachary might make for her: she was thinking of the trouble he might make for himself.

Yet, as soon as she saw him close up, she realized that something was gravely wrong. Here was Zachary Graff – yet not Zachary.

He told her he had to talk with her, and he had to talk with her now. His car was parked in the alley, he said.

He made a gesture as if to take her hand, but Sunny drew back. He loomed over her, his breath steaming. She could not see his eyes.

She said no she couldn't go with him. She said he must go home, at once, before her parents woke up.

He said he couldn't leave without her, he had to talk with her. There was a raw urgency, a forcefulness, in him, that Sunny had never seen before, and that frightened her.

She said no. He said yes.

He reached again for her hand, this time taking hold of her wrist.

His fingers were strong.

'I told you – I can love enough for both!'

Sunny stared up at him, for an instant mute, paralyzed,

....

23

seeing not Zachary Graff's eyes but the lenses of his glasses which appeared, in the semi-dark, opaque. Large snowflakes were falling languidly, there was no wind. Sunny saw Zachary Graff's face which was pale and clenched as a muscle, and she heard his voice which was the voice of a stranger, and she felt him tug at her so roughly her arm was strained in its very socket, and she cried, 'No! no! go away! no!' – and the spell was broken, the boy gaped at her another moment, then released her, turned, and ran.

No more than two or three minutes had passed since Sunny unlocked the rear door and stepped outside, and Zachary fled. Yet, afterward, she would recall the encounter as if it had taken a very long time, like a scene in a protracted and repetitive nightmare.

It would be the last time Sunny Burhman saw Zachary Graff alive.

Next morning, all of South Lebanon talked of the death of Dr Graff's son Zachary: he'd committed suicide by parking his car in a garage behind an unoccupied house on Upchurch Avenue, and letting the motor run until the gas tank was emptied. Death was diagnosed as the result of carbon monoxide poisoning, the time estimated at approximately 4:30 a.m. of April 1, 1959.

Was the date deliberate? – Zachary had left only a single note behind, printed in firm block letters and taped to the outside of the car windshield:

April Fool's Day 1959

To Whom It May (Or May Not) Concern:

I, Zachary A. Graff, being of sound mind & body, do hereby declare that I have taken my own life of my own free will & I hereby declare all others guiltless as they are ignorant of the death of the aforementioned & the life.

(Signed)
ZACHARY A. GRAFF

....

Police officers, called to the scene at 7:45 a.m., reported finding Zachary, lifeless, stripped to his underwear, in the rear seat of the car; the sheepskin parka was oddly draped over the steering wheel, and the interior of the car was, again oddly, for a boy known for his fastidious habits, littered with numerous items: a Bible, several high school textbooks, a pizza carton and some uneaten crusts of pizza, several empty Pepsi bottles, an empty bag of M & M candies, a pair of new, unlaced gym shoes (size 11), a 10-foot length of clothesline (in the glove compartment), and the diamond ring in its plush-lined little box from Stern's Jewelers (in a pocket of the parka).

Sunny Burhman heard the news of Zachary's suicide before leaving for school that morning, when a friend telephoned. Within earshot of both her astonished parents, Sunny burst into tears, and sobbed, 'Oh my God – it's my fault.'

So the consensus in South Lebanon would be, following the police investigation, and much public speculation, not that it was Sunny Burhman's fault, exactly, not that the girl was to blame, exactly, but, yes, poor Zachary Graff, the doctor's son, had killed himself in despondency over her: her refusal of his engagement ring, her rejection of his love.

That was the final season of her life as 'Sunny' Burhman.

She was out of school for a full week following Zachary's death, and, when she returned, conspicuously paler, more subdued, in all ways less sunnier, she did not speak, even with her closest friends, of the tragedy; nor did anyone bring up the subject with her. She withdrew her name from the balloting for the senior prom queen, she withdrew from her part in the senior play, she dropped out of the school choir, she did not participate in the annual statewide debating competition – in which, in previous years, Zachary Graff had excelled. Following her last class of the day she went home immediately, and rarely saw her friends on weekends. Was she in mourning? – or was she simply ashamed? Like

....

the bearer of a deadly virus, herself unaffected, Sunny knew how, on all sides, her classmates and her teachers were regarding her: she was the girl for whose love a boy had thrown away his life, she was an unwitting agent of death.

Of course, her family told her that it wasn't her fault that Zachary Graff had been mentally unbalanced.

Even the Graffs did not blame her – or said they didn't.

Sunny said, 'Yes. But it's my fault he's dead.'

The Presbyterian minister, who counseled Sunny, and prayed with her, assured her that Jesus surely understood, and that there could be no sin in *her* – it wasn't her fault that Zachary Graff had been mentally unbalanced. And Sunny replied, not stubbornly, but matter-of-factly, sadly, as if stating a self-evident truth, 'Yes. But it's my fault he's dead.'

Her older sister Helen, later that summer, meaning only well, said, in exasperation, 'Sunny, when are you going to cheer *up*?' and Sunny turned on her with uncharacteristic fury, and said, 'Don't call me that idiotic name ever again! – I want it *gone*!'

When in the fall she enrolled at Cornell University, she was 'Barbara Burhman.'

She would remain 'Barbara Burhman' for the rest of her life.

*　　　*　　　*

Barbara Burhman excelled as an undergraduate, concentrating on academic work almost exclusively; she went on to graduate school at Harvard, in American studies; she taught at several prestigious universities, rising rapidly through administrative ranks before accepting a position, both highly paid and politically visible, with a well-known research foundation based in Manhattan. She was the author of numerous books and articles; she was married, and the mother of three children; she lectured widely, she was frequently interviewed in the popular press, she lent her name to good causes. She would not have wished to think of

....

herself as extraordinary – in the world she now inhabited, she was surrounded by similarly active, energetic, professionally engaged men and women – except in recalling, as she sometimes did, with a mild pang of nostalgia, her old, lost self, sweet 'Sunny' Burhman of South Lebanon, New York.

She hadn't been queen of the senior prom. She hadn't even continued to be a Christian.

The irony had not escaped Barbara Burhman that, in casting away his young life so recklessly, Zachary Graff had freed her for hers.

With the passage of time, grief had lessened. Perhaps in fact it had disappeared. After twenty, and then twenty-five, and now thirty-one years, it was difficult for Barbara, known in her adult life as an exemplar of practical sense, to feel a kinship with the adolescent girl she'd been, or that claustrophobic high school world of the late 1950s. She'd never returned for a single reunion. If she thought of Zachary Graff – about whom, incidentally, she'd never told her husband of twenty-eight years – it was with the regret we think of remote acquaintances, lost to us by accidents of fate. Forever, Zachary Graff, the most brilliant member of the class of 1959 of South Lebanon High, would remain a high school boy, trapped, aged eighteen.

Of that class, the only other person to have acquired what might be called a national reputation was Tobias Shanks, now known as T. R. Shanks, a playwright and director of experimental drama; Barbara Burhman had followed Tobias' career with interest, and had sent him a telegram congratulating him on his most recent play, which went on to win a number of awards, dealing, as it did, with the vicissitudes of gay life in the 1980s. In the winter of 1990 Barbara and Tobias began to encounter each other socially, when Tobias was playwright-in-residence at Bard College, close by Hazelton-on-Hudson, where Barbara lived. At first they were strangely shy of each other; even guarded; as if, in even this neutral setting, their South Lebanon ghost-selves

. . . .

27

exerted a powerful influence. The golden girl, the loner. The splendidly normal, the defiantly 'odd.' One night Tobias Shanks, shaking Barbara Burhman's hand, had smiled wryly, and said, 'It *is* Sunny, isn't it?' and Barbara Burhman, laughing nervously, hoping no one had overheard, said, 'No, in fact it isn't. It's Barbara.'

They looked at each other, mildly dazed. For one saw a small-boned but solidly built man of youthful middle-age, sweet-faced, yet with ironic, pouched eyes, thinning gray hair and a close-trimmed gray beard; the other saw a woman of youthful middle-age, striking in appearance, impeccably well groomed, with fading hair of no distinctive color and faint, white, puckering lines at the edges of her eyes. Their ghost-selves *were* there – not aged, or not aged merely, but transformed, as the genes of a previous generation are transformed by the next.

Tobias stared at Barbara for a long moment, as if unable to speak. Finally he said, 'I have something to tell you, Barbara. When can we meet?'

Tobias Shanks handed the much-folded letter across the table to Barbara Burhman, and watched as she opened it, and read it, with an expression of increasing astonishment and wonder.

'*He* wrote this? Zachary? To you?'

'He did.'

'And you – ? Did you – ?'

Tobias shook his head.

His expression was carefully neutral, but his eyes swam suddenly with tears.

'We'd been friends, very close friends, for years. Each other's only friend, most of the time. The way kids that age can be, in certain restricted environments – kids who aren't what's called "average" or "normal." We talked a good deal about religion – Zachary was afraid of hell. We both liked science fiction. We both had very strict parents. I suppose I might have been attracted to Zachary at times – I knew I

....

was attracted to other guys – but of course I never acted upon it; I wouldn't have dared. Almost no one dared, in those days.' He laughed, with a mild shudder. He passed a hand over his eyes. 'I couldn't have *loved* Zachary Graff as he claimed he loved me, because – I couldn't. But I could have allowed him to know that he wasn't sick, crazy, "perverted" as he called himself in that letter.' He paused. For a long painful moment Barbara thought he wasn't going to continue. Then he said, with that same mirthless shuddering laugh, 'I could have made him feel less lonely. But I didn't. I failed him. My only friend.'

Barbara had taken out a tissue, and was dabbing at her eyes.

She felt as if she'd been dealt a blow so hard she could not gauge how she'd been hurt – if there was hurt at all.

She said, 'Then it hadn't ever been "Sunny" – she was an illusion.'

Tobias said thoughtfully, 'I don't know. I suppose so. There was the sense, at least as I saw it at the time, that, yes, he'd chosen you; decided upon you.'

'As a symbol.'

'Not just a symbol. We all adored you – we were all a little in love with you.' Tobias laughed, embarrassed. 'Even me.'

'I wish you'd come to me and told me, back then. After – it happened.'

'I was too cowardly. I was terrified of being exposed, and, maybe, doing to myself what he'd done to himself. Suicide is so very attractive to adolescents.' Tobias paused, and reached over to touch Barbara's hand. His fingertips were cold. 'I'm not proud of myself, Barbara, and I've tried to deal with it in my writing, but – that's how I was, back then.' Again he paused. He pressed a little harder against Barbara's hand. 'Another thing – after Zachary went to you, that night, he came to me.'

'To you?'

'To me.'

. . . .

'And – ?'

'And I refused to go with him too. I was furious with him for coming to the house like that, risking my parents discovering us. I guess I got a little hysterical. And he fled.'

'He fled.'

'Then, afterward, I just couldn't bring myself to come forward. Why I saved that letter, I don't know – I'd thrown away some others that were less incriminating. I suppose I figured – no one knew about me, everyone knew about you. "Sunny" Burhman.'

They were at lunch – they ordered two more drinks – they'd forgotten their surroundings – they talked.

After an hour or so Barbara Burhman leaned across the table, as at one of her professional meetings, to ask, in a tone of intellectual curiosity, 'What do you think Zachary planned to do with the clothesline?'

The Book Lover

IVAN VLADISLAVIĆ

I first came across Helena at the Black Sash Fête. Of all the second-hand book sales in Johannesburg, this one has the finest catchment area – good, educated, moneyed, liberal homes. Thanks to the brain drain and death itself there is always a large and varied selection. The venue is a suburban garden and, weather permitting, the books are displayed outdoors, gift-wrapped in leafy shade. They have already been sorted into labelled cardboard boxes – Biography, Fiction, Classics, Industrial Psychology, Judaica, to name a few – and the boxes are on trestle-tables with generous spaces in between. These arrangements are a godsend: one does not have to endure the crush of human bodies one associates with jumble sales or, worse, the intimidating configurations of book-lined walls in the second-hand dealers.

I came away from the fête last year with a satisfying haul. Perhaps my favourite among the half dozen was a battered little *Quattro Novelle* by Pirandello, in Harrap's Bilingual Series, published in 1943, with a dun cardboard cover and grey paper that more than warranted the declaration on the copyright page: Book Production War Economy Standard. This ugly child was crying out for love in Italian. There were English-speakers too: *The Culture of the Abdomen* by F. A. Hornibrook, with a personal recommendation from Arnold Bennett, who claimed it had relieved him of his dyspepsia and thirty pounds avoirdupois. And *Non-Sporting Dogs: Their Points and Management* by Frank Townend Barton MRCVS, with a dedication to the author's mother.

....

A couple of South African works I had been hunting, Huddleston's *Naught for your Comfort* and Millin's *The Burning Man*, also gave themselves up. I hesitate to call these publications Africana – they are still too plentiful and too reasonably priced – but I was pleased to have them.

I should mention in passing that I also netted a jar of pickled onions entitled STRONG on a gummed label of the kind made for school exercise books; and a peace-in-the-home in a terracotta pot from the plant stall. Beat them both down to give-away prices.

I hurried home to breakfast and the pleasure of going through my finds more thoroughly. The Pirandello parallel text is endearing. Recto: 'And Teresina slipped away into the dining-room, a rustle of silk.' Verso: 'E Teresina scappò via in sala, tutta frusciante.' I can't speak a word of Italian, but that did not stop me from declaiming a paragraph or two in rich tones, through a mouthful of Fruitful Bran. (The manufacturers, the Kellogg Company of New Era, Springs, call it 'fruitful', but I'm sure they mean 'fruity'.)

Naught for your Comfort was worth buying for the dust-jacket alone. Father Huddleston reaches out from the front cover with both hands. He is making a telling criticism of apartheid, no doubt, but the gesture puts me in mind of a fisherman showing the size of the one that got away. Perhaps it's the background the portrait is floating on – wavy lines of clerical purple, a cartoon Galilee.

There was a signature on the flyleaf of Millin's book: Helena Shein, Johannesburg, 1956. I'd seen that light and airy hand somewhere before, with its buoyant loops and wind-swept ascenders. I turned to my other acquisitions. To my surprise I discovered that *The Burning Man*, *Naught for your Comfort*, the *Quattro Novelle* and *The Pocket Book of Poems and Songs for the Open Air*, fully two-thirds of my haul, pulled from their scattered pools on the Black Sash trestles, had all once belonged to Helena Shein. The coincidence banged a window open in my mind and the present billowed out like a lace curtain in a sudden breeze. Through

....

a gap edged with geranium leaves I glimpsed a vanished world: a cool room with a high pressed-steel ceiling and a picture rail, a pile of books on the arm of a chair, their ghostly echo in the varnished wood, gleaming copper fire-irons, a springbuck-skin pouffe, a ripple of piano music on the sepia air.

What held these books together, I wondered, apart from glue and thread and the name written with a fountain-pen in ink now faded to sky-blue?

The blurb of *Naught for your Comfort* said that Trevor Huddleston first became interested in missionary work during 'Oxford vacations, spent with the hop-pickers in Kent'. After his ordination he became curate at St Mark's, Swindon. 'I met, and immensely liked, the railwaymen of England,' Father Huddleston said. In 1939 he joined the Community of the Resurrection and took the three vows of poverty, chastity and obedience. Later he came to be Priest-in-Charge of the Anglican Mission in Sophiatown, where he became a legend, 'a legend that will endure long after his departure and perhaps intensify.' Black people christened him 'Makhalipile', the Dauntless One. 'Those who have seen Fr Huddleston in action say he owes his success among the Africans to his great sense of humour and to his joyous nature, which are such strong characteristics of the African.'

The book had been bought at Vanguard Booksellers (Pty) Ltd, of 23 Joubert Street, Johannesburg. Harry Bloom's *Episode*, due for publication in April 1956, was advertised on the inside flap of the dust-jacket. There was a quote from Alan Paton, who must have read the book in manuscript. 'It is the location itself (that part of every South African town set aside for the African people) which is the real character of the novel,' Paton said, 'and Mr Bloom portrays it with a fidelity and a skill that command my admiration. His story never happened, yet every word of it is true.'

The Burning Man, the second book on the pile, had also been purchased at Vanguard Booksellers. There was an

....

inscription in the front cover: To my dear Helena, With love, From Julius P. Lofsky. It was dated September 1952. According to the blurb, this novel told the story of Johannes van der Kemp, 'a soldier, a scholar, a philosopher, a mystic, a rake, a gentleman in sackcloth'. Van der Kemp, it said, had come to South Africa to preach the Word of God to the heathen, but had failed miserably: '. . . he was one of the first causes of South Africa's difficulties today, in that he was the leader of those missionaries whom the Boers, when they trekked northwards from the Cape, accused of bringing the hatred and odium of the natives upon their heads. Nevertheless, like Spinoza, he was "God-intoxicated", and also intoxicated with sex. Thus his tempestuous life makes an admirable subject for Mrs Millin's art; once again she shows herself a mistress of her scene and subject.'

Next was *The Pocket Book of Poems and Songs for the Open Air*, which came to me at third hand. It had belonged first to N. Morris, who had acquired it new in 1933. Twenty-three years later it had fallen into Helena's possession, and she had added her name below Morris's. (I have since added my own book-plate and the year 1990 below these.) I brushed the husk of a fishmoth as delicately veined and pretty as a pressed flower from page 286 with the nail of my little finger, and read the second verse of 'As I Walked Forth', which was marred only slightly by a faded bloodstain. (I wonder whether one ought to refer to the vital fluid of an insect as 'blood'? I suspect that it is not 'blood' so much as 'haemolymph'.)

Poems and Songs for the Qpen Air was part of Jonathan Cape's Travellers' Library; it was number 97 in that series, according to the numerical index published with the text. It was a self-proclaimed Pocket Book. But it was clear at a glance that it would not fit my pockets. I tried it in my shirt pocket anyway, but it was much too big. I tried it in the rear pocket of my trousers, but it would not fit there either. Among my jackets I found an old-fashioned blazer with an inner pocket that was large enough. It must be true that

....

pockets have been getting smaller over the years. Disappearing altogether in some cases.

At the bottom of the pile was the Pirandello parallel text. I paged for the passage about Teresina, but before I arrived there the breeze dropped and the curtain settled. I found myself in my own breakfast nook again, hot and bothered, with the pungent scent of crushed geraniums on my hands.

As a rule I avoid bookshops. Books *en masse* repel me. I dislike crowds of people too, even relatively small gatherings of strangers in which everyone speaks at once. I find intolerable the babble that assaults my ears as I enter a bookshop. Especially the less discriminating sort of second-hand dealer, the so-called 'book exchange', full of shabbily dressed, ill-proportioned, abused bundles of pages with their shameless hearts burbling away on their sleeves.

I only have to approach such a place to feel enfeebled and upset. There is a buzz in the air, a shrill of pages rubbing against one another. Hemmed in by those abrasive strata I cannot hear myself think. Dullness envelops me like a dustcloud. I have to focus: I must find a crooked seam and mine it to an uncertain conclusion, up and down, up and down, prying out the occasional nugget. It is undoubtedly true, as Augustine Birrell says, that the best books are necessarily second-hand – but what trials one has to endure to acquire them!

So it was nearly two full months after the Black Sash Fête before I ventured again into a purchasing situation, and then only because it was necessary to obtain some reading matter for the Christmas holidays. The shop I chose was Yeoville Books of 28 Rockey Street, because the South African literature shelves are close to the door. A sensible arrangement, I think, which allows a decent amount of air to waft in from outside. Sometimes I am able to satisfy my needs there; but if I am compelled to go on, I treat this part of the shop as a decompression chamber in which I accustom myself to the arid, book-moted air that awaits me in the interior. If

....

my will or my lungs fail me, I can quickly retire to the street, where there is a large supply of air, tainted by exhaust fumes but nonetheless quite breathable.

Prepared though I was, my Christmas shopping expedition nearly ended in disaster. I had hardly set foot in the shop when I was overcome by the contentious racket of the book mob. My sense of self – I believe it was that – rushed to the backs of my hands and pulsed like a rash of quotations. The layers of books on all sides drew themselves up into verso and recto of a colossal tome, and tilted to swat me like an insect. I reeled about in the doorway with my eyes screwed shut, until I bumped up against the laminated gondola of new acquisitions and clasped it. As I crouched there, trying to remember what had brought me to this pass, I heard a small voice muttering my name. Opening my eyes, I found them focused on a book in the South African fiction section: Harry Bloom's *Episode*. It was calling me. The spine showed a black man, a riotous person of some kind, brandishing a blazing torch, and in its flames the title and the name of the author spelt out in white bones. I stumbled to the shelf and seized the book in my left hand. It was surprisingly cool to the touch and I pressed it gratefully to my burning forehead. The noise in the shop faded away momentarily, and in the hush I became aware that a woman in a pink tracksuit, the sort of garment that has no pockets whatsoever, was looking at me compassionately. I turned my attention to the books again, fumbled at the shelf to comfort the aching gap where Bloom's *Episode* had stood a moment ago, and found that a copy of *Cold Stone Jug* had somehow appeared in my right hand. I remembered that I was looking for that too. I pressed the two books together in a crude sort of cross, as if the stone in the title of the one could somehow extinguish the fire on the spine of the other, reeled to the till, threw some money down on the counter and fled.

I paused on a bench in Yeoville Park to regain my composure. And there I discovered that my new purchases had also come from Helena Shein's library.

....

36

But somehow the coincidence was less interesting to me now that it had become more pronounced. When I got home, I put the books aside and reached for *The Cricket on the Hearth* instead. I always read one of the Christmas Books over the festive season. I must make it clear, I suppose, that my own library does not have the same disconcerting effect on me as the bookshops. On the contrary, I feel at home among these familiar few. 'The man who has a library of his own collection,' says Augustine Birrell, 'is able to contemplate himself objectively, and is justified in believing in his own existence.' I agree with this statement, and I have no doubt that it applies with equal force to women. (Birrell and I differ, however, on the question of numbers. He hesitates to call a collection of two thousand books a 'library', whereas I suspect that two *hundred* books might more than deserve the title.)

In my own modest library there is silence. The books speak only when they're spoken to. In their silent company, I believe that I exist.

Harry Bloom's *Episode* had been bought at the Methodist Book Depot, corner Pritchard and Kruis Streets, Johannesburg, and inscribed in May 1956. You'll recall that on *Naught for your Comfort* the projected publication date for *Episode* was April 1956. So the book appeared on schedule, and Helena acquired it immediately.

Between pages 234 and 235 I found a fragile notice from the Automobile Association to a Miss H. Shein of PO Box 4134, Johannesburg, reminding her that her annual subscription to the value of £1 11s 6d was due on 1 July 1956. It was signed by J. H. C. Porter, Area Secretary. I myself have never been a member of the Automobile Association.

On page 235 was a reference to Father Huddleston, Nelson Mandela and Mulvi Cachalia, which I couldn't help but notice.

Bosman's *Cold Stone Jug* had been purchased at the Pickwick Bookshop, 45 Kerk Street. Quite against the odds,

....

or so I thought at the time, there was a card tucked into this book too, which showed that it had been a gift. On one side of the card was a guarantee: 'Mr Pickwick cordially invites you to call in and exchange this gift, in its present clean and new condition, if for any reason you are not satisfied with it.' Alongside the guarantee was a drawing of Mr Pickwick. On the other side of the card was the following message: With my very best wishes for a Happy New Year, from Muriel.

I turned the card over on the flyleaf and studied Mr Pickwick. Then my eye was drawn to the logo of the distributor – the Central News Agency – on the flap of the dust-jacket: two naked black men playing bows. Mr Pickwick, with his hat concealed behind his coat-tails in his left hand and his chin propped in his right, gazed at these men through his little round spectacles across a field of yellowed paper. They looked in the other direction.

Incidentally, my book-plate is based on a woodcut by Dürer: St Jerome in his cell.

Although Helena Shein's books were doing their utmost to attract my attention, I might still have turned a deaf ear to the call. But a fortnight later, as I paused on the threshold of The Booknook, 42 Bedford Road, and raised my knuckles to the glass door, meaning to summon the female proprietor out on to the pavement for an emergency consultation about my New Year reading, a voice hailed me from inside. It was a clear, hollowed-out voice, like the tone struck from an empty goblet, but it had an oversweet edge to it like sugar crystals on the rim. It was quite detestable: my immediate impulse was to fly. But at that moment the door swung open all by itself and a shaft of light that seemed to be refracted through the top of my head slid from the doorway to a far shelf and rested on a tatty hardback. My name rang out again (I don't think it's necessary to go into detail here, except to say that my Christian name was used in a way I found overly familiar). Screwing up my courage I tumbled headlong down the shaft and plucked the book from the shelf. It turned out to be Barbara Cartland's *A Ghost in Monte Carlo*. I bought it, a little shamefacedly; indeed, I threw in a copy of *Cry, the Beloved Country* which happened to come to hand, simply to raise the tone of the purchase, and scurried home.

An examination of *A Ghost in Monte Carlo* left me with two questions. The first was a question of quality: what was Cartland, a writer of romances, doing in Helena Shein's library, rubbing shoulders with the likes of Huddleston, an archbishop and patron of the Anti-Apartheid Movement, and Bloom, a lawyer and serious novelist? I am not a snob, you see, but I am a stickler for standards. At that point I was reminded of Birrell's comment that it is better to collect a library than to inherit one – 'Each volume then, however lightly a stranger's eye may roam from shelf to shelf, has its own individuality, a history of its own' – and felt rebuked. How could I know what had moved Helena to keep the book (I say 'keep', rather than 'buy', for reasons that will soon become clear).

The second was a question of morality. This copy of *A Ghost in Monte Carlo* was the property of the Johannesburg Public Library. The slip pasted to the flyleaf, with its teetering stacks of rubber-stamped dates, said so clearly. Ever since the book had been published in 1951, until it had last been date-stamped on 5 March 1956, scarcely a week had passed during which someone had not taken it out. But despite this popularity, despite the letters JPL stamped all over the title page, despite the attached printed notice that the book had to be returned to the library within fourteen days and that there was a fine of sixpence for every week it was overdue, Helena Shein had kept it. She had written her name on it. She had even dated it March 1956, a little superfluously under the circumstances. I had been forming an impression of Helena Shein, and she did not strike me as the kind of person who would steal from a public library.

....

Yet I held the evidence in my hands. I think it was precisely this uncomfortable sense of ambiguity that caused me to become enamoured of Helena Shein and her books.

I did a quick calculation. The book was 1,815 weeks overdue. Allowing for inflation and an unfavourable exchange rate, Helena owed the JPL about twenty-seven thousand rand.

JPL? It rang a bell somewhere . . . and at last I caught the echo: Julius P. Lofsky.

'All Monte Carlo was talking! The winter of 1874 was the gayest, most profitable and most brilliant season since the opening of the Casino. Yet among the Royalty, aristocrats and millionaires from every country, two women caused a sensation.

'One was elderly, her handsome face malignant and secretive; the other was exquisitely lovely with huge dark eyes in strange contrast to the shining gold of her hair.

'Registered at the hotel as Mademoiselle Fantôme, everything she wore was grey, including a fabulous necklace of grey pearls. But only one person learned that "the Ghost", as she was called, had come straight to Monte Carlo from a convent.

'In that glittering, sparkling throng three men played desperate and decisive roles in her life – the sinister Rajah of Jehangar, the debonair Prince Nikolai of Russia and Sir Robert Stanford from England.

'It is a story of good and evil. How Mademoiselle Fantôme walks to the very brink of the abyss of evil, how she is saved and finds happiness through her own intrinsic purity is told in this thrilling, exciting, unusual forty-second novel from the pen of Barbara Cartland.'

My fall was all the more precipitate for having been resisted so long. I went to sleep that night with *A Ghost in Monte Carlo* under my pillow and Helena Shein on the tip of my tongue. When I awoke the next morning they were both still there. I rose in a daze, dressed in serviceable flannels,

. . . .

walking shoes and the blazer with the large inner pocket, and went out to look for Helena Shein's books. I began to collect them for no other reason than that they had once belonged to her.

In the beginning, they were few and far between. It took me two weeks to find the first dozen. But the more I found, the more I wanted. Conversely, the more I wanted, the more I found. In the end, they were everywhere. Sometimes the chorus of demanding voices as I strode through the doorway of a second-hand dealer was almost harder to bear than the unintelligible muttering of days gone by. It seemed as if every second book called out to me, as if every penny dreadful wanted to make my acquaintance. (For 'penny' read 'twelve rand ninety-five'.)

I was obliged to overcome my aversion to crowds. I had to harden my heart by plunging it repeatedly in the raucous air. I learned to circulate among the shelves, brushing a spine here and there with my fingertips, like a personality at a cocktail party. How are you? So glad you could make it. There's someone I want you to meet . . . now where's she hiding? *There* you are!

My question still resounded: What holds this library together?

As Helena's books piled up, patterns that promised to reveal everything kept emerging and then fading away before my eyes. Take Ilya Ehrenburg's *The Fall of Paris* and Alexei Tolstoy's *Road to Calvary*, for example, found at flea markets on opposite ends of the city. Note how the titles echo one another. Note how both carry the War Economy Standard certification, inscribed on the same open book and guarded by the same little lion. Both books were published by Hutchinson & Co. Both had won the Stalin Prize. Both were purchased at the People's Book Shop, Africa House, 45, Kerk Street, Johannesburg. Have you noticed that people don't use that comma any more? I mean the comma after the number. Have you noticed that the People's Book Shop and Pickwick Bookshop have the same address?

. . . .

The Fall of Paris was translated from the Russian by Gerard Shelley. But *Road to Calvary* was translated from the Russian by Edith Bone.

Mistral, who was the only English girl in the convent, arrives at the home of her Aunt Emilie in Paris. Emilie announces that they will be going to Monte Carlo. She summons Madame Guibout, the couturière, to measure Mistral for 'travelling gowns, morning costumes, ball dresses, robes de style, manteaux, dolmans, paletots and casaques'. Madame Guibout's assistants come bearing 'satins, velvets, cashmeres, failles, muslins, foulards, alpacas, poplins, rolls and patterns in every texture and colour'.

Some people lounge about in the book they're reading as if it were a bed in a cheap hotel, dropping cigarette ash and biscuit crumbs between the sheets. Someone has slept here before, you think, tucking in the crumpled flap of a dust-jacket and brushing away a strand of blonde hair. There are initials carved in the margins, NBs and asterisks, obscene propositions, faint praise and futile rejoinders.

Helena was a light traveller, the kind for whom a single photograph lodged in a crack of the dressing-table mirror must stand for home. She had passed through with a quick eye and clean hands. There were no annotations, no underlinings. But there were signs of her everywhere, mementoes pressed flat between the leaves: letters, cuttings, invoices, receipts, playing cards, ticket stubs, banknotes. She had scattered so many papers behind her that I began to feel she was leading me on.

And I followed her: to the tea-room at Anstey's for tea and scones, and then to Sportswear on the first floor, where she purchased a swimsuit, a Mary Nash original, in sea-going cotton, shell pattern, with shirred front panel, 'Butterfly' bra and tuck-away straps, for only 69/6. To the Colosseum to see James Stewart and Doris Day in *The Man Who Knew Too Much*. (She was alone: Julius P. Lofsky was out of

....

town.) To the Belfast for a poplin blouse marked down to 19/6. I even crept up to the window of her room, with the eight of hearts in my left hand, and watched as a pale woman dressed in flickering shadows sat down in a chair turned away from me, took up a book from the armrest and tried to find her place.

All these scattered signs were added proof that her books had been read. The pages fell open smoothly, the spines didn't creak, there were no uncut sections. On the contrary, the rough edges of pages 129 to 160 of *The Lying Days* suggested that they had been slit open with the edge of a ruler. It was among these pages that I found the following letter, typewritten in red ink on paper the colour of bone.

Sunday, 15th

My dearest Helena,

I was extremely sorry to hear about your mishap yesterday over the 'phone. I do hope you will soon recover from the shock you must have sustained and that it will have no ill effects. I had not written you previously as I had thought you might have been away somewhere over the holiday season. I thought yesterday I would take a chance with a 'phone call to see if you were at home, but I was very sorry to have your news.

You will be interested to hear that Mrs Porter is returning to her house in August (it has been let for twelve months) with a husband, a local optician. It has been in the offing for quite a while.

Did I tell you that Mrs Tishman passed on during June? She had a long spell of suffering. Mr Tishman is not too good at the moment with bronchial trouble, and we have had one or two very cold days lately.

I did not have any luck on the July. There were so many 'certainties' before the race that one got a little confused as to what to back. Last Ray saved me a little, as I had backed it for a place when it was in the 20s, so I made a fiver there.

Well, my dear, I hope you are going to get back to complete normal soon. As I mentioned yesterday, I leave here by car next

....

Sunday or Monday, and I shall 'phone you from Bernie's as
soon as I arrive. I had hoped to see you at once, not thinking of
anything that had been likely to upset you.

I believe Muriel's mother has returned to Port Elizabeth. I
could not see her visit lasting.

With a warm affection for you,
J.P.L.

I would have relished something more personal, but one was
able to read between the lines too.

Sir Robert Stanford meets Mistral in the public gardens at
Monte Carlo, at dawn. 'She was wearing a grey cloak of
some soft material which fell from her shoulders to the
ground, the hood shadowed her hair, and in the pale light
he could just see the outline of her face – delicate features,
wide eyes dark-lashed, and beautifully moulded lips which
were parted excitedly as she looked out to sea.'

The signs say: take nothing but counsel, leave nothing but
bookmarks. This particular bookmark, which I discovered in
Persuasion, said: Don't let UNWANTED HAIR cast a shadow
over your life! Have it REMOVED BY ELECTROLYSIS – the only
medically approved, permanent way. Lisbeth Lewis, 302
Safric House, Eloff & Plein Streets, Johannesburg. On the
left of the business card was a line drawing of a woman's
face, and below it the caption: Be FREE of unwanted hair by
the KREE method.

Naturally I wondered what the Kree method was. Are the
Krees not a tribe of Algonquian-speaking Indians? But what
held my attention was the drawing: in a few deft lines the
artist had captured a heart-shaped face and a soft blonde
permanent wave, pencilled eyebrows as neat as brackets, an
impudent scoop of nose, lips glossed with sweet nothings.
The face was bisected vertically by a dotted line, and the
left-hand side was veiled by a half-tone screen.

As I examined the drawing my fingers began to tingle: I

....

felt Helena's gaze skimming over the lettering in an amorous glissando from the cool and supple limbs of Electra to the warm hollows of Poliphilus. I tucked the card back into the book and turned the page. But the tingling continued. I smelt the incense of the ink fuming from the print, mingling with the scent of orange-blossom from her blue-veined wrists. I saw her right hand on the page, taking flesh around my own, then her downy arm, and then her freckled shoulder spilled over by yellow hair, one thing leading to another like the rhymes of a love-song. She raised her right hand to her mouth, licked the tip of her forefinger deliberately, lowered the hand again. The paper sucked the spit from her finger with a thirsty gulp.

I wanted to know everything about Helena Shein, but I refused to set about it properly. I went back to the beginning and asked myself sensible questions. I gave myself sensible answers too. Why had her library been dispersed? She had left the country. Or, more likely, she was dead. And even if she were still alive, and living in Johannesburg, she would surely be old enough to be my mother. I myself am a youngish man with a normal sense of regard for the aged. I could have cleared up the mysteries easily enough, I suppose, by consulting the relevant authorities. Certainty was possible. But I declined it. I wanted to know *this* woman, the one who had inscribed her name in these books. Did I mention that her g's were like party balloons with dangling strings, that her i's had soap bubbles revolving over them instead of dots? I wanted to touch the hand that had smoothed open these pages when they were new. I wanted to turn it over and read its palm.

A book lay open before me, verso and recto curving voluptuously away from the spine. I put my nose into the fold and breathed. The pages smelt of caramelized sugar. I opened my left eye. Slightly blurred, gigantically magnified, I read the following words: 'All in grey she seemed to move like a ghost across the room; and as she drew level with Sir

. . . .

Robert's table, he could see that, wreathing her hair, where other women would have worn flowers, were the softest grey velvet leaves almost like shadows among the dancing gold.' I had opened *A Ghost in Monte Carlo* in the middle of the scene in which Mistral makes her first entrance into the dining-room at the Hôtel de Paris. Aunt Emilie and Mistral, or rather Madame Secret and Mademoiselle Fantôme, are the talk of Monte Carlo.

There seemed to be no end to Helena's books. As far afield as Boksburg and Benoni, insistent voices called my name when I stepped into the swap shops and charity kiosks. My powers amazed me. In the tawdriest of a string of Bookworm Book Exchanges, a dismal place in Primrose wedged between a pet shop and a hairdressing salon, I found a copy of Firbank's *The Artificial Princess* that I *knew* she had read, even though her name was not in it. There was an unmistakable trace of her on the pages, like a whiff of hair-lacquer on a second-floor landing.

In time the dealers, who had never valued my custom much, began to despise me. I suppose I did make a nuisance of myself staggering around in the aisles, groping at the books, even those dumb ones that turned their backs on me, and mumbling through them. On one occasion I had to snatch one of Helena's books from the clutches of a browser. 'Browser' is not a term I would apply to anyone lightly, and least of all myself, but it suited this one to a T, with his rude hands (as Birrell would put it) and champing jaws. The book was *The Way of All Flesh*. God knows what would have become of it.

It pained me to think that with every passing day Helena's precious books were being swallowed up by the libraries of perfect strangers. I redoubled my efforts.

Occasionally I gave myself a day off, and spent it visiting the sites of the vanished bookshops. First stop on my itinerary was always Vanguard Books, Helena's favourite, long since obliterated by an insurance company's high-rise. Gone, they were all gone – Pickwick's and Vanity Fair and Random Books and L. Rubin, Booksellers and Stationers. City Book Shop had become Bob's Shoe Centre. Resnik's was now the Reef Meat Supply.

I breathed freely in these spaces emptied of books. Marrowbones and cleavers and the tinkling bell of the cash register made music for my ears. But in the lobby of Africa House a foul smell rose up from the floor, as if a long-forgotten bestseller was rotting under the marble flags.

Aunt Emilie takes the life of Henry Dulton to prevent him from revealing that she is really Madame Bleuet, proprietor of a house of ill fame in the Rue de Roi. Mistral, confined to her room while the body is disposed of, remembers how lonely she was at the convent, and how Father Vincent saved her by giving her the freedom of his library. 'She read a strange and varied assortment of books. There were books on religion, travel, philosophy, and books which, while being romances, were also some of the greatest achievements in French literature . . . There were dozens of others which at first she liked because they were English, but which later became, as books should, real friends and often closer than the real people in her life.'

The relics yielded by Helena's books I filed away neatly in a Black Magic chocolate box that had once belonged to my mother, but the books themselves mounted up in odd corners of my house. I began to worry that this disorder would prevent the essential unities of the library from manifesting themselves, so one evening I carried all the books to my study and sat down to make a list.

To my way of thinking, alphabetical is still the order of choice. I created the categories A-I, J-R and S-Z and began to sort the books into them by author, constructing three ziggurats on the end of my desk as I went along. This arrangement, though architecturally sound for the first

....

tower, proved to be impracticable for the others when a statistical imbalance was revealed. The first tower (A-I) contained just a dozen books, but the second and third (J-R and S-Z) had 111 and 77 respectively. So I razed the first tower, spread the books out in an alphabetical fan, slipped a sheet of Ariston bond into my Olivetti typewritter, and began.

BIBLIOGRAPHY

Austen, Jane, Persuasion (J. M. Dent, London, 1950)
Birrell, Augustine, Obiter Dicta (The Reprint Society, London, 1956)
Bloom, Harry, Episode (Collins, London, 1956)
Bosman, Herman Charles, Cold Stone Jug (A. P. B. Bookstore, Johannesburg, 1949)
Butler, Samuel, The Way of All Flesh (Collins, London, 1953)
Cartland, Barbara, A Ghost in Monte Carlo (Rich and Cowan, London, 1951)
Dickens, Charles, Pickwick Papers (McDonald, London, 1956)
Ehrenburg, Ilya, The Fall of Paris (Hutchinson, London, 1943)
Firbank, Ronald, The Artificial Princess (Duckworth, London, 1934)
Fowler, Gene, Schnozzola: The Story of Jimmy Durante (Hammond, Hammond & Co., London, 1956)
Gordimer, Nadine, The Lying Days (Victor Gollancz, London, 1953)
Huddleston, Trevor, Naught for your Comfort (Collins, London, 1956)

This last was among the first volumes belonging to Helena I ever found. You will recall that I was particularly taken with the dust-jacket. I flipped to the copyright page to check the date. Then I ran my eye down the inside flap: This is the testament . . . burning questions of the day . . . burns like a

. . . .

beacon . . . challenge which no person of conscience can ignore . . . Jacket design by Kenneth Farnhill . . . Price in Union of S. Africa 15/- net. I groomed a dog-ear with my fingernails. And it was then that I noticed a small white triangle protruding from between the black-edged board and the dust-jacket. I tugged it, and three photographs tumbled out.

I arranged these photographs under my reading-lamp. They were black and white snapshots, about six centimetres by eight, with wavy edges. Two of them were snaps of the sort people feel obliged to keep even though they're practically worthless. One showed a babe in arms with its face obscured by the fringe of a shawl. The other showed three men in swimming-trunks forming a pyramid, two standing side by side and the third straddling their shoulders. The pyramid was on the point of collapse, all three men were moving, all their faces were blurred. Even so, I could tell at a glance that none of them was Julius P. Lofsky.

Have you noticed that snapshots have been getting larger over the years? Very few of them will fit in a wallet these days – not that I'm the sort of person who would carry a snapshot around in a wallet.

The third photograph showed Helena and her parents. There was no caption on the reverse side, just the number 9056/3 written in pencil and the word EPSON, the trade name of the photographic paper, repeated in red ink seven times (and an eighth EP with the SON cut off), but there was no doubt in my mind that it was Helena. She looked nothing like my imaginings, and yet I felt an acute pang of recognition; in fact, the argument between these two contradictory certainties was what persuaded me that it must be her.

I gave the photo a sniffing, but all I turned up was the faintest hint of glue. It may be true, as I've been told, that the human nose is an organ in decline, habituated to stenches and increasingly incapable of drawing finer distinctions.

Helena and her parents are posed on a speckled tile path

. . . .

that runs at a diagonal across a patch of lawn. On either side of the path are beds of impatiens kept in check by toothy brick borders. The garden wall, angling away to left and right like the arrowhead to the pathway's shaft, is made of pale brick, solid for a dozen courses, then surmounted at intervals by square posts half a dozen courses high, with the spaces in between filled by panels of twirly wrought-iron. The gate at the end of the path, visible as broken corkscrews and drill-bits in the spaces between the three figures, has a matching design. From the disposition of the houses in the background, and two streetlights shaped like morning glories on delicate stems, I can tell that Helena's house is on a corner stand. Those houses are made of the same brick as her garden wall and have corrugated-iron roofs. Their windows are set into frames of chunky white concrete and dimmed by cataracts of venetian blinds. One of the houses has a porthole in the wall next to the front door. Another has a hedge as smooth as a concrete quay and a ragamuffin palm-tree.

I know these bricks, these houses. Although the photograph is black and white, I can see the marmalade colour of them, the glazed rind of brick and the plaster thick and white as pith. This is a Highlands North house, a Cyrildene house, an Orange Grove house. The streetlights nod against a wan blue sky, crossed in one corner by telephone lines.

Helena is a head taller than her parents, who stand on either side of her. Mr and Mrs Shein are middle-aged and look like immigrants. Mr Shein wears flannels, a loud tie, a bristly pullover. The cuffs of his shirt are pulled up with sleevebands, and this has the effect of enlarging his hands, which dangle in hollow fists at his sides as if they are dreaming of pushing a barrow. His pants are too short: you can see his socks, and shoes as round and shiny as aubergines. Mrs Shein wears a dark skirt, and a cardigan with raglan sleeves over a white blouse buttoned to the neck. She has strappy wedge-heeled shoes and a boy's haircut. Her left hand seems to be holding in her stomach. Her right hand

....

rests on Helena's hip, disembodied, severed from the encircling arm.

It is hard to believe that two such dumpy, badly dressed Europeans could produce this statuesque beauty of a daughter, looming over them despite her flat black pumps. She is wearing a sleeveless halter-neck top in a dark colour, brightened by a chain and locket. Her skirt, which is soft and full, falls to mid-calf. The skirt is a moon colour with circular motifs – flowers or cogs – scattered over it. I imagine that they are earth colours.

What I have failed to imagine is her black hair, her dark eyes, her olive skin. She is no wispy blonde. With a name like Helena Shein, I might have known.

I saw her cross a tiled lobby. At the foot of the stairs she stepped out of her shoes and then quietly ascended. I followed, scooping up the shoes as I passed, watching her brown feet and the heart-shaped prints they left on the polished treads. On the second-floor landing it dawned on me that the photograph had been lying undetected for all these months. How many times had I held the book in my hands and failed to feel the warmth beneath its skin? The books had blunted my curiosity by surrendering their treasures too easily.

I'm ashamed to say that I fell upon the other books in a frenzy, ripping off their jackets, fondling their boards and flaps, turning them upside-down and shaking them, thrusting my fingers into their spines, squinting into their pockets. I became so engrossed in the search that I forgot my Bibliography entirely. The search failed to turn up anything new.

The Rajah of Jehangar abducts Mistral with the intention of turning her into his concubine, but she escapes.

The next day I was reminded of the Bibliography and sat down to it again. But I think I was never meant to complete the task, for as soon as I ran my eye over the twelve entries on my list I was struck by a peculiarity so obvious that for

....

the life of me I cannot explain how it had escaped my notice before (it surely cannot have escaped yours): the predominance of the year 1956.

I looked through the rest of the books. Scores of them had been published or purchased in that year too. Why had Helena read so much in 1956? Historically speaking, it was not the most memorable of years. The Soviet invasion of Hungary came to mind, and the Olympics in Melbourne. Of course, I was born in 1956 . . .

Then it hit me like a ton of books: we were brothers and sisters, the books and I, Helena's offspring. Helena's abandoned children! Cast out into the streets, thrown upon the mercy of strangers. A sense of kinship with the books overwhelmed me as I gathered my long-lost family into my arms. 'They are mine, and I am theirs,' I said with Birrell.

When I had regained my composure, this new understanding of my relationship to the library made me a little uncomfortable about my feelings towards Helena and the rather overwrought way I had been burying my nose in my siblings. I resolved to adopt a more proper attitude towards them all.

Aunt Emilie reveals to the Grand Duke that his son, Prince Nikolai, is in love with Mistral – who is the Duke's lost daughter! 'There was so much bitterness and spite in Emilie's passionate declamation that instinctively Mistral turned towards the Prince as if for protection and found him beside her. He took her hand in his and held it tightly. She clung to him, thankful for his strength. She knew that he was as astonished as she was at what was occurring. Yet neither of them could say anything. They could only cling together, two children lost in a wood of terror and bewilderment.'

Naturally I now began to take a special interest in the books published in 1956, my peers. But close as I felt to them, there was one with which I acknowledged an even deeper rapport, and that was *A Ghost in Monte Carlo*.

. . . .

I examined the triangle formed by *A Ghost in Monte Carlo*, Helena and myself with a profound sense of disquiet. I had seen the Cartland clan huddled together in the shops, under signs that said EXCHANGE ONLY, chattering away. It amazed me to think that a book of their persuasion might be the one that held the key to our impossible love story – especially when there was so much other good literature to choose from.

A Ghost in Monte Carlo was Barbara Cartland's forty-second *Novel*. She had also published one *Political Novel*, called *Sleeping Swords*, under the pen-name Barbara McCorquodale; a work of *Philosophy*, called *Touch the Stars*; and a work of *Sociology*, called *You in the Home*. This precocious fecundity notwithstanding, who could have fore-seen then that another four hundred and seventy-five books would issue from her imagination?

I neglected to mention, I think, that the photograph of Helena and her parents contained a priceless piece of information: leaning into the picture from the right, on a striped black and white pole, was a white sign with the words BUS HALTE painted on it in black, and below them the stencilled number 15. I hardly need to stress how important such a route number might prove to be in locating the house in which Helena grew up. But perhaps I could add a tangential comment: I believe that this bus-stop was for the exclusive use of whites. The sign for a black bus-stop would have included the words SECOND CLASS. The sign is beauti-fully painted. The question of whether the pole is white with black stripes or vice versa I leave to those with an interest in natural phenomena like the quagga.

Mistral, awakening from a six-day swoon occasioned by her aunt's death, finds that the Grand Duke has claimed her as his daughter and that her wardrobe has therefore been filled with clothes. 'Never had she seen such an array of lovely clothes. There were gowns of every colour and description,

....

and their hues rivalled the very colours of the flowers in the garden. There were dresses of blue, pink, green, rose and yellow. Mistral stared at them with wide eyes . . . The one thing she had noticed immediately was that there was nothing grey amongst them. There was not even a pair of shoes of that colour.'

I came round, at last, to certainties. I took sensible steps. Inquiries at the Information Office on Van der Bijl Square revealed that bus route 15 went through Orange Grove. I was not surprised. Whether the route had remained unchanged since 1956 no one could say, but I was optimistic.

One morning in May, at 9.45, I boarded a number 15 double-decker outside the magistrate's courts in Main Street. I sat at the top, in front, and had the entire upper deck to myself. As luck would have it we went up Rissik Street, and so I obtained unusual new perspectives on no fewer than three vanished bookshops. When the bus turned into 10th Street, Orange Grove, I alighted and began to walk. My plan was to follow the bus route through the suburb, paying special attention to corner houses in the vicinity of stops. If I did not locate the Sheins' house in this way, I would start a more wide-ranging search in the neighbouring streets and, if necessary, the adjacent suburbs.

I felt confident: considering my aptitude for finding books, turning up something as large as a house seemed relatively simple. Even so, it was laughably easy. I had not gone more than four or five blocks when I spotted one of the houses in the background of the photograph. The palm-tree louring over house and garden gave it away at once. I was almost disappointed.

Helena's house was exactly where it was supposed to be, although it had vanished behind an eight-foot wall. Where the twirly gate had been there was now a wooden door with a yellow and white striped awning and an intercom. There was a sign that said the property was protected by 24-hour armed response. Another sign gave the address of Mr Paving.

. . . .

I sat down on the bus-stop bench facing the door and opened *A Ghost in Monte Carlo*. I had been saving the final pages for this moment.

Madame Boulanger tells Mistral that Sir Robert still loves her: he has called her name in a delirium. Mistral seeks him out at the Hotel Hermitage. 'He held her closer to him, his lips against her hair. He knew then that this was what he had searched for all his life, that his search was at an end, his goal in sight. With a sense of urgency at the passing of time he sought her lips. "I love you," he whispered against her mouth and knew there was no need for words as she surrendered herself to the passion behind his kiss.'

As I raised the book to my lips the door opened and Helena appeared. I gazed at her over the top of the book, while she double-locked the door behind her and secured an enormous bunch of keys in a shiny blue handbag.

She didn't look a day older. She was wearing the skirt she wore in the photograph, but I was delighted to discover that it was a sunny yellow, and splashed with whorls of bright blue and green. A white poplin blouse set off her brown skin to perfection. There was a chill in the autumn air, but she didn't feel it. She swung her bag over her shoulder and walked in the direction of Louis Botha Avenue.

I stowed my book in the pocket of my blazer and followed, like a blind man, the tapping of her heels along the pavement. I floated in her fragrant wake, light-headed with the scent of orange-blossom and patent leather. At every step the book in my pocket thumped like a heart against my chest. On the cool fabric of her blouse, between her sculpted shoulder-blades, I saw in English Times the legend: THE END – and I walked towards it.

....

Folding

MARY FLANAGAN

PIERS

is my best friend, but sometimes I can't stand him.

He used to come up to London and take over my tent, sleep in it day and night, then borrow money for art materials and mope about his sadistic Dad or moon over some girl. His contribution to our livelihood consisted in what he called cooking. Can you believe it, he once made me a dish that consisted of nothing but chillies. Oh, maybe there was a little rice. But not much. All the money I gave him had gone on the hot stuff because 'the colours were so acidy'. Naturally he ate the lot. And I was really hungry.

When he dyed his hair green, I didn't think much of it, being a carrot-top myself. What did annoy me was not being able to budge him from the tent which is silver (my favourite colour) and the product of very advanced engineering. Everyone's jealous of my tent. There's no space for visitors here, so I use it as a guest room or sit in it when I'm gearing myself up for a new painting. Hermione's another one who's plotting a takeover. She claims it improves her dreams. It's the shape, she says. I'll tell you about Hermione in a minute.

Piers had to drop out of art school in his first year because his Dad wouldn't give him any money, and the council wouldn't give him a grant because his Dad was too rich. A typical contemporary dilemma. The reason his Dad's so mean is that A. he has five kids, all boys, and B. he didn't go for the green hair, and C. he blames Piers for what happened to the twins.

They're disturbed, can't go to school and live in this sort

of private world. So Piers (you've got to admit this was pretty altruistic of him) spent weeks teaching them to draw cartoons of extra-terrestrials, and now that's all they do. But I have to say they're brilliant, you'd be amazed, maybe some kind of idiots savants, and okay, so no school will have them, but at least they don't watch as many video nasties as most eight-year-olds. And the fact that they don't talk except to each other might be regarded by some parents as a blessing. I think Piers' father ought to be grateful to him instead of throwing him out on the street. I guess the last straw was when he lent him some money to pay off his Barclaycard and Piers spent it on a pair of Roller Blades and moved up to London for good. For a month he careened around Brixton, a menace to pensioners and small dogs, and was known locally as 'No Brakes'. It would have gone on indefinitely if he hadn't been relieved of the skates by a gang of highly dangerous ten-year-olds. After that he went from roller blades to Iceland. Read dozens of books about it, saw films, wouldn't talk about anything else.

So you're probably getting the picture: Piers is obsessive. Obsession runs in the family. Look at his mother, having nothing but boys, all blond and all bananas. She just didn't know when to stop, so now she's on an express train to the locked ward. And his Dad – a repulsive goulash of frustration and greed. No wonder Piers is weird. With that angel face and scraggly green hair growing out to its original white-blond, and his trousers too short and his clothes a mix of charity shops, he looks a bona fide flake. But I'll tell you something – and we all believe this – he's special, maybe even brilliant. Other people, mainly adults, just dismiss him as lazy or brain-damaged. But we think he may be the most interesting of us all. We can't explain why, so don't ask us. We just know. And if you're wondering who we are, we're the

PYGs
which stands for Promising Young Geniuses, though of course that's an irony. We're a family, and we've been a

....

family for years. Since we were little kids: Comprehensive, then Grammar day students (admitted on our brains), foundation course and now art school. We've been closer to each other than we've been to parents or step-parents or siblings. The group is basically me (I'm Sam), Hermione, Piers, and Louise, who wants to be an actress when she grows up. We're the vortex around which the rest of them rotate – old school friends still trapped in Kent, art school friends, and the sort of trainee friends we make at work. We all have part-time jobs in cafés and pubs and boutiques because our grants are so small. The government's whittling off ten per cent every year cause they think we'll value our education more if we have to starve and beg for it. Most of us already owe money since we've taken out student loans to pay our rent in a panic or our bills at the London Graphics Centre.

And I bet you thought art school was a doddle, full of piss ants and poseurs. We may be mere aspirants, but we work our arses off. It's tough, and it means there's not much clubbing any more, except for the school dances which are okay but so crowded that sometimes you can't get in. So it's lucky we've got

HER

to generate social stimulation. Her being Hermione, aka Herricane, the woman in my life, my other best friend. We all hang out mainly at her flat in Covent Garden. She's very idealistic, wants to make cheap fashion for the masses, thinks they'll all be better people if they have something fun to wear. And she has this talent for in-home entertainment. She'll switch into high gear over any excuse for a party. And she's wildly inventive, insists on fancy dress. There was The Fig Leaf Party, The Storms Party (I was a cyclone), The Fleurs du Mal Party, The Plant Party. Now this is difficult, given our limited means, but it keeps our imaginations fit and sharp.

When they first meet her, people suspect her of being on speed, but she's not. She's naturally high, doesn't take anything at all. Some girls I know think she's a bimbo or

....

that she's imagining she's on *Absolutely Fabulous* cause she wears these daft glasses, but they're wrong. It's true she practically has to do a colour study to get dressed in the morning, but that doesn't mean she's an air head. For Her every day is special; every day is a fashion statement.

She was great when I Came Out. She went with me and my boyfriend to the Gay Pride March to show solidarity, even though she's a flaming hetero and likes vanilla sex. Whatever you're doing, you get her entire support. And she's not restricted by conventional good taste. For instance we went to see *Boxing Helena* which was really the pits and we knew it would be, but that's the point. It's our principle to investigate everything. Besides, we like laughing at bad art. But don't worry, we've seen *Wittgenstein* three times because Her's Mum pays for her ICA membership.

Sometimes she annoys me deeply and I tease her about her surreal gear and her affairs with the Irishman or the Albanian or the Jamaican (Her prefers foreigners), and make her life a quick season in hell. But I really love the way she's just so alive and open and off the wall. So I admit I was baffled when

KYOKO

moved in. I couldn't see how they'd ever get on. But Her and Louise needed another flatmate fast, and, like I said, she's keen on foreigners.

Kyoko was sweet and all with her baby voice and an accent like she had a satsuma in her mouth. You'd catch about every fourth word. And she had this sexy way of tossing her hair from one side to the other, almost as if she were doing it in slow motion. (I don't know what it was supposed to signify, but probably they have a name for it in Japan.) She was very formal and secretive, the dead opposite of Her who always says exactly what she's thinking. I've got a rep for being a bit inscrutable, but Kyoko surpassed even my cool. She kept her bedroom door permanently locked, and you got the feeling she thought our behaviour could do

....

with a lot of improvement. She complained that Her had too many men in the flat and that Louise smoked too much. She wanted visitors restricted to two hours a week. Well, Her sorted Kyoko out pretty smartly on these issues, and soon she was part of our parties and having a good time in her subdued way, though she abstained from the fancy dress.

She worked at the Osaka Diner slinging sushi and went to English classes three days a week. She said she'd come to London because she was fascinated by English culture, and we said what's that, but she didn't see the joke. (Though she smiled a lot, she didn't have much of a sense of humour.) She said she wanted to know everything about England, and I have to admit she was very up on her Seventies Retro and took us to a couple of clubs that even we didn't know about. They were seedy and sort of comfortable. Unfortunately they too were beyond our means.

Kyoko wasn't making a bundle either, and we thought she was as financially embarrassed as the rest of us until one day she appeared with three pairs of shoes that sent Her into orbit and which Kyoko confessed had cost *only* £90 each in the Sales. She was proud of her bargains, you could tell. She had a good haircut too (styled especially for throwing back and forth I guess) though she wore it in bunches a lot of the time and also plaits, which made her look about twelve. She was sort of cute.

In her spare moments she'd sit at the kitchen table doing Origami. She said the folding process was good for Stilling Your Mind. But since we weren't interested in stillness in any form, it was hard to get excited about it. She was also a great cook and began making us shrimp cakes, and tempuras and noodles. She didn't mind assuming the domestic burden and produced her Oriental din-dins without any sign of resentment or boredom. Inevitably

PIERS
joined us for one of them. We hadn't seen him for a while. Hard to imagine, but he'd been working in a pet shop.

....

They'd fired him after two weeks. He confided to me that his Iceland phase was over and that black moss and hot geysers and films about the threatened life styles of fisher folk and even Bjork didn't thrill him any more. He was terminally depressed. Since he'd lost his job he didn't have enough money to work on his hand-made comic books. He'd been hoping to turn these into a cottage industry and peddle them at dances and demos. (They were a combination of post-cyberpunk, German fantasist kitsch circa 1905 and Rupert Bear. Actually, they were bloody good.) The only hope of regaining psychic health, he told me, was Japan. He'd been thinking a lot about Japan, Japan was looming, he might be going to get a Thing about Japan. Now you see where all this has been leading. I'm not just rambling, you know, though I've been accused of it.

Their relationship surprised us all and we are not, especially me, easily surprised. (People telegraph their intentions. It's a kind of body language. I pick it up.) Her told me that one afternoon she came back from a day in the Dyeing Room to find Piers and Kyoko at the kitchen table folding and unfolding little squares of coloured paper. As we already knew, she was brilliant at it. She could do Swallow in Flight and Mountain Village. (She had these tiny immaculate fingers that were fascinating to watch.) The two of them weren't saying much, just sipping pale green tea from cups so small they could have been thimbles. They barely said hello to Her, they were so into it, and it wasn't long before, as the instruction book put it, they were

'SPENDING PLAYFUL TIME TOGETHER'
on a serious basis. But don't interpret serious as sex. There didn't seem to be any of that. Kyoko retired to her locked room alone and stayed there until seven in the morning. So if they were doing it, they'd have to be pretty discreet, and pretty quick. But I'm sure they weren't. They were focused exclusively on Her's kitchen table. I mean it was impossible to sit down and have a coffee any more, especially for poor

....

Louise, who was reduced to blowing smoke out of the window of the freezing bathroom. (Her had made one or two concessions.) So we'd go into the sitting room and huddle on the floor in front of the gas fire like a Neolithic family in its cave.

Meanwhile the kitchen had become this *bon ton* nursery school. Piers should have been looking for a job; how could he make his comics otherwise? But as usual he had opted for Never-Never Land.

Kyoko started him off on the basics: Envelope, Boat, Pinwheel, Flounder. He'd come into the flat – no one knew where he was living; we hoped it wasn't a doorway – whenever she wasn't at the Osaka Diner, and they'd get straight down to their Paper Folding Projects.

'3. Fold A upward towards the midline and fold wing B to the diagonal line.' (I peeked at the kiddy's instruction book she'd bought to help him practise when she wasn't around.)

'4. Turn form. Pull out wing C, unfolding that side of the fin so that corners D and E can be folded backwards.

5. There is your flounder.'

And so it was. Happy little flounder.

Kyoko, Japan and the playgroup atmosphere were allowing Piers to remain the child he wanted to be. Was this healthy? We analysed at length. We speculated. We watched spellbound as the two of them made little green frogs jump around on the kitchen table. Kyoko would press their paper bottoms with her tiny fingernail and – boing! But it was clear they only wanted us as an audience for their accomplishments. When they were deep in their paper projects they preferred to be left strictly alone, like a sick cat.

Once in a while they'd take a break and go off to play Frisbee in the park, returning home happy as toddlers. Then it was straight back to the stacks of coloured paper. Louise complained that they were depleting the rainforests, it was totally irresponsible of them and did Kyoko know that Japan had destroyed the Indonesian hardwoods? They should be

....

planting at least fifteen trees to compensate for the damage they were doing. They said they were very sorry. They hadn't meant to upset her. Kyoko looked as if she'd never heard of Indonesia. They were undistractable. We were worried about Piers. Her complained that she had to gobble her muesli in mad haste before the kitchen reverted to an occupied zone no one dared disturb. When they were at it, the silence was like a church. It could be damned intimidating.

Kyoko guided Piers on to more complex forms: Butterfly, Pig, Gondola. And she was cooking for him too. And we were no longer welcome. Those precious little meals were now for Piers' exclusive delectation. He who subsisted on a diet of vegetable samosas and Bourbon Creams and made dinners that consisted of nothing but chillies. She was endowing him with a palate. They'd whisper over their noodles, do the washing up, leaving the kitchen as immaculate as an operating theatre, then carry on with Stork in Flight.

'7. Turn form and repeat step six.
8. Fold point E to point F.
9. Turn and repeat step 8.
10. Fold points G and H to meet in the middle.'
Christ.

They were relentless. They worked straight through the Satanic Knickers Party which lasted until five a.m. and was extremely rowdy. Piers did his best not to let the side down and wore Her's green satin shorts, a camouflage jacket and a pair of Edna Everage glasses. As usual, Kyoko wore a tight little blue dress and bunches. They didn't really participate. They'd moved on to Grouping Animals and Other Figures.

Piers was now living in the flat, sleeping when Kyoko was at the diner or at school, waking up when she came home. Then the flat was like a sombre nursery. Two good clever children quietly keeping busy. He continued to bed down on the Lilo while she stayed locked in her room, safe with

....

her secrets. Their achievements were everywhere: animals, trees, houses, pinwheels, butterflies and birds covered every surface, so that there was no space to throw your books or jacket or set down a beer glass. Her was beginning to feel claustrophobic. She told me as she was backcombing her hair into a beehive (a style she planned to reintroduce) that she was staying with the Albanian for a few days then going to one of her step-parents where it was warm. (I think it was the Camden step-parent.) She said she was beginning to feel like Tippy Hedren in *The Birds*, and I understood what she meant – all those paper beaks and paper snouts turned towards you, seeming to follow your movements. They were taking over. It was creepy. Soon there wouldn't be room for us.

I didn't intend to come round while Her and Louise were away. I had a new lover who needed a lot of attention. The women and I thought maybe if we left the Toddlers alone they'd finally Do It and break the Origami spell which, we'd concluded, was nothing but sublimated lust. I didn't antici-pate the

HALF-TERM HYSTERIA
that was to wreck my romance.

I'd decided not to go back to Kent and my usual holiday job at 'The Happy Eater'. I'd swapped the Garden of England for Brixton Hill. My parents were doing their nuts but I convinced them by some deft reasoning that ten days in London would be better for my art, and that anyway I'd found a job in the men's department of Harvey Nichols, which wasn't true. Madness, since I was desperate for dosh. But Robert was very seductive.

Eleven forty-five p.m. and we're entwined in the silver tent watching *Goodfellas* on my eight-inch television when the phone goes. Should I answer it? Don't, says Robert. I answer it. Fucking idiot.

It was Kyoko, crying and spluttering in Japanese so that she sounded sort of dense and explosive at the same time. I

....

couldn't make out what had happened but I did understand that she was insisting I come round to the flat. Immediately. She was terrified. She couldn't be alone. Was the problem Piers, I asked? Yes. Who else?

I explained to Robert about Piers being my best friend and that he'd done something crazy and that Kyoko was very upset and that, reluctant though I was, I felt obliged to go and sort the matter out. Now. Robert was unimpressed by my devotion and expressed no wish to join me in a tube ride to Covent Garden which would involve a sprint for the last Victoria line train. So I left him brooding in the tent. Friends come first.

When I arrived Kyoko was in full Madam Butterfly mode. It took me quite a while to understand that the focus of this drama was the answering machine. She was expecting me to translate a lengthy and incoherent message from Piers. The part she thought she understood had already sent her into a tail spin, so I wasn't very keen to tell her the rest.

Well, he was drunk. Other substances may also have been involved. There was some loud Techno in the background and a lot of excited people. I had to replay the tape three times, flinching frequently. How was I going to break this to her? Best be blunt.

'1. He says he's in love with you.' Tears rose in her eyes. I assumed she was touched.

'2. You are the only woman in the world for him.

3. He thinks you should get married – to each other – and live together.

4. If you say no he will do something terrible to himself. I wouldn't worry too much about that bit.

5. He's waiting for your answer.'

In between were sentiments so treacly that even I am embarrassed to put them to paper.

She was looking at me like a confused hamster. Then she started to scream.

'It must *not*! It must *not*!

She was running around the kitchen as if searching for

....

65

shavings to burrow in. Her hair was sticking to her wet cheeks. I felt sorry for her.

'Can I make you a tea, Kyoko? What about a Pepsi? I'm sure I have an old pill here somewhere.' I searched my pockets half-heartedly. I wasn't awfully good at this.

Still, when she begged me to stay the night at the flat I couldn't refuse. It was too late to go home to Robert anyway. He'd just have to understand. She was terrified Piers was going to show up and commit some atrocity. I said she must know him better than that by now. He was incapable of violence, bless his heart. But it was like Mummy's perfect darling had turned into this *enfant terrible* who was threatening to murder her with love. I slept on the Lilo while she triple-locked herself in her bedroom. What the hell does she keep in there, I wondered as I often did. No one had ever been inside. I hoped Robert would be pleased to know that my last thoughts were of him.

Of course when I got back to the flat the next morning he was gone. No note, the ingrate. But I didn't have time to moon about Robert. I had to find Piers. I called everyone I knew, the entire extended family, but no one had seen him. So I decided to go back to my new painting. The one with the X-rayed silver bodies being nibbled by pink rats. (I'm calling it *Rat Love*.) The flat was freezing so I had to work in a woollen jacket, scarf and hiking boots that I've had since I was thirteen. I'd like to live somewhere else, I really would. I don't enjoy being a starving artist, but what can one do with the Tories' slash and burn policy on housing grants. I suppose they figure that only the fittest will survive.

I worked all night. I forgot about everyone, including John Patten, Kyoko and Robert. The next morning my beloved rang, all reproachful, and we made a date for that night. Then Kyoko called, marginally calmer since Her had returned, with the Colombian this time, and she now felt protected. Finally Piers phoned, reversing the charges as usual. He was at the Bagel Bar outside Charing Cross

....

station; everything was 'sort of freakily peculiar'; he didn't have any money. Could I come and get him?

Since he looked like an exhumed corpse, I escorted him to the crypt of St Martin's for a tea. We sat as far away from the food counter as possible, so as not to be tempted. Where the hell had he been?

He said a guy he'd met in Brockwell Park had invited him to a transvestite party in Peckham, and he thought maybe this guy had given him something he really shouldn't have had (Piers has a low drug ceiling) because he'd passed out and woken up in a pink Fifties girdle and a pair of wedgies. He'd felt very cold. It wasn't really his scene. No comment. Anyway, I said, taking a stern tone, what about Kyoko? Did he realize how upset she was? Was he toying with her affections? (I was feeling protective of her.) Her reaction to his message had been quite extreme. To which he replied,

'What message?'

God he's a nightmare. You see why I can't stand him. Even if he is my best friend. I told him he was a dweeb and that he had shit for brains. But all I got was incomplete sentences, something about amnesia and that fallen angel look. I took him back to my flat and put him in the silver tent to chill out. He thrashed and moaned for a few hours while I worked on my painting. At ten the phone rang. I'd completely forgotten my date with Robert. I had a lot on my mind was my only excuse, though it was a true excuse. I told him to come round, and he agreed. He was radiating a lot of bad vibes. Bor-ing. When I went back to the bedroom, Piers was awake and drawing comic strips. This seemed hopeful. I looked at what he'd done (with my materials) and thought maybe he really was a genius, though I realize that's an outmoded concept.

By the next morning he'd remembered. He ran the pathetic scenario past me over a bowl of my Raisin Bran, with a surly Robert as audience. (I'd decided I liked him surly. It's something about me Her doesn't understand. She just wants to be happy. There really is no accounting for

....

67

taste.) Piers said it was all a misunderstanding. Yes, he did love Kyoko, more than anyone, probably, but as a mother, or a sister. Yes, he did want to be with her for ever, but as a friend. He wanted them to go eternally on, doing Origami and eating noodles. Was this a whole new kind of love? Sounded like it might be, I said. He claimed he couldn't recall the marriage bit, but if that was what she now expected, he'd be happy to sacrifice himself. You dork, I said, she doesn't want to marry you, she never wants to see you again. You've offended her delicate Japanese sensibilities; what the hell is wrong with you?

As the magnitude of his crime became clear he grew more despondent until finally he was crying. Robert left in disgust, and we agreed to meet that night to see *Jurassic Park* for the second time. Piers' penitence was touching. How could he make her forgive him and take him back into the flat? And she'd been teaching him The Peacock. He couldn't proceed without her. He'd lost interest in everything else, even his hand-made comics.

Well, I knew what the next question was going to be: would I go round to the flat and explain to Kyoko, say he was a jolly good fellow, despite his eccentricities, and how excruciating Origami cold turkey was. I was to report that he would rather have died than distress her. (I told him he was going too far here and would only frighten her.) I said I really felt I'd done enough and that it was now up to him to either repair the wreckage of his life or kick the Origami habit for good.

In the end I went round, of course I did. Louise was there, in despair because she'd just been fired from her job at the King Tut sandwich bar. Just like that – out. It was what we all dreaded. And it was the third time in five months that she'd got the boot. No recourse for the part-time employed.

Her, wearing a purple sort of Tennessee Williams satin dressing gown and Doc Martens boots, was feeding Louise bickies and cocoa. She's quite maternal really. So where was Kyoko, I asked. I'd been delegated to say a few words to

....

her. Piers needed help. We had to reinstate him in her affections and in her paper projects. He was in terrible shape. Funny you should ask, said Her. Kyoko's expecting

A VISITOR

from Japan. Who? They didn't know. We speculated about the mystery guest and discussed Her's Design and Make for the rest of the afternoon. Then Her suggested we nip round to the Polo before the queue built up, so off we went. I noticed that the flat was now an Origami-free zone. No beaks, snouts or fins. It felt a bit empty without them.

We got back about nine. Just as we were approaching Her's doorway, a primrose-yellow Mercedes pulled up and out stepped Kyoko and this extremely well-heeled Japanese dude. She introduced us all to Mr Ishiwara. She looked hideously embarrassed. We followed them up the stairs in silence, and they immediately made their excuses and said good-night. Mr Ishiwara must rest. The flight from Tokyo, you know, is very long. Then they retired. *To her bedroom.* We heard the locks go click, click, click.

Then we all started to talk, or rather whisper, at once: lots of I don't believe it's and I told you so's. We were so engrossed we forgot to check the answering machine. Among about a dozen messages for Her were two for me. One from Robert, who said he'd been waiting for an hour and a half at the bar at the Clapham Picture House, and what was I playing at; another from guess who, begging Kyoko to release him from his Origami hell. We agreed Kyoko would probably be happy for Mr Ishiwara not to hear that one, so we erased it.

Events went very fast after that. Robert agreed to give me one more chance. We made a date and I waited two hours in the ICA bar, nursing a beer and reading. I guessed he was making a point. Okay, I thought, fair enough. At least I'd finished *The Foucault Reader*. But I had a feeling Robert and I were history. I walked to Green Park and caught a south-bound Victoria line train just as the doors were closing.

....

I could hear the phone ringing as I climbed the stairs. It had an insistent sound. I answered. It was Hermione in tears. They'd been burgled. But what have you got worth stealing – except your art, I added, to be polite. It wasn't her loss, she said. It was Kyoko and Mr Ishiwara, and it was extremely serious. I had to come right away, the police were there. If I hurried I could catch the last Piccadilly line train at Green Park.

I went to the bedroom and put on the new jumper Mum had sent me, and there I found Piers curled up in the silver tent, clutching the Origami book in his right hand. I didn't have time to ask him how the hell he'd got into the flat, so I left him in foetal bliss and set off for Covent Garden. I felt like a sort of bushwhacked Superman.

My powers of cool were tested to the limit because I met with a scene of such social chaos that I began to think I had wandered into the last act of *The Bacchae*. The police were questioning Louise. Her and Kyoko were in the kitchen crying and slagging each other off in English and Japanese. Whatever had happened I was defending Her, because Mr Ishiwara was sitting at the table – in Piers' place – looking very unpleasant. Why don't we *all* sit down, I suggested, firm but fair, we can work it out. And I thought of that little git Piers all cosy in my silver tent, and I have to tell you I felt annoyed. Very annoyed.

That was the night

THE KYOKO MYSTERY
was solved. And Piers was noticeable by his absence. The rest of us suddenly seemed to be actors in his very compli-cated dream. And Jesus, was it complicated.

I worked out, through the women's tears and hysterics, that serious accusations had been made.

'They think I'm a jewel thief and that my friends are jewel thieves,' shrieked The Herricane. 'What makes them think I'd want to wear their stupid jewels? I'm sure they're totally ugly, and I didn't even know they were in the flat!'

....

Mr Ishiwara maintained his implacable, minatory calm. His cufflinks gleamed in the overhead light. I couldn't help inspecting the print on his silk tie. Her and I exchanged looks. She'd been doing the same thing.

I made the women sit down. I told Kyoko not to talk rubbish. I asked her to explain what had happened. I put the kettle on. The two policemen came and went, checking and re-checking the kitchen window. Nothing was broken, the flat was on the first and second floors. How did the thieves get in was the question. I didn't think these particular plods would be providing any answers. But it was clear to yours truly that it had been a credit card job.

Reader, I will keep you in suspense no longer. It turned out Kyoko had been the princess with the treasure all along, because what she'd been guarding in that triple-locked bedroom was a suitcase full of loot – all presents from Mr Ishiwara – and a substantial amount of cash, also belonging to Mr Ishiwara. Sweet little Kyoko, I thought, so he's her sugar daddy. In addition more cash, which he'd brought with him, a camera and a Game Boy so advanced it wouldn't hit the UK market until 1996, were all missing. Her said this was the first she'd heard about their stupid Game Boy. (Her is a bit of a technophobe.) The fight was in danger of escalating. I reminded Kyoko of all she'd said about Stilling The Mind, but she didn't seem to know what I was talking about. Mr Ishiwara certainly seemed to know about Stilling The Mind, but in a sort of deadly way, like he was concentrating on my absence or even my demise.

I reasoned that it was impossible for Her to have been involved in the robbery, attempting every so often to make eye contact with Mr Ishiwara. I wanted to persuade him of my integrity, but he continued to regard me as a low type. I'm sure he thought I was the criminal. Finally everyone was too tired to carry on, so Her helped me blow up the Lilo and we all went to bed. We needed strength for the next instalment.

I heard the front door bang about 6 a.m., but fell

....

immediately back to sleep, exhausted by my efforts at mediation. Now I know how poor old Edward Heath feels. I was awoken at eight by more raised female voices coming from the kitchen. All I could think was that I must protect Her from any further harassment. So I leapt up and rushed to her defence in nothing but my Y-fronts. And it was bloody cold. Kyoko took one appalled look at me and fled. I felt her modesty was a bit *de trop* in light of recent events.

I asked what the hell was going on now and was told to cover my nakedness, the fingerprint man was coming at eight-thirty.

When I returned, dressed, Her and Louise were sitting at the table, their heads in their hands. Louise said she was getting a migraine, could I get hold of any morphine. Even Her looked knackered. Then they proceeded to fire off more revelations. Christ, how many can you take? I remembered Piers. He, more than anyone, would be interested to know that Mr Ishiwara was Kyoko's

HUSBAND?!

'They don't live together,' Her explained. 'I don't really understand their arrangement, but apparently lots of Japanese girls do it. They've got to be married. Isn't that *horrible*?'

It then turned out that Mr Husband was furious about the loss of his lolly and had stormed back to Tokyo without even visiting Madame Tussaud's. Kyoko was prostrate. What would Piers dream us all into next? I rang my flat, and he was still there, probably eating my Raisin Bran and drinking my Nescafé.

'Oh hi,' was all he could say.

I got abusive. I mean I know this is the wrong approach with Piers; names will never hurt him. But I'd decided it was time he sorted out his miserable life, and that I was the person to make him do it. I ordered him to appear at Her's flat on the double. Naturally he didn't have any money, so I had to tell him where my emergency £5 note was stashed. Now *I* was broke. But at least I could maybe stop being a

....

character in a lunatic's dream. Then I announced to Her and Louise that we were all leaving. The wretched Kyoko could deal with the fingerprint man. Who knew, maybe he liked Origami.

Her was going to work, so we all went round to The Café Blah. She managed to sneak us a cappuccino and a chocolate muffin. I could not remember when I had last eaten. Now we felt sorry for Kyoko. After all, none of this was really her fault. She should not have bullied Her, but then she'd been traumatized. (Of course Her had already forgiven Kyoko, like the good girl she is.) And Hubby's impending visit explained some of her reaction to Piers' proposal. And Ishiwara was clearly a shit. We hoped Kyoko would stay in the flat long enough to run 'accidentally' into Piers. This might be his only chance to mend the rupture, and he'd certainly come off better in the light of Ishiwara's abrupt departure. But would Kyoko allow Piers to console her?

After another purloined muffin I went home. I needed some time in the silver tent. I needed to work on my painting. I needed to feel real again. Sometimes you just have to get away from people, especially if they're your best friends.

At seven Her telephoned. Everything, she whispered, had returned to normal. They were at it. She was showing him how to do The Peacock. The paper animals were back on the shelves. No one could get into the kitchen. I was a

HERO.
Could she come over and sleep in the tent?

The paper folding projects continue. Piers and Kyoko are spending playful time together again, but are chaste as ever, it seems. Kyoko cannot break the habit of locking her door, though there is now no treasure to guard but herself. Piers retires to the Lilo. Her gobbles her muesli and dresses funny and entertains good-looking in.migrants wherever she can find the space. She says language isn't important, as we all know. Louise has another job in another sandwich bar and is taking bassoon lessons at a special cut rate. Unfortunately,

....

she has nowhere to practise, since the kitchen and sitting room are always occupied and everyone complains. So she practises here. What can you do? I have a new lover. With a sense of humour this time. It was good fun pitching eggs at Michael Portillo.

The Linseed Gallery has taken Piers' hand-made comics. They are selling. Soon he will have some money. (Didn't I tell you he was brilliant?) The thing is, he hasn't done any new ones. He and Kyoko sit in silence for hours, good busy children. Occasionally they smile at each other or munch an Umiboshi Plum. They fold and they unfold and they fold. They are doing it now, even as I write. I, Sam, carrot-top, artist, gay hero and founder member of the PYGs.

The Anxieties of Desire

JAMES HAMILTON-PATERSON

That a musician should be haunted by sounds seems only proper; that they should have been the sounds peculiar to his exile is equally right. They come to me in my memory as frontier noises, for the outskirts of Algiers in the early 1930s formed a frontier between city and desert, modern and ancient. My nearest muezzin had perfect pitch: five times a day he began his melismas unfailingly on E♭, varying the chants with improvisatory flourishes of his own. At dawn the sound would rise, richly decorated and trembling against the eggshell sky like a single peacock feather. Soon afterwards the copper beaters began work in the souk. At night, sounds of violence and travel. Every few weeks the police would round up the stray dogs which slunk in from the desert's fringes, herd them into my alley and shoot them more or less accurately as a measure against rabies. The snarling and shrieking and gunshots were terrifying; and even though the corpses were immediately thrown into carts to be burned the alley was always black with vultures next morning, pecking at stains and gulping fragments. Most nights, though, long after the radio and flutes had stopped in the little café whose name I can't now remember, that silence fell which is, as Mozart observed, the most beautiful thing in music. It was the voice of a wilderness which began only a couple of streets away. Sometimes in those still hours I would hear a caravan arrive as though on tiptoe, the velvet shuffle of camels and a tinkling like loose change.

Had I not committed myself to strange territory? I was a thorough European on both parental sides, born in Antwerp, raised largely in Berlin and having attended the Paris Conservatoire (Prix de Rome, 1922, for *Les Jardins Mystérieux*). What had such a man to do with deserts and muezzins? What had I known of Algiers, except that Saint-Saëns had died there of a fever? Well, it's a shocking enough story for it shows that the muses, far from being the handmaidens of high art and encouragers of those prepared to sacrifice a life in their service, are in reality traitorous hags, as fickle as schoolgirls and of an equally brainless cunning.

You too, perhaps, hypocrite reader? You who have just reached down your damned encyclopaedia and found – aha! – that in 1922 the Prix de Rome was *not awarded*. Oh yes it was; but it was taken away again from me by the vilest imaginable machinations. The spectacle of those academicians – whose vellum scalps sported withered laurel in place of hair – snarling like curs behind the iron gates of their own entrenched opinions was more than an artist could bear. Normally ponderous professors scuttered about, robes flapping, marshalling votes and writing malicious squibs to members of rival cliques. Never had the Académie so humiliated itself in disharmony. And why? Because my beautiful *Jardins* were too unfashionable for it, too *mystérieux*, too talented. I had failed to put into them enough evidence of the professors' own teaching. These academics didn't want strange scents and uncanny perspectives. They wanted heavy hints that behind the delicate colours was a technique like pumice, something grey and hard left over from the volcanoes of a former age. Not a set-piece canon, maybe, but at least some thoroughgoing counterpoint in the orchestra, a mock-learned and witty fugato (say) while the singers wailed earnestly on. Anyway, as all the world knows it became a *cause célèbre*. The jury of nine composers gave a six-to-three verdict in *Jardins*' favour, those from the Institut being unanimous. Then, thanks to vicious lobbying on the part of my detractors – including, I later discovered, approaches to the illustrious J-J – the Académie vetoed it. So: no performance of the work that October; no four years'

....

government pension; no residence in the Villa Medici. Very well, then, so be it. None so deaf as those who will not hear! I turned my back on them all, the so-called musical establishment, those tight little circles of dullards and perverts who simply played each other's works and sniffed each other's farts and gave each other fawning reviews. In any case, who ever heard again of any winner of the Prix de Rome? Debussy, Massenet, Bizet, Gounod . . . Four real composers. That's about it for a prize which has been awarded annually (or not) ever since 1803. René Martens, then, was a name destined to rise from ranks other than these.

The wilderness: that's where all true artists go to lick their wounds and recover their strength in order to return like lions. Even as I headed for it, not knowing where it was, I moved about Europe, a job here, a job there. If there is such a crime as puellicide I came close to committing it on many occasions as I sat listening to some hapless child with plaits and freckles massacring a Bach Two-Part Invention. But I learned to congeal. Coolly I told them I wasn't paid to hear them practise but to hear them play. Like ice I took the envelope left for me on the brass salver in the hall. Slowly the lions' breath entered me, undeniable, thrilling as strychnine. My paws itched. All this while I was working, studying, scribbling and tearing up, swallowing and swallowing pride and feeling it gradually turn to the breath of lions down among lights and bowels. René Martens was biding his time. I think now he was shucking off the Conservatoire and replacing it with more Teutonic influences from his Berlin adolescence. That tradition certainly supplied heartening examples of composers pacing themselves, making themselves prowl their cages. Bruckner was over forty before he began his list of great symphonies; Brahms didn't complete his own First until he was forty-three. This was fit company for René Martens. The essence of desire is waiting.

Yet just as it had taken Brahms so long to learn how to step from the dense shadow which Beethoven cast, so it took me most of my wandering thirties to overcome Paris' perni-

. . . .

cious hold. If I'd heard it once, I'd heard it a thousand times when I was a student: 'But the symphony is dead, Monsieur Martens. It belongs to another age' (the elegantly cocked eyebrow, the dismissive flutter of the hand). Oh how I wish I could have cast Messiaen in their teeth at the time. Young Olivier did the right thing, of course: all those first prizes at the Conservatoire in the late 1920s – harmony and counterpoint, fugue, improvisation and organ playing, composition . . . But we're all different and we have to run our own courses. Mine turned me into the lone and humble student of my own academy. I hired and borrowed instruments, made myself passably competent on several. Never again would I write a non-existent note for a French horn – the occasion, I remember, for quite exaggerated scorn and calumny on the part of one of *Jardins'* savagers. Hadn't young Schumann made just such an error in the very first bar of his very first symphony, the *Spring*? Genius goes where it has to and is sometimes careless of details in the overwhelming rush of inspiration.

Slowly I fell away to the south. I ran my tongue around Vienna for left-over pockets of musical sweetness, sucked at Florence for its lingering taste of blood and brilliance, swept the streets of Rome for useful dust (such handsome little Fascists!). While there I would make a point of passing the Villa Medici at a mocking lope, regal with scorn and disdain, wondering what pampered and cosseted expatriate *Wunderkind* was holed up behind the tall shutters, making a bid for Parnassus at French taxpayers' expense. And I . . . I was free of such things! Thank God! And so at length I reached Algiers, having run innumerable gauntlets of whining creditors, prurient landladies and miffed policemen. I arrived with a growing bundle of score beneath my arm, needing only a neutral African sun to shine on the completion of that first, great symphony of mine.

So it was that the tawny breath of the Sahara scorched into me like big cats at my back as I sat in a whitewashed room

....

and wrote while five times a day the muezzin shook his peacock feathers in the rectangle of sky. The café's flutes and wailing radio, the metal beaters and even the shot dogs are there in the score for anyone to hear, while the slow movement's tread is the velvety pad of camels bearing from unimaginable lands strange and disquieting bounty. It was, in fact, to this very movement that I was adding a late inspiration, an intermittent soft jingling like harness buffed by windblown sand, when I happened to catch sight of a copy of *Le Mercure du Sud*. Normally I barely glanced at the Arts page, at those syndicated reports of the distant, parochial goings-on in the world's so-called artistic capital. If one deigned to notice them in all their lickspittle pretension it could only mean one felt excluded – and you surely know me well enough by now to realize that idea's absurdity. I was all too happy to be working my work, free at last of a metropolis which, like a child, considered herself both the universe and its centre. Yet on this occasion glance I did. There beneath the headline '*Début éclatant*' was an account of the dazzling première of René Martens' First Symphony.

My instant reaction was a thrill of joy. At last, you pigs! *Now* will you . . .? before thought overtook it like a javelin, piercing it through the heart. Feverishly I read the piece, bewildered, aghast. René Martens had last Sunday himself conducted the first performance of his symphony. L'Orchestre de Paris had given a sumptuous account of a work which, from that moment, had become the talk of Europe. No lesser laureates than Poulenc and Milhaud had hailed it as the most original, most beautiful, most . . . Beyond the window the muezzin hit his usual smug E♭; I flung the paper from me, at him, at the world, at Allah. It fluttered through the aperture and vanished. A donkey added its tortured mockery from the alley below. *There was another René Martens*. I couldn't believe it. I clung to the table. Once more, by some malignant joke which the muses must have hatched in helpless stitches, my success had been stolen from me. My very name had been stolen from me. I could have

. . . .

79

believed a jealous rival had crept in by night, taken my score off the table, had published it under his own name.

That night the curs were culled again. I lay awake on my mat, staring at the flickering ceiling with a snarl so fixed it ached, hearing the bullets crash through skulls and brains, ribs and hearts, seeing the stranger who had stolen my life die a thousand times over. It was his body I heard tossed again and again into the cart until it rolled off the heap and had to be stuffed ignominiously behind the tailboard. Trundled to the edge of the desert, this huge stack of the fake René Martens was doused in waste oil and piled around with his spurious manuscript. A match flared, the orange flames leapt up and sent heavy, stinking smoke into the absolving African night. How his fat sputtered and melted, dripping blue flames into the sand! How his brains bubbled and seethed! How his internal gases expanded until slowly he raised himself to a sitting position, blackened arms seared into an imploring boxer's defence, puny against an obliterating blow! And how, released by the cleansing flames, his crotchets and quavers and bar lines took grateful wing, fluttered upwards and were lost for ever. Oh, I lay awake that night; and never once did I take my eyes off the play of those distant orange flames on my chamber wall; and never once did my grin cease until wearily I sat up and kneaded my face back into an expression fit to meet dawn's light and the world of human commerce.

Sayeeda on her splayed ankles couldn't bring me coffee hot enough, thick enough, bitter enough. I cursed her puny brazier and cheeseparing ways, hurried off through the souk and via a succession of mewing and sullen cafés was fortified until my heart raced and ears sang. Normally I avoided *Le P'tit Panthéon*, that predictable outpost of fart-sniffers, but today it would serve me by having copies of all the major Paris newspapers, flown over from Marseille in a rickety Latécoère which honked and wallowed outside the harbour twice a week like a tubercular goose. The papers were there. Three of them carried reports of the concert, one of the

....

columns included a photograph of 'the composer'. My hand was shaking too violently for his features to be legible so I dropped the paper on the table and stared. My usurper was shockingly young, which accorded with a description of him as twenty-one. This was awful. A sharply intelligent, good-looking – no, no, I was able to revise this as soon as it was thought. He reminded me – got it! – of the young Mendelssohn, a certain Hebraic cast . . . *Flashy* good looks, then, shall we allow? A drop of sweat fell from the tip of my impendent nose and obliterated this other René Martens with scribbles of reversed print bleeding through from the back of the page.

What to do? We biders-in-the-wilderness have our resources. Over the years I had regularly practised callisthenics and to these exercises I turned now. With a vengeance, one might say. I had never allowed myself to fall into that trap of degeneracy which sucks at and claims so many artists. With flour paste I stuck the photograph of the toast of Paris to my chamber wall so he was forced to watch the ominous intent as I drove my body inexorably towards physical superiority.

Meanwhile, of course, it wouldn't have done to allow this fellow to get on top of me so I wrote him a perfectly graceful letter in which I enquired if he was aware that he had a rather older and better-established namesake? He had only to ask around the Conservatoire and *l'affaire Martens* would assuredly be recalled, not least by Maître F— and Professeur de Faculté H.E., together with their testimonials to my single-minded career. (For never make the mistake of thinking that because one isn't constantly there, impertinently beating on their gates, the figures of the establishment don't know of one's existence. They know, all right, just as the firelit circle of roistering tribesmen knows that at their backs, beyond the bonhomie and the furthest reach of the flickering light, prowls the lion.)

In due time I received a reply: civil, though not – I thought – over-respectful, saying that he had of course no idea there

. . . .

was another René Martens who composed. ('Who composed' was cheeky. He made it sound like a hobby.) Further, he claimed, nobody at the Conservatoire whom he had asked could remember an *affaire Martens*, and F— and H.E. had both been dead for years. (It was an obvious pretence never to have heard of either of them.) However, he ended, he was sure there was room in the world for two composers named Martens, given that there were about thirty-three called Bach. In any case (oh, breezy and winsome puppy!) mightn't we agree to turn the situation to our advantage? If ever we wrote something which displeased our respective publics we could always claim 'that other fellow' had written it . . . And so signed off with a flourish.

The muezzin sang. There was not a moment to be lost. The muezzin sang again. All moments were equally lost and had been from the beginning. Better to beat out copper pots all day than attempt to make a new music, practise an old art. I forced myself back to my poor symphony. The score was dog-eared. The opening pages had a weary, travel-stained look to them. I'm not ashamed to say I wept at my table for many hours, re-living the sundry defeats and hardships of a life which had, after all, been undertaken for nothing but the greater glory of art, in celebration of beauty, without a thought for self-advancement. Could a man of my talents not have advanced himself had he chosen the easy road of wooing the public? Naturally he could. And why hadn't he chosen that road? Because that sort of success was too easy, too flimsy. One had to work hard in order to be as unsuccessful with the public as I, a truly finished composer in private. So be it, then. I would at last begin my public career.

Even I, in my distress and anxiety to hear my symphony, to promote its glories, could see that another First Symphony by a second René Martens (although of course really the first) would be a little hard for that public to take. When in tears a despairing father goes upstairs to remove his beloved infant's life with a straight razor, he does so with no less

. . . .

murderous mercy than mine as I surgically extracted my symphony's slow movement. I made a fair copy, added a title ('Tone Poem: *Nuits Mauresques*') and sent it to a good acquaintance in Berlin, Count Shuker d'Iffni, with the request that he place it as soon as possible with Peters or Breitkopf in Leipzig, or similar reputable house. This, I felt sure, would cook this little Hebrew's goose for him. It is easy enough to be a big frog in the little pond that is French music, but German music is what counts, as everyone acknowledges.

When these publishers rejected the work I was at first incredulous. On thinking about it further I assumed there might well be an angle to this which I, in my innocence, hadn't considered. Despite the best efforts of Germany's leaders at the time, members of this other Martens' tribe still reached their tentacles into the most diverse concerns – the arts, sciences, banking – and music publishing was clearly no exception. I wrote again to the Count, warning him to consider this probability and to use his best offices to ensure my score reached only men of unimpeachable *reliability*, or else . . . Of course I never wrote 'or else'; but there are ways and ways whereby someone who is light on his feet need not laboriously spell things out. This Count, this Shuker d'Iffni, was someone I had known here in Algiers. I believe his title was genuine enough, as, presumably, his fortune. He had lorded it in a huge crenellated villa in the hills – a lot of very young, willowy servants, a well-known enthusiasm for photography, need I say more? – and I felt sure his social status in Berlin, no matter how solid, would be considerably shaken if certain details of his *garçonnière* pursued him thither. Especially in such an unforgiving and puritanical climate.

And yet even this attempt proved fruitless. Well, I thought, *nil desperandum*. More irons! More fires! I sent off *Nuits Mauresques* again, this time to Paris (sooner or later the nettle would have to be grasped) and at once saw my symphony's ebullient Scherzo, too, might well stand alone. In fact, with its virtuoso brass writing in the Trio section it

. . . .

would do admirably as an orchestral *bonne-bouche*. Off it went, accordingly, entitled 'Entr'acte'.

I discovered I'd broken a lifetime's habit and was taking a sudden interest in the newspapers these days. I can now see that like everyone else I was gripped by the hypnotic approach of war which we all sensed in 1937. Since it is as easy to take up a newspaper for one thing as for another, I found myself turning from the politics of the front pages to things of lesser note. The second time I saw the name of René Martens (a piano concerto) was awful. The third time (a *Cantata Profana*) worse. His impertinent face even began to rise up and interpose itself between the peacock feather and the sky, eclipsing both. Wherever I looked his presence obtruded as a dark cast compounded of his face and my name, like a blot on the retina which floats over every scene. In exasperation I wrote to him once more. Were we not both professionals? Surely there must be some sensible accom-modation we could reach? This was a situation which could only harm us both . . . He never responded.

René Martens, René Martens, René Martens. Have you, my reader, ever repeated your own name to yourself until you were no longer sure what it meant? Or thought its ownership might as well be in other hands? I had Sayeeda steam his face off the wall and for a month I exercised brutally, *perdu*. I was crouching to spring so I built up my springing muscles in private, even as my manuscripts were finding their way like time bombs into the hands of some of Europe's most influential musicians: agents, conductors, fellow-composers. I had given this pretender more than enough warning. Yet one morning when I leaned my shaven skull against the wall, panting from an exacting set of flexions, I glanced up to see his face still there. Evidently my stupid peasant's steaming activity had somehow managed to transfer his image indelibly through the newsprint and on to the whitewash. Well, a few strokes of paint would soon deal with *that*, but for the moment there was work to do. I was even then finishing a fair copy of the symphony's first

....

movement. It was, as I had discovered, imbued with a feverish sense of expectation, almost of anxiety. This, of course, was entirely deliberate and the following three movements had been expressly designed to satisfy this unfulfilment, those hopes so exquisitely raised. It was hardly my fault that the idiots would be getting arousal without resolution. Off it went to Adrian Boult in London as 'Fantasy Overture: *Le Désir*'.

And now came news of fresh impertinences. A René Martens string quartet premièred in Antwerp, my own natal city. A 'Jazz Concerto' (inevitably, and for the usual modish collection of saxophones, percussion, *Ondes Martenot* and banjos) which Copenhagen 'adored'. I found in this a tiny crumb of comfort. The rocket had surely peaked and any moment now would descend, a feebly glowing stick. No serious composer would waste his time on those ham-fisted Negro syncopations in order to be fashionably 'in the swim'. But then after what was surely no time at all I read of the Paris première of his Second Symphony. Clearly, this was a vastly overblown affair – double orchestra, organ, double choir, everything but the kitchen sink – and had immediately become known by the title of Martens' own poem, of which the last movement was the setting: 'The Diaspora'.

Does there not come a time, my friends, when from beneath the successive hammer-blows of injustice a man may no longer complain of injustice? To cry injustice predicates redress; and there is no redress possible for the theft of time, theft of one's being. One day I was René Martens, lion-in-waiting, listener to an inner voice, attentive to every sound which life gave off. The next I was a nobody of the same name. One by one my teeth were pulled. Note by note the inner voice faded away, my only companion, my love. On the table where once my precious symphony had lain was nothing. A little dust. Stains of ink. It had flown, fatally dismembered, in stout yellow envelopes to all points in the musical world. And not an envelope alighted in some grand and distant city but the night before had seen one more

....

triumphant concert in another René Martens' career. Precisely thus had my own last movement (which I had wanted to call 'The Sands of Time' but which I'd consigned to the postal abyss as 'Introduction and Allegro for Orchestra') been overtaken, eclipsed, ruined by his Second Symphony. No, this was not mere injustice.

But if not injustice, what? Anyone living in my alley would have known at once. Stupid old Sayeeda herself would have come up with an immediate reply. '*Le destin, m'sieur.*' The Will of Allah. Karma. Kismet. Crap. In my little private chamber on the outskirts of nowhere I began to believe something far stranger. I won't deny it took me many months to recover from my symphony's death. Maybe I never really have, any more than I have got over the waning of an inspiration which once was so vivid and fertile. I would sit for hours, listening and listening to hear if this stranger's attrition had left me anything I could call my own and found it hadn't. I could hear only the café, the tinsmiths; only the children's squeals as they played among the pigeons, the washing, the heaps of goat-fodder on nearby roofs. And the muezzin, remorselessly hitting E♭ and sending up his freshly minted platitudes punctually into the unheeding sky.

It was when I realized that René Martens had stolen my soul that the strangeness occurred and I began to look at him differently. To my initial disbelief I found myself taking the beginnings of an interest in his career. To say I rejoiced in his successes would be pitching it a little strong – then, at least – though by the time war broke out the idea of his distinction had a certain pleasurableness attaching to it. I can't put it better than that. Not a day went by on flashing wings, like the pigeons circling beyond my window, without my taking my usual walk at dusk (oh! those North African smells at dusk: dung fires, mint, olive oil, orange blossom, excrement), without my thinking of him, fondly almost, relieved nearly. For that was it. He had taken away from me a vast burden so that I could view his imaginary presence with something of the benign farewell one might bestow on

....

a heavily laden caravan padding away as over a carpet spread towards the sunset. Mauve distances. Somewhere else the hucksters and bazaars.

Everyone knows of his tragically early death, of course. Or rather, of his arrest and disappearance when the Germans occupied Paris. The exact circumstances will remain for ever unclear but it is known he ignored his friends' urgings to flee to London or New York in order to finish rehearsing his Third Symphony. After that, who knows? An informer, a someone who wrote an anonymous letter? They were crazy and terrible times in which youth and promise – even genius, yes – were no protection. But no matter; his music is played today, which is what counts. Ever since the war my deafness has shut me off from that world entirely, but I gather that his Second Symphony, especially, is nowadays often played (I am writing in 1959). The name René Martens is spoken of with pity, affection, reverence. In a sense I had always known it would be.

In Jealousy

LISA TUTTLE

I've always liked ghost stories without believing in them. But this one I believe, because it happened to me.

In 1985 I went to China on a tour organized by the Society for Anglo-Chinese Understanding. I went not so much because I was deeply interested in China as to get away from London where everything reminded me of my estranged husband. Even after six months I couldn't stop brooding about what had gone wrong and how I might have handled things differently and saved the marriage. I had just finished a book, I had a little money, courtesy of my ex-, so I decided to go somewhere far away and utterly different.

It was mostly couples on the tour, which I hadn't thought would matter as I wasn't looking for a new partner; but it did matter, there seems to be a powerful instinct in human beings towards pairing off, and if you don't do it yourself, others will do it for you. David and I were the only singles under fifty, so we kept getting put together on the tour bus or at table.

Under other circumstances we would not have been drawn together. He was in the catering trade, wholesale side, with no interest in my kind of literature. Physically, he wasn't my type: very tall, big-boned, pale-skinned, with that faintly raw look you see in some Scandinavians. He wasn't Scandinavian: his father came from Scotland, his mother from Manchester, and he was a Londoner by birth and choice. He had big teeth and his blue eyes showed a lot of white. He was gloomy but witty, politically conscious and opinionated, and his reason for going on the tour was similar to my own.

He had been involved with a woman called Jane for nearly four years, the same length of time as I'd been married. It was over, she had ended it, finally, by refusing to see him again, and, fed up with glooming around their old haunts in London, mourning what was lost, he'd decided to try to get her out of his system by doing something completely different.

Yet neither of us really wanted to forget. What we wanted, and what we found in each other, was a sympathetic, non-judgemental listener to give us the chance to talk about our feelings.

We became very close very quickly, in the way that people sometimes will in a new environment, away from the usual cautions and distractions. China itself, so overwhelming and strange on first experience, faded into the background, of less importance than the old, London-based events we were recreating for each other, of less interest than the internal drama which was developing, the intimate heat drawing us closer and closer.

Did he listen as closely to me as I did to him? I thought he did, but maybe, while his blue eyes were fixed so attentively on my face, he was mentally rehearsing his next revelation about Jane. Or maybe he took it in at the time and then jettisoned all that unnecessary information. He must have had a greater talent for forgetting than I do, to judge from his later behaviour, or maybe, being a man, he was able to do what men are always advising women, to listen, to understand, but not take it personally.

We became lovers in Shanghai, on an evening when we should have been at the theatre watching acrobats. We'd both cried off on grounds of ill health. Some sort of tummy bug had been sweeping the tour so this was a readily accepted excuse, but I felt guilty, certain that the disease would strike us for real now that we had invoked it. David laughed at me for my superstitions; he claimed to have none himself. He believed in neither ghosts nor gods.

....

In Shanghai we had rooms in a very posh hotel, far more elegant than anywhere else we went on the tour or than anywhere I'd ever stayed before. Nixon had stayed there during his visit to China. Staying there made me feel very grand and yet uneasy, as if I'd strayed into someone else's life. When the others had departed for the theatre, David came down the hall to the room I shared with Miss Edith Finch – it was all shared rooms; his room-mate was another pensioner – flourishing a bottle of vodka. We giggled like naughty children as we mixed the vodka with some of Edith's orange and toasted each other.

This may sound horribly naive, but at that point I still hadn't realized why we'd stayed behind together, why we were there in my room. I was so interested in his life, in his past, that I was waiting for still more revelations about Jane. I thought we would go on talking for ever.

I took a sip of my drink and smiled at him expectantly. He took the glass from my hand and set it down beside his on the bedside table. Then he placed his hands very gently on the sides of my head, over my ears, tilted my face up to his, and kissed me on the mouth.

I was astonished and flattered. That must sound odd. It wasn't that men had not found me desirable before – even during my marriage there had been the occasional pro-position – or that this conclusion to our growing intimacy should have been so unexpected. But I had come to think of David, as a lover, only in connection with Jane. Jane, the unknown other, whom he called 'genuinely beautiful'. This was not a phrase anyone would ever use about me. 'Not bad', '*quite* attractive', even 'cute', but never beautiful. Yet he wanted me, this man who had loved a beautiful woman.

Did I want him? I'm not sure. I wanted something, but it was Jane I thought of as he pressed me back on the bed. In some ways I felt I knew Jane better than I knew David. I didn't know her as I knew other women, as a friend, but rather as her lover had known her. I perceived her only and entirely through David, and tried to imagine him through

....

her eyes. I don't know if I identified more with David or with Jane, but I scarcely felt like myself at all as we made love for the first time on the bed in the posh hotel room in Shanghai. Outside it was raining, had been raining since the afternoon. The window was partly open and the damp coolness and sound of the rain came into the room along with the smell of rain-wet city streets, and the omnipresent sour-sweet faecal smell of China.

After we had made love, after it had grown dark, to the sound of the rain still hissing down, we talked. Or, rather, he talked and I listened. The subject, as always, was his affair with Jane. It was over, we both, we all knew it was over. He said he no longer loved her, no longer cared if he ever saw her again. He didn't say that he loved me, but the implication was that my company and understanding, and this shared act of love, had finally cured him of her. Although I didn't say so, I didn't believe it. I thought it was a kindness he was trying to do me, trying to make me feel that I mattered more than I did, or to salve my jealousy, when it really wasn't necessary. I knew it would be a while yet before he got over Jane. She was too wonderful, and she'd been too important to him. His hurt was too raw, his obsession too intense, for a single sexual encounter to heal. I understood, and it didn't matter to me, I wasn't jealous, only grateful to be involved in something new, taken out of myself and the pain of my broken marriage. I didn't say that, though, I didn't want us to argue, and anyway, there wasn't time. We would have liked to spend the night together, but our room-mates would be returning soon, so he had to leave.

That night I had my first dream about Jane. She looked a little like the actress Jane Seymour and a little like my mother twenty years ago. Smiling and kind, she told me she was so glad David had found me, that she knew I would be good for him. I basked happily in her approval.

All the next day we were discreet, yet discreetly let a few others on the tour understand how our relationship had

....

changed. The day after that, as we left Shanghai, we arranged with the tour leader to share a room. The trip had been transformed, as holidays always are by romance. I still feel a little annoyed with myself sometimes that I experienced so little of China, allowing my inner life to dominate everything. At first everything was coloured by regrets and mourning for my marriage, then the affair with David became everything. We might as well have been in Manchester for two weeks, going from one Chinese restaurant to another and spending all the time we wanted in bed. Sexual satisfaction kept me from seeing anything very clearly. Sometimes I look at the pictures I took and can't believe mine was the eye behind the camera. Only the ones with David in them remind me of anything. Yet at the time I wanted nothing else, and certainly he was a better cure for what ailed me than half a dozen foreign countries could have been.

The first test of our relationship did not come until we were back home in London. We were apart for a couple of days, recovering from jet-lag, and then we'd arranged to meet in a West End wine bar, neutral territory. I was nervous, wondering what would happen. Would we seem like strangers to each other? Would he want to end it? Although he had told me he loved me, I knew that something said in bed, in a foreign country, could be as worthless here as the pretty paper money I had kept as a souvenir. If he treated me coldly I would feel miserable, yet I knew it would be a misery quickly overcome. What we'd shared had happened so far away that it would not be difficult to leave it behind, in the past, in China, and get on with my life alone, refreshed and renewed.

I'll always believe that David had meant to break things off with me, but that my attitude, the mental distance I kept, made him fall in love with me. He had told me how emotionally self-sufficient Jane seemed to him, and how irresistible he found her; sensing a similar attitude in me would have hooked him.

....

Once he became part of my real life, no longer just a story I was reading or a game I was playing on holiday, I was hooked, too. Everything changed. I had been interested in Jane formerly; now, I was jealous.

Yet I had no reason to be jealous any more. He seldom spoke of her now, thought of her only rarely and in a different way. The talking cure had worked: he was over her and in love with me.

But I couldn't stop thinking about her, even if he could. I wanted to talk about her, I wanted to see her. I convinced myself that if we met my jealousy would vanish. I would stop dreaming about her. We might even become friends. I suggested to David that he invite her over for dinner, or take both of us out.

'Are you crazy?'

'Why not? You're still in touch with her.' He had told me that once they'd both realized their affair was definitely over, and had both cooled down a little, they had agreed to stay in touch, to try to construct a friendship out of the ruins of their love. He had even written to her from China.

'We've kept in touch, but we never meet.'

'Well, surely you can't be friends if you never meet.'

'Maybe someday. But not like that. She wouldn't thank me for that, inviting her over to meet my new girlfriend!'

'Why not? How do you know? You didn't leave her – she's the one who told you it was over. That's what you told me. So maybe she'd be glad to see you're settled with somebody, she doesn't have to feel guilty – '

'You don't know her. And you don't want to know her, believe me. You wouldn't like each other; I don't mean she's unlikeable, or that you are, only that you're very different. You've nothing in common.'

'Except you. Why don't you want me to meet her?'

'There's no reason for you to meet her,' he said impatiently. 'It's all over between us. Don't you believe me? Are you jealous? Is that the problem? You don't have any reason to be jealous. She hardly ever crosses my mind. She's

....

in the past. I have no wish to see her, and I don't know why you should.'

It stung, to be told I had nothing in common with this 'genuinely beautiful' woman who had been – as he had told me once and never since altered or denied – the one, great, passionate love of his life. I wondered why he loved me, if he did, when we argued so much and had so little in common.

It was Jane who brought us together, and Jane who came between us. I knew too much about her, that was the problem. He didn't have to talk about her or mention her name for her presence to be summoned. The things which were connected with her in his mind also, as if by telepathy, called her to mine. I don't think he realized quite how much he had told me about her, how many small details I still retained. There were a few songs – 'Jealous Guy' by John Lennon and 'Trouble Again' by Karla Bonhoff are the ones I still remember – which I knew had been special to him and so now carried a particular emotional freight for me. I couldn't sit on his couch (loose covers sewn by her own fair hands), raise a wine glass (set of six, a present after she'd managed to break his last two) or turn on the kitchen light (the art moderne fixture was one they'd found together on a weekend trawl through Camden Lock) without being reminded of the woman whose place I now filled.

He still wore the large, square signet ring she'd bought him for his thirtieth birthday. I wished he would stop wearing it, but he was unresponsive to hints. Once, when we were making love, he hurt me with it very slightly, but even then he didn't remove it, he was only more careful, which in turn made me even more aware of its importance.

No matter what he said or did, no matter how much he claimed to love me, there was always the memory of Jane in the background, in my mind if not in his, keeping me on edge or off balance, bitterly aware that she had been here before me, and that no matter how much he said he loved me, once upon a time he had loved her more.

....

Almost from the beginning we quarrelled a lot, petty disagreements, but they added up. I didn't like his friends and he could tell that mine didn't much like him, so we gave up socializing with other people and just went out to dinner, to concerts or to movies with each other. That was all right, but when it came time to go home we always argued about whose home. By any objective standards, his flat in a mansion block off Oxford Street was more comfortable and more convenient than my bedsit in Chiswick with the drummer next door, but my place wasn't haunted, and his was.

I'm not speaking metaphorically. There was a ghost. I saw her twice. The first time was very late at night. I was coming back from the bathroom and saw a naked woman just ahead of me in the hall, going into the bedroom. I screamed. When David turned on the light, I made him search the room with me. He was first worried, then puzzled, then cross. He refused to listen to any nonsense about a ghost. I must have been dreaming with my eyes open.

The second time I saw her she was fully clothed, a beautiful, dark-haired woman in profile by the kitchen window early one morning as I stumbled in to make coffee. I didn't scream that time, not even when I saw her vanish.

Although I'd still never seen a photograph of her, it seemed to me obvious that the woman was Jane. I thought it very possible that David saw her, too, and took those sightings for brief, powerful memories. I wondered if it was his regret or undying love which summoned her spirit, or if Jane's was such a powerful personality that she left small traces of it behind in places which had been important to her.

I'd once read about a theory that ghosts were not spirits at all but simply powerful impressions left behind by particularly strong emotions felt in that place. If you take that as an explanation of haunting, then there's no reason why it should be the prerogative of the dead. The living should have just as much psychic energy and just as many reasons for using it, consciously or not.

....

I felt very glad that Jane didn't know me, or where I lived. I could get away from her. I've heard people argue that ghosts aren't really scary because they can't do anything to you, and I know now that anyone who says that ghosts aren't scary has never met a ghost. I knew she couldn't hurt me, I knew Jane wasn't even dead, and still the prospect of ever encountering her ghost again was just about more than I could bear. I was so grateful that I wasn't the one she haunted, that I could get away.

David wouldn't listen when I tried to tell him the truth, so I made various excuses, we argued, I was accused of selfishness and of not caring for him, but there was no way I was going to give in. Whether he believed it or not, I was afraid to spend the night in his flat. As a result of my stubbornness and his, we spent fewer and fewer nights together at all.

We were drifting apart. In my concentration on Jane I failed to see that she posed no threat. I had imagined that when he found fault with me David was comparing me unfavourably with her, and that when he was forgetful or melancholy he must be missing her. It came as a very great shock to discover that he had betrayed me with another woman, and that woman was not Jane.

Her name was Vanessa. He was guilty but defensive: he'd felt unloved, I seemed so uninterested, I must be seeing someone else, the way I always made excuses not to spend the night with him.

At that point, Jane was so far out of the picture for him that I knew he would believe in neither my ghost nor my jealousy. The existence of a new woman aroused what his talk of Jane had originally stirred back in China. I can't say that I fell in love with him again, because I no longer think I'd ever fallen in love with him, but something in my heart or my imagination moved again, and I wanted him fiercely.

He wanted me, too, although not quite enough to drop Vanessa. For the next few weeks London became like China, a foreign backdrop to our internal drama. We sat for long hours in cafés and restaurants I'd not seen before nor

....

been in since, drinking endless cups of tea and rolling cigarettes for each other while we bared our souls. We were closer than we'd ever been, desperate not to lose each other.

No longer frightened of Jane, no longer in danger of seeing her ghost, I spent every night in his flat, even staying there by myself that endless evening when he went out to meet Vanessa for the last time. I was there, waiting for him, when he came back and cried in my arms. We drank vodka and orange until we fell over.

The next two weeks were curiously flat. It was supposed to be a time of healing, and we were especially kind to each other, devising little treats. Yet we couldn't go on spending quite so much time together as we had been; we both had our work, which we had let slide recently. Love could not be our whole existence, which was a relief.

Things went on feeling flat, and I began to feel sour and impatient and angry with David. I knew it wasn't fair. I'd got what I wanted. Vanessa and Jane had been vanquished. He loved me the best. I had no more reason to be jealous. I also had no more reason for wanting him.

We dragged on together for a few more months. It was a hard thing to realize, harder still to confess. It was easier just to let things go on, and to think up excuses to avoid seeing him when I could. Finally I realized how absurd it was, and how unfair to both of us, and I broke things off.

It was more difficult, more painful, and much more protracted than that sounds. David took it much harder than I expected. I don't know whether that was egotism on my part, expecting his feelings to mirror mine, or whether it was a fatal lack of ego, that self-denigrating certainty that no one could really love me all that much. At any rate, his response, his hurt astonishment, his pain, his tears, took me completely by surprise. I had hoped I could just stop seeing him, but he let me know how cruel that was, and I had to agree to the occasional evening together, the meeting in some neutral London pub or café for 'a quick drink', followed by dragging,

....

relentless hours in which he tried to talk me back into love with him.

When I refused to see him again, he kept phoning. I got an answering machine, and so he turned to letters. It has always been hard for me to resist words on paper, and the chance to create a neat justification of myself without risk of interruption. Writing seems like the way to truth. If we could each tell our stories unhindered, in our own good time, in our own words, eventually a complete and final understanding would be reached, and we'd be beyond guilt and hurt. Maybe we'd become the friends he said he wanted us to be. But it didn't work. After a while his letters began to seem as much an intrusion as the phone calls had been, and although I still answered them, my replies became shorter.

Then I was invited to spend three months teaching in America. It was only a summer stint, in Seattle, but the money was good and I had friends in California, Texas and New Mexico, and I figured I could spin it out, with visits, to six months at least. I gave up my bedsit, stored the few possessions I couldn't take with me and didn't care to sell, and I was off, leaving no forwarding address for David.

I stayed away for nearly a year. I can't say I completely forgot about David, but he seldom crossed my mind. My affair with him had taken place in another country, and, it began to seem to me, in another era, in a different existence altogether.

Much happened to me in that year, but the only thing it seems pertinent to mention here is that I began to have a recurring dream. It wasn't an interesting dream, it was just me in a house which wasn't mine and in which I felt I didn't belong. I didn't know why I was there but I wasn't worrying about it, my one concern was simply to find a way out. The dream seldom lasted long, and I always woke up before I found my way out. The house was always the same, and it was not one I recognized. Bare wooden floors, architectural prints and old maps hanging on bare white plaster walls, modern furniture, no mess or clutter, just a few leafy green

....

plants in odd corners . . . It seemed like something I might have seen in a magazine, I was sure it was nowhere I had ever been. There was a feeling attached to the dream, a kind of guilty impatience with being there, which I connected with David, because it was like the feeling I'd had about him since breaking up with him. But towards the end of my stay in America I began to feel that the dream was telling me I ought to go home, that America was the place I had to find a way out of before it trapped me for ever. A lot of the houses I saw in California and New Mexico were as soullessly modern and 'designed' as the house in my dream.

I was getting homesick for bad weather and good conversation in damp old cluttered houses. I had stayed away too long. Yet London, when I returned to it, was strange and uninviting. There was nowhere I had to go, no one who needed me. I called around to see friends, and found they'd all changed, their lives had moved them to other places while I was away. One had come out as a lesbian, another had a baby, others had changed jobs, relationships, addresses. At one point, walking down Oxford Street, I took the familiar turning and walked along to David's flat. I had no idea what I would say to him, I just suddenly wanted to see him, but the name beside the bell was not his.

Someone I'd met in America had invited me to visit him in Edinburgh, so that's what I decided to do. He worked for an arts magazine and there was a possibility of some work on it for me; anyway, he said there was a lot happening in Scotland just now.

I had never been to Edinburgh before, and I liked it. I liked the sharp cold gritty air, the lilting voices, the old buildings, the streets and wynds, the whole atmosphere. It reminded me of how I had felt when I first arrived in London, full of energy and possibilities. It was this I had been missing in America. I stayed for a week and considered staying longer. I talked to some people about a job and to some others about a room.

On my seventh night in Edinburgh I was in a bar, waiting

. . . .

to meet someone. I was early and he was almost certainly going to be late, but every time I heard the street door open I turned around to look. On about the fourth or fifth time it was a woman who came in alone. Our eyes met, briefly, she looked startled, and then some kind of excitement sharpened her features.

I felt a sudden cold apprehension. She was about my own age or a little younger, very well dressed, attractive in a groomed, glossy way, with a look of intelligence. She was exactly the sort of woman I found interesting, and if we'd been at a party, with mutual friends, I would have wanted to be introduced. At first, that is. Because as soon as her face changed I didn't want to know. I didn't like the way she looked at me. I turned away, towards the bar and my drink, and wished I wasn't waiting for someone, so that I could leave, or that he'd already arrived, to provide a barrier, because I just knew she was going to come over and talk to me.

'Excuse me – this is terribly rude of me, I know, but I'm sure you'll forgive me when you know, it is quite fascinating, actually – did you ever live in Ann Street?' She sounded English. She was definitely younger than I was. The intensity of her gaze was terrible.

'Ann Street?'

'Number Twenty-seven.'

'I don't even know where it is. No. I've only been here a week.'

'Well, perhaps you had ancestors who lived there? It is quite an old house, although it's been done up.'

'I don't have any connection with Edinburgh. My people weren't Scottish. Sorry. You must have me confused with someone else.' I couldn't even ask her what it was about, I so wanted her to get away from me.

'Well, it's very strange. You see, we have a ghost in our house – I've seen her myself, several times, and she looks very like you.'

I heard the street door open and I turned away, hoping

....

for rescue, hoping it would be my friend. It was David. As I saw him, and he saw me, and the woman beside me said, sounding more annoyed than glad, 'Oh, there's my husband now. He'll tell you it's nonsense, because he doesn't believe in ghosts,' I understood all at once. I was this woman's Jane. It was her house I'd gone to in my dreams, hers and David's. The only thing I didn't know – and I suppose I never will – was whether it was David's mournful love which summoned my spirit, or her jealousy.

Rigging

ADAM THORPE

When the wind blows seaward it's smoke. Otherwise it's fish. High as a bloody kite. Glutinous, all innards. You get used to it. Only rarely do the great rollers rinse it all out. The great rollers of the Atlantic bloody ocean. Too far out and lofty for this peevish little bay, was how he'd put it, holding a spanker steady while the Uhu set. The great rollers of the Atlantic. The foaming rollers. Peevish little goitre of a bay. Fucking little glass-fibre dinky dinghies bobbing and bobbing. Little runts.

I'm quoting.

Holding the spanker steady with a finger. That's how I see him, in my best moments. Me there with my Bournville, the chipped mauve mug, at the door, and he holding the spanker steady as a match to a candle, or an oil-lamp, or whatever, in a Force Tenner like in the films, and mumbling. Swearing his heart out, bless him. Railing. Railing ever so quietly, because if not quietly the spanker'd never set. It helped him, railing. Crouched there under that dirty neon in that little tin-pot shed holding the spanker. Or rather, to be strictly proper, the spanker's spar. Between friends. Or boom. Booms swing, don't they? Out over the choppy ocean, some poor bugger reefing it up like a monkey, clinging to the aft-boom. In all the films.

Him blinking away the smoke from his Benson & Hedges. In those days. Before that it was roll-ups, funnily enough. Navy Cut. In flat tins that clip shut from old Mr Fletcher by the harbour wall. Old Mr Fletcher from St Albans, originally. They all come down.

....

102

That's how I see him. That tin-pot shed. Fish landward, smoke seaward. In the winter months. In the summer you'd get no end of grockles strolling in because they'd have seen the big clipper in the window, never mind the grime and cobwebs and the STRICTLY BLOODY PRIVATE in red on the corrugations, as he'd call them. The sides of his tin-pot shed. The corrugations of iron. Never corrugated. He'd lean his head there in his less lucid moments. Swear the wind had driven them deeper. The corrugations. Lean his head on the shed like a bull and swear they were troughed deeper. I'd tell him it was the sunlight. Shadows. Filth all over his cheek.

They peered in, those grockles, with their ice-creams plopping all over the rush-mat and he'd tell them no end of stories. Tall tales. Holding a finger on the mizzen-mast until the glue had done its bit. Or coating on the linseed while he spun them a yarn. They loved it.

In the old days, anyway. Then it was all truculence. Scowls. The English understood and hopped it but never the Yanks. Not that we had many. I'll come to that. The truculence.

They loved it in the old tale-telling days, though. Especially the Yanks. He was a picture, wasn't he? The old cap, the roll-top, the clutter, the drawl. Fag-smoke. Paraffin stove and that bloody kettle. Fish-nets. Wrack. The works. Digestives sprawled on the work-bench. Swan Vestas. That tin bloody mug of his from the Navy days. And there she was, in all that muck, rising out of all that junk, beautiful and clean and sprightly, as he'd put it: a gleaming three-foot hull with a shower of rigging. His fingers in there. Those bent fingers. Fiddling, carving, fixing, steadying, coating. Lavishing, lavishing, lavishing.

He only did one for a film the once, though. And that went down. It was meant to. He watched her break up on the rocks and said never again. Terrible film. All swinging lanterns and Cornish corn. Yelling under tricornered hats into fog. The smuggling lark. Wreckers. Ten seconds flat it

....

took to smash her up and you could tell the waves were spuming all wrong. Slow-motion and all that. Wrong kind of spume. We had to walk out. It had taken him six months to get her right. Ten seconds flat and she was driftwood.

Yes, in my best moments. Sipping my Bournville. I used to bring him the tea but then he stopped. It was all bottle. Desperate gin bouts. But what I'd not gathered was the secrecy. I'd thought it was the linseed or the paraffin. Old sailors never stop. If they don't drown in one they drown in the other. I don't really blame myself. The worse it got the more he had the worse it got, if you see what I mean. I'll come to that in a minute. It's pathetic watching him now. It's cruel. When you consider it.

The grockles got various versions but this is the most authentic. About as authentic as you can bloody get, anyway. And I slept with him. I'd have sailed to Zanzibar for him, in the old days, if you can sail to Zanzibar. Algiers, then. Rains less at any road. Than this pot-hole. And his fingers were still a mess when I met him on one of those geological lectures. Touring the cliffs of a Sunday with the luminous anorak lot and all strata and faults and fossils. He was the only one who wasn't jolly. Not jolly at all, in fact. Very depressed. I thought he was a divorcee. Or a widower. Who'd got his hands caught in a car-door, probably. Then we bumped into each other at The Frigate's Rest (The Frigger's Retch, he'd call it) when I was doing the meals there and he had a complaint about the Chili Con Carne. We got talking geology but it was obvious neither of us cared a bitch for strata and it was something in his eyes that had me flushing. A far-away sadness. The far-away sadness of the great rollers he was always on about. The great rollers you sometimes see flashing out there, not the mean buggers that sud the High Street from time to time. That you watch on the telly after unless you want to do a Jason Rickards and get swept off, poor sod.

The great rollers.

The grockles loved it. He was on this submarine cruising

....

104

about in the Minch, I think it was, and they came up to the surface, as is their wont, submarines, and he pottered about a bit on top then went over to the hatch to yell something down it, rocking on his heels by the big black hole when the hull's given a helluva kick and in he goes head-first, big dive, hands out, crunch. Flat calm it was, too. The mind boggles. They've seen things out there, the fishermen, you wouldn't credit. Something big enough to jolt a submarine, anyway. Perhaps it wasn't the Minch, given wherever it was was flat calm. Every finger so much matchwood. Steel deck. Fifteen-foot drop, probably. You'd be surprised. Wheeeeee.

Might have been off the Maldives, come to think of it. A bit shaky on names.

Anyway, the surgeons did about twenty ops and inserted little rods and by the time I met him he could grasp, but there wasn't the strength. Given he was a submariner turning big pump-wheels and whatnot, with shoulders like an ox, all sweaty singlet and gleaming skin like in the films, there wasn't a lot of future. Down in the dumps time, wasn't it? I reckon the boozing proper started then. He wanted to be a surgeon, went on and on about his fingers. He'd show us with matches and pins between the beer-mats. Look, he said, you'd never believe what it takes to make a knuckle. I'd feel a bit sick, watching him reconstruct. Then he'd lay his hands ever so gently on the matches and pins and say, it's all in there. I'm a walking bloody miracle of surgical precision. And hc'd lift his hands up off the table and flex. Flex his finger-joints. You wouldn't believe the clicks and squeaks and we all groaned. He liked that. The groaning. We could imagine it all, all the stuff inside. He liked that. Downing his chaser and chuckling, after.

It was Godfrey said, how about doing my yacht to scale. I think it was Godfrey. Godfrey had the nice old peeling one that had been in Dunkirk or something, anyway. Your yacht? My yacht. Okeydokey, if you'll get me another. A joke, really, but he stuck at it. Then it was galleons for the Armada thing and then little fellers in bottles for the grockles

....

and finally clippers. With the odd frigate. The odd frigate. But mainly the schooners. The clippers. Three foot six from spanker to jib. Jib o' jibs. Wet varnish. Crease your eyes up and you could see them clipping a heavy sea. He put Earl Grey in the hold once. Crates the width of your thumb-nail. That was for a Yank. The 'Taitsing' if I remember rightly. Broke the gaff in transit, bloody oafs.

Bloody oafs.

Then it was that one day, that awful bloody morning it was. First I've got to say this: he'd have made a very fine surgeon. It's all in the fingers, isn't it? He'd spend a week just on the bowsprit. Him and his Stanley. He wouldn't read the paper in the morning, he'd read the blue-prints. Rustle rustle. Then there they were smoothed out on the work-bench with a bloody forest of balsa on them before you could say crossjack. I'd tell him, at night, between the sheets sort of thing, that he surprised me. Because he was a bit of a prude, when it came to getting me going. I'd say come on I'm spread up to me royals. Out to me stuns'ls. Drive me.

No elegance, when it came to that. A bit of a bloody dinghy, truly. Yet watch him for ten minutes crouched over some little bowsprit or other, or reefing up a main-mast or whatever and you'd hold your breath. Fingers played those ships. Bent fingers, that much metal in them they could dangle a magnet. Took three years before the last splint came off but it gave him the fascination. The patience. You couldn't see him sometimes for sails and rigging. And he'd always do me on the prow. Topless. His little joke. Blonde. The last lick was always the nipples on the figure-head. A bit bloody cold I'd say. A bit bloody cold and wet stuck out topless over the cutwater, spume all over me lovely locks. I wore it loose then.

One time I bared myself. When he was dipping and dabbing at some nice slim tonnage, as he'd put it. Just set the Bournville down and raised my cardie and slip and stood there. And they weren't unnoticeable exactly when they were out, as you can well imagine. Famed, they were. Then.

....

Bloody hack-saw. Saved me, though. Touch wood. One can't complain.

Just stood there. Ten minutes. Goose-pimples. Then I burst out laughing. He looked up with his little pink tongue stuck out the corner of his mouth as it always was when he was hard at it and he railed. Gold on black and you made me jolt. Stupid cow. Doing the name, would you believe. 'Ariel', probably. One of the big tea clippers, anyway. Gold on bloody black. I felt a right fool. A bit of turps I said. But I knew it smeared. He'd do each bloody nail in Airfix copper. Then I burst out crying. A real weep. Him standing with a brush in the air and a little paint-pot. Stupid cow he said again, but quieter. That bloody great ship with about thirty bloody sails full set next to him all done bar the fancy gold name and me on the prow. A bloody good weep, neon flickering, big bloody ship and him just ogling because I'd still got my top deck showing. The cardie and slip rolled up and stuck up here, they were that big.

They were that bloody big. They had to do both, didn't they? It had got right into both, or something. Though I only felt one. Anyway, ballast. Ballast would have been all wrong. I'd have been rolling over. All styrofoam and rubber or something, these days. Forget it. Too old.

I said you'd better get that neon fixed. Blowing my nose. Bad for your eyesight. That's when I first noticed it. His tremble. Holding that paint-brush out in the air. You couldn't help noticing. Not with the paint-brush emphasizing it, as you might say. Then he sat and got on with it. With that 'Ariel' name. He managed. Did me with the biggest top deck ever. And crying. I said you would be bloody crying wouldn't you if you were stuck out in front cutting the high seas at a clip. Afterwards, in bed. Between the business. He even did a few tears. Sky-blue they were. You'd have to get right up and peer. Lobby of the Hong Kong Hilton, if you're interested. They didn't complain.

That's when I first noticed.

But the worst bloody morning the real one that was almost

....

a year later and I knew all about it by then. Gin bouts but also the secrecy bit. He never took a drop of tea all day. Even the paraffin and whatnot couldn't drown it out. He'd always smell of linseed himself and so on but it mostly showed in bed. Up close. It was coming off the skin. And the business. He could never finish. He'd get all excited and drove himself until he was red in the gills but he couldn't ever spume, as I called it. Believe it or not it was the American muck. I can only stand it with Coke. Go down his gullet like tap-water. Alone in that bloody tin-pot shed with his needle, stitching up canvas. Those tiny bloody reef-points I couldn't even see on his bench with my reading glasses. All that nylon rigging. Like a bloody cobweb. No wonder he helped himself along a bit. The worse he got the more he had, because he knew. And the more he had the worse it got. Get out of that one in a hurry. And his fingers. They never stopped telling him what an idiot he was. Taking a dive through the hatch. He'd moan in his sleep and I'd watch them grasp. Pushing on the Stanley to get the hull curved was agony he said. He couldn't hold a shopping bag if it was tins. Which it mostly was, in this dump. He suffered silently, that was the trouble. And his railing got worse. Scowls.

Then that bloody awful morning with the Yank. The Yank's son, really. I came in with the Bournville and there was this big Yank and his son between me and him. Staring. They were crew-cut, practically to the bone, so I knew they were Yanks straight off. Sort of indecent, all that knobbly stuff. He'd joke about sandpaper, to their faces, but they'd never click. I only came in with the Bournville now for a chat. He was working on the 'Cutty Sark' for Brooke Bond's, I think it was. Conference room or something. I thought he hasn't scowled them out at least. I said Good morning and the Yank said Hi I suppose. Then we both watched, and the son. The fingers were fiddling and he was sticking his tongue out and he winked at the boy. So I thought something was off, straight away. He was on the main topgallant staysail. I'll always remember that to my dying minute. The main

....

topgallant staysail. He told the boy. He held it up and said this is the main topgallant staysail and here we go. Let her blow. Then he started whistling. He had one end of the line and he took it up to the mast, almost to the top, to fix it on. A tiny little hook. Whistling. Those bent fingers. That tiny little hook. Then it was silence, except for the kid chewing. Horrible habit. All of us watching. He couldn't get it on. He couldn't get the bloody thing on. Like threading a needle only worse. It was his hand. It wasn't his fingers. Oh no. His hand. Shaking like a bloody leaf. Shaking and shaking like a bloody leaf. I'd thought actually he'd been taking his time on this one. The 'Cutty Sark'. He'd done her before, though. Went all the way up to Greenwich to smell her, as he put it. Thought he'd been taking his time. But he'd been clever with his hands in his pockets or something and that was when my little trouble had started so I wasn't paying attention.

Then the kid, horrible little kid really, piped up. You ain't gonna get that on mister. *You ain't ever gonna get that on.*

When the wind blows landward it's fish. High as a bloody kite. Fills your mouth. Seaward it's smoke. I've said that already. That day it was fish. I remember exactly. It was bloody fish.

I remember exactly.

Bloody little Yank!

I held the door open for them and made it obvious. In came the wind and the fish. There was bits of sea on it that day, against your cheeks. Lips. Spindrift they call it, off of the wave-tops. Spindrift. I can feel it now. How I felt it then. Bloody awful morning. By the door of that bloody tin-pot shed. Those Yanks going out, ducking. Spindrift and fish. We were right up close, in those days. Blustery. I can feel it now, exactly how I felt. I'd got my results that week but it wasn't that, surprisingly. We all have our allotted span and I didn't know it would be both or even one right off. They can do miracles these days, so Mrs Grove kept saying. It wasn't that, though I was worried. No. It was that bloody main

....

topgallant staysail. It was that. It was the end of it all. I could hardly look in of course but I did. The door only open for a minute but I felt like I'd been out in it for years. In the wind. That spindrift. Fish. I could hardly go back in but I did. I didn't want to look at him. No I didn't. But I did. Oh I did.

Saving Time

JANE ROGERS

Alice Clough spent most of her life in her mother's kitchen. Some might say she was a prisoner; others, that she was doing her duty. No one would have called her a murderer.

The kitchen was painted bright gloss green and yellow. It should have been like buttercups, like daffodils, sunny. But the colours were too strong and the gloss too shiny, especially the green, and the room had the enclosed and sweaty air of a primary school cloakroom. The curtains Alice had made were a large and colourful floral print. The floor, of red quarry tiles, was fresh redded and polished every week, and glowed in the light of the brilliant fire which always burned, come summer, come winter, in the kitchen grate. On the walls a variety of calendars, still supplied by agricultural merchants and purveyors of farm implements (despite the sale of the farmland back in the sixties) showed country scenes, smiling busty girls, and prize-winning shire horses. There was no washing machine or fridge or modern gadgets to clutter the place up. On the windowsills and sideboard stood orange and mauve gauze flower arrangements, which Alice had made following instructions in a monthly handicrafts magazine. The blanket that she had on the go at the time would be draped over a chair, with red and blue and purple tails of wool dangling to the floor.

Despite this wealth of colour, restraint was evidenced in the form of the room itself. The windows were never opened; fresh air was poison to Alice's mother and could set her coughing for hours. Layers of cooking smells accumulated beneath the shiny cream ceiling, jostling for airspace, smells of boiling bones and baking custards, simmering jams and roasting potatoes. There was nothing dirty or old about this – the kitchen was spotless. It was just so hot; so full of things; so oppressive, that the milkman when he called to be paid on a cold morning was relieved to back out again into the frosty air, and the doctor rinsing his hands under the sparkling tap would say, 'Miners'll thank you for keeping them in work, Miss Clough,' with a nod towards the high-banked glowing fire.

Added to the heat and smells was frequently an element of steam, rising from sheets and towels draped over an old wooden clothes horse which stood with its arms outstretched to the fire at night, like a large cold guest. The upper sections of the windows were often misted with vapour, and on Mondays the room would be totally enclosed, windows blinded with heavy condensation. Except that Alice would repeatedly clear a smear, at eye level, with her wet red hand, and peer out (at nothing) many times in the course of the day.

They lived on the ground floor, she and her mother. Upstairs the house was decaying rapidly. The roof leaked, rafters were rotting, plaster was crumbling away and window panes rattled themselves loose and cracked. Lumps of Victorian furniture, furry with dust, stood in the shadows like stuffed bears. The electric did not work.

Downstairs Ellen had for bedroom the old parlour with its generous tiled fireplace and double window on to the garden. Her room was permanently semi-dark, shrouded from light and more pernicious draughts by heavy velvet curtains. The still air was warmed to oven heat by the ever-burning fire in her grate. Along the wall opposite her bed stood the old three-piece suite, waiting stiffly to resume its rightful position in the room. Alice's bedroom, a bathroom and scullery completed the downstairs, lived-in part of the house. The scullery, which was cold, was lined with her jams and pickles, and cluttered with broken furniture.

The state of the house was a reflection not only of Ellen's

....

meanness but also of Alice's conviction that this state of affairs was temporary. There was no point in repairing the roof, renewing the windows, rewiring or replastering. Because soon Ellen would die, and Alice would sell the house. No point in throwing away good money on it. In fact Ellen's grip on her purse strings was so vice-like that Alice never had money, either good or bad, to throw at anything. When father died, he had left everything to mother. When she died, it would be passed on to Alice and her brother Tom. Each would benefit in turn. And Alice waited her turn.

She had waited when she came back from her nursing in '45. Nursed her injured brother and said no to Jack. She had waited while her father's health declined to invalid state, and waiting, had nursed him. Tom married and left home; their father died; and Ellen, suddenly deprived of both her menfolk, threw herself into illness with a determination that should have killed her within months. Alice waited, to nurse her. But Ellen did not die. She continued to be sufficiently ill to need constant nursing, regular doctor's visits, and a lion's share of sympathy, for twenty-five years.

Alice did not know it would be twenty-five years. That's the point about waiting. If you know it's going to be twenty-five years then you go away and do something else in the meantime. Alice lived the twenty-five years in daily expectation of the time being up. Every activity she embarked upon was temporary. Each decision was provisional. Her own life, 'for the time being', was in abeyance; her mother's demands were more justly pressing, for her mother was about to die.

Alice filled her time, while she was waiting. She nursed her mother with such skill and efficiency that the doctor complimented her regularly. Ellen was turned, and washed, and exercised, and her diet so carefully adhered to, that she was almost entirely free from those secondary discomforts of long-term illness which cause so much distress. She never had a single bedsore, nor was she ever constipated. For

....

years Alice forced her to get up for part of every day, just as she forced herself to cook twice a day – broths, custards, fresh vegetables in season. Ellen pointed out that she had no appetite – none – and that standing and moving was sheer torture to her aching bones. But she knew she owed it to Alice to make an effort, and she hoped Alice appreciated what it was costing her.

She had a hatred of light and fresh air, which Alice's training had taught her were great aids to healing. When Alice walked in and pulled back the heavy curtains, threw open the window and allowed the clean spring air into the sick room, Ellen retreated beneath her blankets in paroxysms of coughing, afterwards tearfully accusing Alice of trying to kill her. Eventually Alice was forced to give up, knowing quite clearly that her mother was wrong, and also that her mother knew she was wrong. She believed Ellen not only took satisfaction in behaviour which would increase her own ill health, but also in bullying Alice into abandoning a practice she thought important. Making Alice give things up pleased Ellen. She thrived on it. As she thrived on sickness, and sickness on her.

Alice, growing older, grew bitter. It came on her slowly, as the concertina pressure of years of waiting accumulated behind her to squeeze her forward into a shortened future that could be her own.

Her own life had lasted three years. Until she was eighteen she lived at home with her family. Then (after a row, but Tom had already gone off to fight and Ellen was so busy being devastated over that, she didn't have much energy to spare for Alice) Alice joined a Voluntary Aid Detachment and went south. She went with six other girls volunteering from the neighbourhood, to nurse convalescent troops.

The three years had had to last; the first magical exhausting year in the military hospital, and then her two years at Newcastle General doing her nursing training – broken off by the homecoming of her wounded brother. She had never thought she would still be feeding off those memories, thirty

....

and forty years later. That nothing else at all would have happened. The memories, like old and retouched film, became oddly coloured, unreally bright. She was losing the sense that they had been her own life. As if it had happened to someone else. Another girl with chubby cheeks and long fair hair and a giggly, dimpling laugh. The most important memory, Jack, had been subjected to so many viewings, so many touchings up, that she hardly knew it now. He was handsome. Kind. Funny. American. A hero; he had joined the British Army before the other Americans came into the war. It didn't last long – he was nearly better, and was going back to France. But they went for walks when she was off duty, and he kissed her in the fields. The afternoon before he left they lay down in the long grass; it was hot, he tried to – she was trembling, she nearly –

The poor film was so scratched and faded that she was no longer quite sure what had happened. What lingered like a smell was a nauseating sense of physical loss. Her fears had made her reject what her whole body craved. She had been afraid of getting pregnant. Also afraid of seeming cheap, of losing Jack. And perhaps she had been right there, because he did care for her. He sent her three letters. And when the war was over he wrote again from London, saying he was awaiting passage to the US. Could they meet? Tom was bedridden, the pain in his shattered leg still making him delirious from time to time. Alice braved her mother.

'I have to go to London.'

'To London? To London? What for?'

'I want to see – I need to talk to an American friend of mine – before he goes home.'

'An American?' Ellen said quietly. 'My God.'

'What?' cried Alice quickly. 'What's wrong with it?'

Ellen shook her head.

'Why shouldn't I go and see him? I love him. We might get married.'

Ellen snorted. 'That's what they all say.'

'It's true. Why shouldn't I go? I'm an adult, aren't I?'

....

'Yes.'

'Well?'

'Go. Go on. Go.'

'I – I was going to go and ask Mrs Munroe if she could give you a hand with Tom – while I'm away.'

'You needn't bother.'

'Look – you can't manage on your own, you know that.'

'We'll manage. If it's more important to you to go galli-vanting off with a Yank than to look after your own flesh and blood that's nearly died fighting for your freedom, then we can manage, my girl. I've got some pride left, I hope. And I'll tell you something else, madam. If you go, you go for good. I'm not having you back here, after you've been off whoring down in London. You go – go on and enjoy yourself – never mind about your brother lying here sweating in pain. Never mind us. I just hope you can sleep nights, in years to come.'

Alice in her innocence saw time as elastic, able to stretch to encompass all good things. She wrote and explained to Jack. She would see him when her brother was better. Perhaps Tom would come with her and visit him in the States! She would see him soon, and sent him kisses.

There was never time for her to go. And when she became old enough to realize that she should go even though there wasn't time, it was too late. She looked grey and haggard. Jack had probably forgotten her, married someone else. Besides, he never had, had he? Asked her to marry him. Only to see him. If she had gone then, she knew – she felt sure. But now it was too late.

Alice Clough was always busy. When she wasn't looking after her mother, or cleaning, or cooking, or washing or ironing, she would sit by the kitchen window, sewing or knitting. In summer she worked in the garden. She looked up at every set of footsteps coming along the little lane, and when she was inside she waved at every passerby she knew – milkman, postman, farmworker, farmwife. She knitted squares for blankets for the local old people's home. In

....

season, she made pounds and pounds of jam to go to the church fête for charities overseas. Not that she was a churchgoer – she was needed at home too much for that sort of thing.

'Where have you been?' Ellen would call querulously, immediately, as Alice opened the front door.

'Just to the shops, mother.'

'I needed you and you weren't there.'

'What do you want, mother?'

'You should tell me when you're going out.'

'You were asleep.'

'I shouldn't be left on my own.'

'I can't stay in all the time. What would we eat?'

'You could have the delivery van.'

'He costs more. Besides, am I to be a complete prisoner?'

'I don't know what you mean.' Pause. 'How long d'you think it is since I last went out?'

'You can go out mother – I'll take you out, any day. I'll set up a chair in the garden for you. It would do you good to breathe some fresh air.'

'You don't know how I feel – you've got no idea. You can't have any notion of how I feel, or you wouldn't be able to talk about fresh air.'

'Well I'm sorry but I have to go out sometimes. You don't want me to get ill as well do you?'

'What a wicked thing to say. You should be ashamed of yourself. You go out – go out and enjoy yourself while you can. Don't think about me lying here on my own.'

'I don't go out and enjoy myself. I go out on errands to keep the house running. I go out to collect your prescriptions and buy food. You won't be happy till I'm tied to the end of your bed, will you – till you've removed my last inch of freedom.'

Ellen starts to cry. 'I wish I was dead. I wish to God I was dead and with your father. Then I wouldn't have to endure this. What have I done to deserve it? Nothing but pain, whichever way I turn or look – and being told I'm a burden

. . . .

to my own flesh and blood. Dear God, haven't I suffered enough?'

Alice (calmly, bringing her a drink): 'Stop feeling sorry for yourself, it doesn't help.'

'I wish I was dead, I do. To think that I'm dependent on a selfish slip of a girl who resents every little thing she does for me and can think of nothing but blaming me for my sufferings . . .'

'Mother, I am not a slip of a girl. I'm a middle-aged woman. I do not blame you. I try to look after you. Will you stop it now?'

Ellen crying with increased force. 'Don't leave me, will you Alice? Don't leave me. You're not going to put me into a home, are you? You're not going to leave me?'

The only way to cope was to be efficient. Do what needed doing – meticulously, everything. Be a machine. Alice woke in the mornings with a list of duties in her brain, and the list carried her from one task to the next, one hour to the next, day after day. The wheels went round, spoke after spoke. It was no use wanting anything else, or longing for it – she must go on steadily, day after day, boring on through time as patiently as a worm through a log.

In the winter of Alice's fifty-first year, she became ill herself. She caught a virulent strain of flu and was forced to take to her bed for three weeks. Doctor Carter arranged for a home help and the district nurse to visit them daily. When she recovered, Alice was scared. She had been ill. She was getting old. She might die.

She might die before her mother. All this time waiting, all these chances given up, one by one: friends, romance, marriage, a career – and soon it would be her life. Soon she would have wasted her whole precious life waiting for her mother to die. She had never thought of death before. The very fact that it had yet to happen to her mother removed the possibility of it happening to herself.

But now she knew she could die. Why was there any reason to suppose Ellen wouldn't last for ever? She went on

....

and on always against the odds. Doctor Carter had told
Alice it was a miracle. 'Still alive at seventy-nine, after all
these years of illness? What a miracle! It's thanks to your
nursing, Miss Clough. A pity you couldn't have used those
skills on a few more patients, eh?'

Staring fiercely out of the kitchen window, as the first of
the spring hikers trudged up the lane to the Pennine Way at
the top, Alice's eyes filled with tears. She had waited for it.
Hadn't she earned it? Didn't she deserve it? Just one year –
that's all – just one year to call her own, one year to live her
own life in, before she must give it up. Hadn't she paid for
it, in all those years she'd lived for others?

How to take it, how to grab it before it slithered on out of
her grasp, was the question. How to catch that time and
make it wait for her. In the first days of blind panic, sensing
death's cold breath on her neck, she wanted to smash and
run. Punch her fist through the smeary kitchen window and
run screaming up the lane. Burst, like an overgrown chicken,
out of the terrible confining shell of Ellen's house, and fling
herself on the world.

Gradually she thought of a better way, driven continually
by a strong sense of panic. She wasn't going to steal her
time, or do anything wrong. She would save it. The time was
hers and due to her; she would save it. She would do each
day's tasks more swiftly and efficiently. Not by skimping or
not cleaning in corners, but by working harder and quicker.
So she would finish the washing and the morning cleaning by
11.30 instead of 12.30. Then they could have lunch. In the
afternoon she would do the cooking and bathe her mother
and weed the garden or whatever other chores she had to
do, quickly – so that instead of finishing for tea at 5.30 she
could finish at 4.30. But having already saved an hour in the
morning, that would be 3.30. After tea her mother could be
given her medicines and put to bed. Alice would wash up,
do the ironing, do the darning and bake bread – then she
could go to bed, at 7.30 p.m. instead of 10. That day would
be over. The next day could begin at 5 a.m., and on that day

....

they could have their lunch at 9. That day would be over by mid-afternoon. And so on. Soon she was overtaking days, hustling her mother and herself through time with such exhausting efficiency that she was saving not just days but weeks. She would do next week's work this week, next month's next week – slide up the back of time and grab a year – a whole year of her life – for herself.

Ellen was poorly now. She rarely spoke, and spent most of her time dozing. The doctor really was astonished that she had lasted the winter. The old woman clung to life like a barnacle. It was no surprise to him that she gradually became comatose over that spring, and when Miss Clough asked for a repeat prescription four weeks early he assumed she had simply mislaid her mother's tablets.

Alice, exhausted by her determination not to skimp on any of her self-appointed tasks, lived in a trembling frenzy. There was a terrible underlining to the business of saving time, because it seemed to exhaust her (and so lessen her own possibility of surviving to enjoy it) more and more, each day she saved.

In April, the old lady died. Alice went in to turn her in the morning (it was in fact 2.30 a.m., and according to Alice's reckoning, a date several weeks after the actual one) and switched on the bedside lamp, as she usually did. She stirred up the fire and added fresh coal, before turning to her mother. As her fingers touched the wrinkled skin of the old woman's neck, she realized it was cold. Ellen must have been dead for hours. Her face was perfectly composed, as if she were still asleep; her hands still rested neatly on the overturn of the sheet, like a doll in bed. Ellen was dead.

Alice put the drink down. 'Mother?' It sounded odd. She had not spoken to her mother for days. There was no point. 'Mother.' She sat on the edge of the bed. The dead woman was small, she did not take up much space in the bed. Alice sat and stared at her.

She sat there for a long time, because when she finally

....

stirred and went to the window, the darkness outside was lifting. Carefully, not making a noise, Alice pulled back the heavy curtains. A chill grey light filled the room, expanding it to twice its normal size. Alice stood uncertainly by the window for a minute then carefully closed the curtains again. The room folded in on itself, dark and reassuring.

Alice went quietly to the kitchen, and, sitting at the table, began to make a list of things to do.

Doctor.

Tom.

Vicar.

Undertaker.

Mother, wash and dress.

She was cold, she shivered and picked up the cup of tea on the table. But that was cold too. She'd made it when she got up at 2 a.m. Mechanically she put on her coat and set off for the phone-box, shutting the front door silently behind her so as not to disturb the sleeper.

When she returned an hour later she went straight into Ellen's room. Her mother lay still. She was dead. Alice went back to the kitchen. It was cold. The fire had gone out. Moving slowly she boiled the kettle, filled a bowl with warm water and carried it to her mother's room. Carefully she stripped her mother's stiffening bird-boned body and rolled her on to a towel. She washed the familiar wrinkled flesh and dried her carefully. The skin was hard to dry. It wouldn't stop feeling cold and wet. Then she dressed her in her underclothes and a dress which Ellen hadn't worn for years. She rolled her over on to her back, and combed her hair. Then she spread a clean sheet over her. Ellen was ready. Ellen was dead.

Alice sat on the sofa opposite the bed. She would empty the dirty water in a minute.

She was sitting there still when Doctor Carter arrived that afternoon. He greeted her kindly, offered her some sleeping pills, and enquired when her brother was coming. For the funeral, she replied, on Friday. Another doctor came in

....

from the car to sign the certificate, then they both left. Alice went back to the kitchen and sat at the table. It was very cold. She would have got up to make a cup of tea, but it hardly seemed worth the bother.

In the night she roused herself from her chair, and hobbled into her mother's bedroom. The cold had sent her feet to sleep. Ellen was still there. She hadn't moved. She didn't need anything. There was nothing to do.

Alice returned to the kitchen. She switched on the light, but the curtains had not been drawn and anyone could have seen in, from that blackness outside. She switched off the light again, steadying herself against the cold wall in the dark. Perhaps she should go to bed? But she couldn't remember what hours today was running to. And if she went to bed – when should she get up? And what do then? Ellen would not want changing, or giving a drink. The fire would not need making up. Nappies would not want soaking, nor sheets washing, nor food buying. There was nothing that needed doing. There was nothing for her to do.

When Tom arrived on Thursday night the house was in darkness. Alice must be in bed, but it was thoughtless of her not to leave a light on for him. The door was not locked but he tripped and hurt his gammy leg because he forgot the way the door sill stuck up out of the floor. The house was chilly. Rubbing his ankle irritably he switched on the light and called her. There was no reply. He went through the house room by room, switching on all the lights. In the kitchen he paced up and down, swinging his arms together for warmth, waiting for Alice to return. He'd had a four-hour journey, for God's sake. The grate was full of cold white ash. Angrily he riddled it, sending choking clouds of dust into the air, then laid and lit the kindling stacked in the fireside basket. The flames were reluctant and he spread a sheet of newspaper over the fire to draw it up. A fine bloody mess. Maddy might have come with him, instead of leaving him to sort it out all on his own; his mother dead, this filthy old ruin of a house, and Alice playing at silly buggers.

....

The roaring fire sucked in the paper and it blackened and burst into flames before he could let go of it. Shaking his hands in pain he stumbled back. A car drew up outside. Tom opened the door as Doctor Carter came up the path. 'Mr Clough! Glad to see you. Is your sister here?'

'No. I don't know where the devil she is.' Carter followed him into the kitchen. The fire had gone out again and the charred wood smoked sullenly.

'She phoned me,' the doctor said. 'About an hour ago. She sounded upset. I thought I'd come and see if she was alright. She's not on the way up from the phone.'

'I haven't even seen her.'

Carter nodded. 'She was saying that she'd killed Mrs Clough. Overdosed her with painkillers.'

Tom stared.

'There's no truth in it, of course,' the doctor said sharply. 'Your sister kept Mrs Clough alive for many years longer than she would have survived in hospital. She was an excellent nurse. Her reaction to your mother's death is one I should have predicted.' He paused. 'I blame myself.' Tom rubbed his leg and tapped his feet, which were like blocks of ice. 'So what happens now? Where d'you think she's gone?'

The doctor shrugged. 'We'd best notify the police. My guess is she'll make her way back here, though.'

'I suppose she's upset,' Tom said. 'She'll get over it.'

The doctor tested the door handle, as if he were about to repair it. 'In my experience, I doubt it. My guess is she'll follow your mother fairly quickly.'

The doctor and Tom stared at each other.

'Well she could come and live with us. My wife used to be good friends with her,' said Tom defensively.

Doctor Carter shook his head. 'This was her world, Mr Clough. It's like those Egyptian mummies that last for centuries in air-tight tombs. Perfectly preserved, good as new. As soon as you open the door and let in the fresh air they disintegrate – they simply fall apart.'

....

He opened the door and looked out into the black garden. 'I suppose you could say your mother did her a favour – lasting so long.'

Lists

MICHÈLE ROBERTS

OCTOBER 1ST
Start to plan Christmas menus. Venison? Goose?
Supermarket.
Rake leaves from orchard.
Buy daffodil bulbs.
Speak to Father Damien about changing flower rota.
Speak to Cedric about his snoring problem.
Drycleaners – my silk suit.
Look thro Chr. catalogues for presents for the girls.

OCTOBER 7TH
Rake leaves and keep for mulch.
Start new slimming diet.
Supermarket extras: low-fat marg., low-fat fromage frais,
low-fat mayonnaise, sweeteners, bran.
Invite Father Damien to dinner this week.
Minutes for Women's Inst. meeting next week.
Ring the girls about their Christmas plans.

OCTOBER 14TH
Raking, mulching, pruning.
Ideas for Christmas décor. A small Christmas tree in every
room? Great swags of greenery laid over the mantelpieces?
NB get book from library on Renaissance palaces, garden-
ing, etc.
Whist drive at church. Do sandwiches.
Supermarket: large tubs of low-fat cottage cheese.
School Governors meeting. My silk suit? Hat?

....

OCTOBER 21ST

Cedric's snoring: mention herbal pillows as a possibility? *Gently*.
Resolve keep up *positive* approach!
Order Christmas presents for Sophie and Angela from catalogues.
Check bank statement again. Check with Cedric?
Finish bagging leaves for mulch.
Christmas trees. Use the medium-sized ones from bed in kitchen garden? Yes. Check holly, mistletoe.
Aerobics class.
Church cleaning rota. Mention can't come this week.
Mention to Father Damien I'll provide all greenery for church Christmas decorations.
Supermarket: low-fat plain yoghurt.

NOVEMBER 1ST

Yeast pills.
Spring clean – autumn clean!! – guest rooms for girls' visit this coming weekend.
Take Hetty to vet. Father Damien says fleas but can I be sure? Check with vet.
Ring council about caravan parked in lay-by next to church. Gypsies?
Make appointment with GP for Cedric.
Buy large sacks compost, peat, lime.
Talk for Young Catholic Mothers group. Tweed suit?
Silk suit to cleaners.
NB special offer of tinned chestnuts in supermarket. Stock up for stuffing. *None* for me of course!!
Search diet recipe book for low-fat stuffing recipe.
Cancel Cedric's GP appointment and make one for me.
Resolve to stay *calm*. Do *not* get angry with Cedric. Snoring minor problem really.

NOVEMBER 7TH

Buy relaxation tapes Sophie told me about on phone.

....

Ring Sophie and Angela back and suggest another weekend for visit. Mustn't harass them! Just come for Christmas? What about New Year?

Suggest to Cedric he could try hypnotherapy for snoring? NB Angela's good experience with nailbiting. Be *tactful*.

Plant bulbs in garden.

Buy extra compost.

Plant extra bulbs in pots as extra Chr. prezzies for those unexpected visitors!

Buy squared paper. Do design for garlands on hall banisters, wreaths for doors, swags for mantelpieces.

Do designs for festoons around crib in church, vases on altar, hanging baskets in nave.

Cleaning rota. Can't do this week.

NOVEMBER 14TH

Supermarket: celery, low-fat milk.

Buy three hundred stamps for Chr. cards.

Check store cupboard for ingredients for Chr. cake, pudding, mincemeat.

Substitute cottage cheese for suet? Check with Sophie when asking about her Chr. plans.

Go to confession.

Invite Father Damien to Chr. drinks.

Buy gold braid, gold paint, silver paint, glue, corrugated paper, tissue paper, crêpe paper, gold paper, silver paper, gold and silver stick-on stars, gold and silver string, white cartridge paper, white cardboard, gold glitter, silver glitter.

Get out fir cones, dried flowers, dried thistles and grasses.

Wire.

Start novena to St Jude about Cedric's snoring.

NOVEMBER 21ST

Jiffy bags, brown paper, airmail stickers, staples, stapler.

Post all presents for abroad.

Make Christmas cards.

Make pudding, mincemeat, cake.

....

Invite Father Damien to tea. Mention I'm only too happy to take *sole* charge of Chr. decorations in church.
Aerobics!

DECEMBER 1ST
Suggest separate rooms to Cedric just as temporary measure while I recover from last week's collapse. Stay *calm*.
Renew library book on Medici palaces and gardens.
Weedkiller?
Cleaning rota. Mention I still feel too weak.
Knights of St Columba Ladies Night Dinner Dance – check gold shoes, handbag. Send balldress to cleaners. Write speech.
Order goose from butcher.
Find recipe for goose rillettes.
Substitute cottage cheese for goose fat?
Buy boxes of crackers, oatcakes, Earl Grey tea, cranberry jelly, champagne, sherry, gin, brandy. Wine.

DECEMBER 7TH
Confront Cedric over blank stubs in joint account cheque-book. His Christmas presents to me and the girls?
Resolve to try to be more trusting.
Go to confession.
Give talk to Women's Institute on dried flowers and grasses arrangements for Christmas lunch-table centre-pieces.
Buy exercise bicycle, new leotard, sweatbands, workout video.
Attend primary school nativity play with other Governors. Silk suit, hat.

DECEMBER 14TH
Book Hetty into kennels for New Year.
Book airline tickets, hotel in Rio. Insurance. Check passport.
Wrap Christmas presents for Cedric and the girls.
Post all Christmas cards.

. . . .

Finish making all Christmas decorations.
Get out damask tablecloth and napkins and check.
Buy candles for tree, wreaths, table.
Try massage for migraines?
Go to confession.
Primary school carol concert. Tweed suit.
Silk suit to cleaners.

DECEMBER 21ST

Make canapés, pâtés, dips, croûtons, for Christmas drinks party. Bridge rolls, cocktail sticks, cocktail napkins, cocktail sausages.
Decorate church with lots of lovely old-fashioned holly and ivy and mistletoe from the garden.
Decorate house ditto.
Organize primary school children's carol-singing house to house.
Dig up twelve small Christmas trees from bed in kitchen garden and decorate.
Ring Angela and Sophie back and wish them a happy Christmas with their boyfriends' families.
Try one last time to convince Cedric of health dangers of snoring: lack of oxygen!
Buy disposable syringe.
Look forward to Christmas!

DECEMBER 30TH

Inject Cedric with fatal air embolism while asleep snoring after lunch.
Dispose of syringe and plastic gloves.
Get Father Damien to help me move corpse to prepared trench in bed in kitchen garden. Cover with lime, then with compost and peat. Replant Christmas trees on top, mulch well with prepared rotted leaves. Plant a few bulbs here and there.
Take Hetty to kennels.
Put away Christmas tree decorations.

....

DECEMBER 31ST
Leave for airport with Father Damien. Silk suit, no hat.

JANUARY 1ST
Make New Year's resolutions: try to tackle this obsession
with lists; help Damien choose title for article for *The Tablet*
on why he's leaving the priesthood; start novena for Cedric's
soul.

Ode To Boy

(*Whitman at a Mall*)

....

ALLAN GURGANUS

I Sing how their socks fall down.

I Sing the amount of mousse you can get on hair this short and have it make absolutely no difference. I sing how plain they show their secret worry with their hair, touching its sides, checking in every glass storefront. They cruise their mall. I sing their defeatist loyalty to others 11–14. I sing how they groan, a chorus, when the mother picking them up in the stationwagon from the Chevy Chase flick says, 'Was the movie cute?' I sing their satiric vision of those governing lumps, the rest of us. I sing how wrong they are about the rest of us; I sing how right.

I Sing how they need a belt because there's nothing extra keeping Levis up, nothing on the hips but hipbones; (O, at forty-four years old, the miles I've jogged, knowing I will never run back that far, ever!)

I Sing how their socks are still falling down; bucking the tide of how everything else is so often standing up.

I Sing the contents of the pockets of that blond one, The Boy on the left. In his linty P-coat pocket: a single housekey chained to a blue Grandpappa Smurf he's owned and loved since age three; eighty cents worth of grape bubble gum; one peek-a-vu stolen from his father's dresser that, if lifted toward daylight, or mall-skylights – shows Jayne Mansfield with her nipples re-touched in a red that's lurid beyond most any other red this side of blood or fire departments; his mother's work phone number written on blue lined children's school paper; ninety-seven cents in change, plus a single condom, mint flavored, user-friendly.

....

I Sing how I, at fourteen, I tucked one condom in my wallet and kept the damned thing safe right there till college; I sing how this kid's mint rubber is his third replacement one since Thursday; I sing that, their unawareness of my early suffering.

I Sing their valor in the video arcades, a valor resented by parents (one quarter at a time), a valor admired by their own sort, esp. that dufus who's at the next machine for ten minutes and has only scored eight hundred points at the next machine. I sing their short attention spans at school, short for anything beyond each other. I sing their not quite needing to shave yet, though their mothers nag about the mingy silver-blond moustache. I respect their child-reticence at committing to any daily deodorant: I sing their scent – part wet-puppy, part vanilla extract, add one drop of motor oil, part snakes, part snails, part ninja turtle tails, part stone, and partly stick. A smell now bitter as a child on waking, but somedays bloomy milky as a bride, lying down.

I Sing how girls their age turn heads and literally stop traffic in the mall's vast lot, esp. those girls who're prodigies at makeup. I sing how same-age boys live hidden, grouchy under tentsized khaki coats, eyes safe back of bangs like purposeful awnings; and beneath bangs, behind the best of their extensive sunglass collection, they themselves lurk; formulating, a stern and groggy hibernation as they come to reproductive life. Or having arrived there, decide what to do about it . . . The new beauty is a secret even from the Mom of each. (Except recently, when she forced him into a blue blazer for Sis's graduation and everybody oohed so much about the handsomeness it made The Boy, like, barf). I sing an unwillingness to change the bedsheets, ever. I sing the hatred of underwear and especially pajamas. And how quick socks bag out on you. The No Trespassing sign, emphasized by a 'I LOVE THE DEAD' decal, nailed to his bedroom door, that I also chant.

I Sing boys' worship of usually-worthless heroes, 'Bruce' means Bruce Lee, 'Sly' or 'John' means Stallone/Rambo,

. . . .

hopeless, wrong heroes, bigchested, low-cerebelumed, visible and lumberish as totempoles of lats and pecs – target GUYS. I sing how heavy and how light boys are.

I Sing how they can actually spell Donatello, Leonardo, Raphael, and Michelangelo. I sing the five swiped porn mags hidden underneath The Boy's bed and the uses of the magazines and his knowing them, like catechism, page by page. I sing how the woman bending over on the bottom of page forty-six is named 'Verna.' Because The Boy decided. And then what could Verna, like, say?

I Sing the boys' contempt of any pop music except bootlegged Liverpool or Hamburg workingclass-inspired heavy metal. The heavier the metal the better, with decibels as the one sure proof of artistic seriousness. And yet I sing their singing something else. I sing how, grouped pirate-like near the mall fountain and goldfish pond, they can utter nothing for twenty minutes, beyond 'Weed?' (when requesting a Joe Camel) or 'Fire?' (a Bic lighter). Only nodding toward the backview of young housewives busying their strollers and their credit cards all morning in tight jeans, often a fashion mistake. Then The Boy will suddenly pitch into a Whitney Houston ballad. And his whole gang, despite their professed disgust with slick market-research pulp trash, his whole gang joins in, eyes closed from so knowing all the words. Crooning whole choruses, they hardly notice doing it. Their falsettos hope to make their usual come-and-go-soprano-blurts seem sent up there by choice. I sing their singing like forlorn alley-animals in some disney animation; they choirboy over the fakey fountain's real roar:

'Where Do Broken Hearts Go?
Can They Find Their Way Home?
Back To The Open Arms Of A Love That's Waiting There.
And If Somebody Loves You, Won't They Always Love You?
I Look In Your Eyes And Know That You Still Care,
For Me . . . Oooohhhh.'   'Weed?'   'Fire.'

*

. . . .

I sing how the cartilage is stretching him on a rack marked
ADULT SIZES. I sing how rapid growth can make your
joints ache; I sing how growth, like, hurts him.

Plus it makes his socks fall down again, goddamit.

I wish to sing their love of parents but really probably
cannot, just yet; I wish to sing their future promise but that
too, from this mall, seems sometimes sketchy. I wish to sing
their skill at drawing, tabletalk or knowing more than the
four chords required to play the rudiment plumbing of so-so
garage band rock; I can't promise. They know about all
Hendrix; they know whole pages of 'Grinch That Stole
Christmas'; they know about oral sex tricks (when in doubt,
breathe through yer nose); about a kind of African music
called Ska – part reggae, part tribal drums, part French pop,
and that's supposed to really be drop-dead cool: but they
can't get the mall's jerkoff CD store to order any (partly
because the boys don't know the name of any artist or
recording of it, of Ska; but they know it's outstanding,
probably). They know who sells your best dope in hitch-
hiking distance. They slouch around the mall, unpopular
with merchants, waiting to be discovered, not having yet
discovered what it is they'll be discovered FOR, but patient
in a fatalistic herding way.

At home, behind the No Trespassing 'Dead' Sign, The
Boy's bedsheets feature Captain Marvel doing wondrous
lifting chores and projects involving flying, etc. These same
bedsheets were requested when The Boy was nine, just four
years back. He wanted them in earnest and for real, because
– with their canary yellow background and the 'Pow' 'Zap'
in jagged speech balloons – they seemed just plain old Great.
In the years since, these sheets have become a source of
shame, have gone through being so 'out of it' they're like
ultra-in once more. Captain Marvel sheets now seem an arch
put-down of just what made them seem so rad and right,
way way back then. The sheets haven't changed – (except
colors' slight sun-fading, plus some sudden scallop-edged
stains that no detergent, not even Captain Marvel himself,

....

could lift out). What has changed is four years' way with the body of a child.

His pals' Dr Smith brogans rest on these sheets now, friends slumped here in early dark, no lamp lit. Door is locked, and they are waiting for something, waiting for something other than themselves, to happen. The buddies will sometimes mud their way through the house and back here, grabbing cracker boxes and drinks as they traverse an unsuspecting kitchen. The Boy's Mom still at work. Plush dinosaurs still crowd every ledge but all wearing sunglasses now. The tyrannosaurus rex sports, beneath its granny glasses, a mint-flavored ribbed rubber that masks its cartoon smile, that binds most of its crook neck. Somebody pulls out the skin-mags and shows Verna and others and a gross three-way involving two guys in (then out) of postman's uniforms, men who look no better or worse than your average old guy in a postman's outfit, sad – men the boys' Dads' ages 39–41, sick-o. Pals situate for a smoke or a talk or a nap before heading back out to do . . . what? to see what's going on at Big Elk Browse 'n Buy Mall or the little woods beyond it, back and forth, forth and back . . . tiring.

One guy goes: 'Nothing to do down here in Nowheresville. Earth to Captain Tommy, no, Earth to, like, Earth, come in, Earth? Earth, where's the party? Verna? Earth? party-animal earth, come in, please?' (Laughter).

One poster, found in his dad's attic footlocker, then scotchtaped to The Boy's wall, shows a group called Three Dog Night (!). And they're, like, sitting in a 1945 house-trailer, guys with their hair blowndry but trying to look ruff anyway; and they're in these acqua corduroy bellbottoms whose bottoms are wider than any woman's skirt since Gone With The Wind times and then real tight at top so their crotches are strangled up into knots you can't miss, and probably with socks stuck in to poke it all out more boss-like, and their arms are crossed in t-shirts to show off their pretty-dweeby biceps, and they're thinking they are the hottest shit, ever. (deeper longer Laughter). And the trailer

. . . .

is pathetic (leopard throw pillows! dig it) and The Boy and his friends can get stoned and sit here and just collapse with cackling, 'Look at this dickbreath, with his mouth like . . . and his arms like boing boing and his prod trying and get in the picture and thinking that women will do an instant-wet from being, like, even NEAR this,' and they keel over and sometimes, if feeling full of incentive, will take the poses themselves and then check out the poster and just crack up to see if they got it right. I sing their righteous contempt for the hype of bygone ages; but is there any glory in their own, beside the joke of hypes past?

(I also wish to sing the fact that, even when this particular group was popular when I was these kids' age, I never bought even a forty-five by Three Dog Night. Dig it?)

I Sing the Mall that serves as blank frame for Youth that notices only itself, and makes jokes at the expense of everybody older and everything else, till more Youth comes along. I wish to sing their desire, a force making them feel even larger than their own enlarging frames predict. Marvel is the Captain; they are flown, not piloting. Puppies get judged by paw-size, and those two seated there on the end, though just eleven, wear size ten converse all-stars already.

I Sing the crazed appetites that fuel their bitter jokes and I sadly sing Time itself. The time that will turn these critics into the bottomheavy middleaged men they mock. 'Catch a load of Mr Forties In Sweatpants – real jock, right? He must be dangerous, why? because he's got on grey sweats priced to, like, move at the fuckin, like, Gap! Yeah, real Olympic medal winner, going for the gold in "Having a can bigger than his wife's, even" and look at the lard bouncing on her one! Yschhh.' I sing the snobbish Yschh of a kid eleven who could eat the earth and remain innocent of weight-gain. I sing that metabolism and wish for it. I even sing the hope that singing may itself prove calorie-reducing.

I Sing how, at eleven, you don't know that you're in Gravity or Time. And I blessedly lack a republican wish for them to find that out fast. 'Abstinence till marriage' say the

. . . .

millions of aging male amnesiacs who hate the young so much, they act as if they never really WERE boys first. I sing a wish for these kids to stay free. And free to hang out, do nothing, learn rock lore and fuck lore via word of mouth; I want them to stay safe from the gravity and time that now has me.

I Sing their shoplifting of fine-grained sandpaper and then retreating to the mall parkinglot, back by the dumpsters, to stand there as a group and sand the crotches of their new Levis; to show everything good off good. I wish to sing the thirteen year old, owner of the Captain Marvel sheets, our host recently, who, four months ago, stuffed a sock in his jockeys so everything shown off would look like more of a good thing. And I really wish to sing the fact that last week, he put the same sock on his left foot, no longer needing it elsewhere. But, overdoing as boys will, while being boys, he soon sanded at his front so much, tore right through. Had to go back and heist a whole new pair of jeans and start over, a lot more gradual, a little more loving.

I Sing these overlooked ones, in their black and khaki, grouped like crows on backless (don't get too comfortable) benches at their mall. They drift around here because they're now too old for their backyard swingsets. (They've grown so big they bent the swing's crossbar last time they trooped out, on a Mom's dare, and sat there, but only as a goof.) They are too young to get drivers' licenses. They are waiting, between.

I resist knowing how they too must someday become, like me, citizens of mere matter and occupant time. Look, must they balden like me? Must these children thicken as I have, as I am, work out though I do, sometimes? Will biology and clocks force even these marginally wild ones to someday choose a favorite chair, seek tax shelter, stay home more, even weekend nights?

I fear I must sing Yes. And yet, ex-boy myself, how readily I recognize my fellow scrawny mongrel beauty outlaws.

....

The young, it is said, look forward.

The old, it is said, look backwards.

And the middleaged, I say from my chair in my sweats, we look around.

So, even from here, I see them around, unnoticed or ignored. I see them looking forward to something and, managing to expect it, and even at The Mall. But they know to expect only in sideglances, the way they check out their own hair, savage with mousse, using the mirrors and plate-glass that, if you're vain enough (young enough), can turn even a mall into a reflecting chamber, a walk-in closet's wrap-around view of you.

I ex-boy, ex-snot, ex-punk, former-scourge, ex-shoplifter, ex-backtalker, ex-sex-pistol and curfew buster, former fever blister, ex-hex perpetual, ex-eternal boner, am still here, mostly.

I yet recall the purifying rage of being so new here and this impossibly sexy (was it possible to be, if not this sexy, then this sexed?) and yet so utterly overlooked. I, grown, overgrown, stride past their bench in Gap sweats. Hoping nothing jiggles much. They are visible to me because I am invisible to them. But some founding sixty-eight pounds of me, the boy starter-culture, still knows. Can still guess each guy's name and rep. Still wants to hang with them. Still fears they will outscore me at the arcade, still hopes to get my initials up there in lights forever: Highest Scorer, this machine, this mall, like, ever . . .

And finally I sing how, when they leave each other, even to go and snag some unwatched pizza wedge at the Mall's International Food Court, they mumble to each other, 'Later?' 'Later.'

If they only knew how true that is! (Thank God, they don't.)

'Weed?' 'Fire.'

*

....

I sing socks fallen down so long, so far, they've taken
socks off.

At forty-four, I sing how it can all fall down, how it all
comes off. (you know that too, don't you . . . well, thank
God you can briefly forget).

How light and heavy boys are.

From where I sit, to where they loiter, I just sing just
Them – all glum, tough and touchy, the cherubs posing as
Hell's Angels, untamed, terrified, each one Captain Marvel's
chosen sidekick-mascot though less powerful than he, but
loyal – suddenly a major eater, a product and a product
defacer, non-washer except the hair, a sneer disfiguring a
dimple, so smugly doomed, but, in side-glances, hoping.

For all those boys who are All Boy,

But not, alas, for long,

        I sing.

Fluids

KIRSTY GUNN

She always was a particular girl. Like the way she wore her hair, for example, that was particular. Brushed out to a pale brown fan on her back, it settled upon her as a trimming. In the same way, her breasts seemed removed from her, items that she wore. There was the particular way she held them out, as if balancing precious cups on them, or practising for a quiet but intricate Japanese show.

Quite in addition to these garnishes, she had a way of doing things that was also neat and fine. All twenty-four coloured pencils sharpened to points and returned to their plastic case after use. Sums answered by rows of little soldiers, eights and sixes and elevens, corrected. And, instead of crusty Tipp-Ex scabs on her homework, clean pages carrying the smoothness of her thoughts, the ink running from the nib like a finger on velvet.

Still, when I saw her again, after all the years, the thing I remembered most was her way with cake. Her proficiency in that area, with the fatless sponges, jammy gâteaux and the rest. After our awkward first greetings, the two dry kisses, she was the one who suggested, quaintly, that she bake for me.

'Prepare,' I believe, was the word she used.

Then how the memories birthed, with her greasing and sifting. Those clouds of ivory all-purpose flour drifting into the mixing bowl from the past, a veil, with no mean little wedding guests, no lumps. There was that familiar way she wiped herself carefully between each cooking part: her commitment to crumb and batter, to lightweight crust, unbroken.

....

140

I always had a queer feeling that these cakes were just for me – though I knew in my head it wasn't so. It was the way she fancied in front of me with her utensils, promising sweetness. Her cheeks were two pinks, either side, her mouth moistened like a delicate female part. Together, we were so private. In the fine hairs that clung to her dampened upper lip was the secret whisper that cooking was even taking place. When she pulled the risen cake triumphant from the oven the heat of it bloomed and rose. My special little muscle twinged; I loved her.

That was it, being best friends, the particular memory of our times together. Seeing her again was like the stone unrolling from the tomb, those little ways not lost to me after all.

'Don't tell me you don't recognize me,' she said, when I opened the door. 'After all this time, I'd still have known your old face anywhere . . .'

She put her arms up, like a little girl, to be kissed and hugged. 'You're still too tall,' she said, after her pursed mouth had brushed mine. 'I suppose you still have trouble getting the boys to like you . . .'

It's true, she'd always been the promiscuous one. The one with other friends, boys too, if she wanted them. It was her pretty hair that did it, her charming, charming ways. Later, even when I didn't see her any more, I could guess how perfect she must be between the sheets. Lush, Eve'ish, insinuating her little round body for pleasure, those breasts aloft. How clever, I used to think, her caresses and unbuttonings, the way she would use the space between skin and hair. Even those afternoons at her place, when I felt so special, I knew were not just reserved for me. Others sat with her too – you could see it in her face the next day. She'd always allowed herself to be shared. Nibbling at her iced cake in the way shy animals take food from a proffered hand, she was only using habits and manners to conceal her true, particular appetites. Of all the others, the boyfriends she would have, over and over, of all her hot men and adoring little girls, I

....

believed I was the one who would always know her best. After school and on Saturdays we sat in her mother's warm kitchen and talked, secretly, about sex, yellow buttercake crumbs under our fingers, penises mostly.

Here was a girl with a dialogue of nakedness that made my insides swivel. Testicles, parts, what you did with the blood after your first time . . . She missed nothing. With her pursed lips, considering, she was relentless. Together we pored over oils, bedlinen and what we would look like lying underneath.

We rivalled each other with textures and tastes, out-guessing the feel of it, going in and out, in and out, like that, and like that . . . It would be bruising, to start with, I said. Too hard. She replied no, more like marshmallow. Like something solid going into melting. A liquidity.

'You don't know the beginning of it,' she said to me then.

We met at school, in the first week of term, both the sort of girls who didn't like sport. I'd managed a sore foot but she had the wit to produce a period and false pain. The PE mistress eyed us as we sat in the changing rooms, white legs, liars, and in the minutes that passed under her consideration, I heard my new friend's breathing rise and fall beneath her uniform. Our sides touched. While the rest of the form ran violently about in the playing fields, we escaped to the library and looked up books of classical statues, got hot as we traced the shape of David with our fingertips. He was so *broad*.

That first afternoon together and the broadness of David was the foundation of all future talking. Body types, hair . . . Easily and naturally we moved on to perfectly shaped men and how they would press themselves upon us, naked. That would be us lying there in the sentence, mouths parted, waiting for a tongue to come sliding in. The man's finger, insistent . . . We found, in the early months anyway, that these details bent more easily to description than actual erections. They were altogether harder to explain, harder to imagine. A dog's pointy bit, I suggested. A horse's pipe, she

. . . .

maintained. Similar to that, to the touch. Perhaps difficult to handle.

By the time ready men had a shape we could have taken on five or six of them at a time in our wombs. Fourteen to fifteen to sixteen we continued to sit in her kitchen after school, drinking jasmine tea and eating different kinds of cake. The hems of our uniforms were let down as low as they could go and we wore dark tights as fashion. All I could think about was fucking.

In real life, things weren't so glamorous. Sore pimples ravaged the faces of the boys at school dances, they were too small. Their hairless arms made useless advances as we shuffled over the newly waxed floor of the assembly hall. A kind of phlegminess hung about their speech as they tried to come on in slow numbers up against my ear. What a joke, those weasel bodies and their little moustaches that they couldn't stop touching. How could they even attempt it? When in dreams I squirmed and heaved under tree trunk rugby players with thick ramming forearms, slid over the washboard bellies of mercenaries, did myself harm. For succour, I watched the serene movements of my best friend. In the distance I could see her breasts sailing calmly beneath the ceiling of bobbing balloons. She would be dressed in an outfit of organza and tulle, with roses, dainty shoes strapped fast – so perfect. When our eyes matched we made a sign and when the band took a break for refreshments, snatched our things from the cloakroom and left. Caught the late bus back to her house and stayed the night with each other, awake until dawn talking, getting a bit sweaty.

What time has passed between then and now. What giant space. I went to one university, she to another, and that's how it began, our teenage falling away. We wrote of course, but I never did learn properly how she lost her virginity. Her letters didn't give me any meat. After we graduated, she moved abroad and though I left messages on her machine, the time was all wrong: when I wanted to call I knew she'd be sleeping. There were Christmas cards of course, and

....

strange presents, like chocolate or bracelets, at birthdays –
but by the time she gave up her job and came back to
London it had been months chipped into years since we'd
last really talked.

The voice on the phone sounded slightly foreign, but the
impetuous little shake of the head was still in her sentences.
She thought we should see each other again; the phrase she
used was 'for old times' sake'. Had I changed? she asked.
Was I better looking? Did I remember David and the stuffy
library? Was I stupid enough to think I was in love?

The years between her mother's kitchen and the present
closed like a seam. The way she combined intimacy and
formality in one quietly spoken sentence – for me it was like
hearing a mother tongue, it made me want to talk again.
Tell her everything about my life, split my legs, show off,
use the old language.

'I've got a few bottles from the Duty Free,' she said. 'Do
you like to drink?'

'Of course . . .' I said, my voice could have been shaking.

'On Saturday?'

'Saturday's fine.'

'Hold tight 'til then,' she said, and hung up.

When I saw her the following week, the particularness of
her seemed less noticeable. That gesture with the chest, for
example, I didn't see it any more. She was thinner, there
were more bone outlines in place of soft mounds, there was
an edge to her eyes. Still, her face was the same oval, the
lips set against it, the same pale brown hair was brushed out
into its girlish fan. It seemed the most natural thing in the
world to have her ask to see my kitchen, to reach for a bowl.
Measure flour and sift it. 'Sweets for the sweet,' was how
she put it. 'My fatted calf . . .' I didn't feel overweight, just
tall, big-boned.

'Where's your chocolate? Your vanilla? Let me make
something to suit your special taste . . .'

She was composed, even, a nun in my pantry. She'd
always been that bit older than me.

. . . .

'Talk to me,' she said.

So it began, she loosened my tongue. There were the duty free gins, of course, me drinking again, that helped my answers, my long lines of talk. She went about her quiet business at the sink, the delicate little self-contained body of old, full of its secrets, politenesses . . . And still I persisted with my sentences. How she carried herself, humming quietly, as I told her about the men I knew and my habits, my own proclivities, gates, entrances. The paths taken, over the years, between my legs, roses around my bloody cottage door. I was pouring, and the old teenage phrases were out of hiding. She, naturally, only sipped. But it felt like my turn, didn't it? After all the years of being the ugly one? My turn to tell her that I was craved too, with enough semen to still taste it in the back of my throat. I was taking great plugs of my drink, even in love, I said, despite her warnings. With a boyfriend of my own, I was finished. Completed. All grown up.

It took me an ugly length of time to realize that she hadn't been saying anything at all. The ice was melted and the cake baked and eaten before I heard her silence in my head. I'd been sharing my intimacies like we were still best friends, like after all the time that had passed we were still bound together by conversations and fact. Yet she hadn't disclosed once, this new quiet one. Always just that bit older than me, clever. All-knowing, a flower, pale against the window's dark light. It was late. My own limbs suddenly too big, drunk, hot. The bottle done, cake to crumbs . . .

With sex, in females, one of the pair will survive, the other crumples. It has to be that way, it's our nature. Needles, thread, our nests. Lips, eyes . . . We know the particular ways to do damage. She'd always been the promiscuous one, with shining utensils. Adult. When she finally spoke, that afternoon, after the years of our separation, of our competition, she was my cruellest opponent. Her voice came out in a whisper.

'How open you have been,' she said. 'Your body such a

. . . .

145

crowded house . . .' She smiled, such a fine, fine smile. 'And you, poor booby, inside it.'

She was composed, her hands folded on her lap, a little lick to the corner of her mouth, a little cat.

'For my part,' she said, 'I won't allow it. I push their heads down, until I'm satisfied there . . . But I would never let them put their terrible things inside me.'

The phone was ringing, I was sober. It would be my boyfriend on the line.

'And then?'

She shook the pretty, pretty hair. The breasts were set apart, high. 'I never let them come . . .' She brushed her fingers along the edge of her plate, careless, as if along the edge of a blade. 'I can't bear at all the feeling of their fluids inside me.'

Her voice was a whisper, the petal face gone to darkness, disappearing before my eyes . . . And in the next room, the phone, my boyfriend was calling. I roused myself, I stood up.

She was always such a particular girl. Looking back on her, that face I loved, flushed with cake, how lovely she seems. Her plump and creamy hands, lace edging on all her handkerchiefs – that's how I'll remember her. As little dollhouse ways, another pretty child. After all, when my thighs part today I'm still opening one of her sentences, I still touch against her verbs. Today, my sex uncurls from a phrase she began years ago. She taught me everything I know.

The Echoes of Puncak

ADAM LIVELY

There was once a land covered entirely by forest. One dark night, a man was limping through a remote region of that land. Above him the wind tore at the clouds, revealing from time to time a small moon far away in the darkness. Rain dripped from the trees on to the long grass, soaking his heavy trousers. His eyes twitched nervously, his bearded jaw was set in an expression of determination. Other men were spread out far and wide through that forest-covered land. They too tramped the forest tracks, tugged by the restless wind. They were searching for the bodies to which their spirits belonged. For each man in that land had been born into an alien body. Each sought to be united with his true body, so that soul and body could be one. They moved uncomfortably in their unbelonging bodies.

Towards dawn, the man with the limp came to a crossroads and entered an inn that was dwarfed by the broad trunks of the forest trees. Logs crackled slowly in the grate. Travellers sat on benches around the walls, gazing sadly out through the windows of their alien eyes at the others in the room, disappointed that none was the one for whom they always searched. None of them had slept that night. Each was engaged on his own wakeful dreams of Perfect Union. None of them would ever find peace in their lives or an end to their wanderings through the dense forests. For even if they discovered their own body, it would be inhabited by an alien soul that was itself searching for its own body. Thus he who had found his own body could only follow it at a distance, never to be united with it. Only by a miracle – and no living

....

person claimed to have seen such a thing, though it was passed down in myth and song – would there be a perfect match on both sides, where body fitted soul and soul fitted body. These miraculous occurrences were known by the most sacred word in the language, whose translation is 'Perfect Union', and the places where they were reputed to have taken place had become shrines.

The man with the limp gazed around. Everything in the room was made of wood. The walls were wood, and the long benches at which the travellers sat. The candleholders were wood, and the plates on which the food was served. One of the travellers was singing quietly. The songs of this people were sad and intricately constructed, as intricate as the tracks that wove through the thick forests, or as the carvings that decorated their furniture, made from the wood of the forests. Everything seemed intricate and sad in that land, like the knots and grains of the wood, damp from the rain that fell softly and ceaselessly on the forests. The singer strummed a wooden guitar whose ivy strings sounded with dull thuds.

O listen to this song of an unhappy man
Born to suffer, born to wander
His name was Remek, but his body had none
All his life he had searched and sought
The body with which he could live at peace
He'd heard stories of the Perfect Union
The singers had sung of that mystic One
But never could he find it, never could he rest
O listen to this tale of an unhappy man!
Then one day his dream seemed to happen
At the inn at Vilyuy he saw a vision
For there stood Tak, whose body was Remek's
And Remek was filled with unbounded joy
But Tak, too, was on his quest
And could not give Remek the Perfect Union
The pain was made worse, the hurt was harder

....

For Remek's body was both near and far
For years he trailed Tak, through mud and through water
And his misery piled up like the clouds on the hills
Till one black day he could bear it no longer
And took himself up to the heights at Puncak
Where the forest is broken by the cavernous cliffs
And so high are those cliffs, so far is the fall
That three days will pass on that dreadful journey
He threw himself off, he made that journey
And as is the custom, the journey was marked
In all of the inns by fasting and vigil
Three days and three nights the people stayed up
Till Remek had reached his final rest.
This tale is just one, there are so many more
Of the sorrows and wanderings of unhappy men.

The man listened to the song and chewed his food. Soon he would begin to suffer the empty dreams of Perfect Union, those hallucinatory forms without content that afflicted him every night. He was about to surrender to them, when the door of the inn creaked open and another traveller entered. The travellers on the benches hardly raised the weary heads they inhabited. Only the man with the limp stopped chewing. A shock of recognition was running through his spirit. And the new traveller stopped dead still in the doorway, while the mist from the forest swirled about his feet. He stared back across the room at the man who had limped in just a short while before. Neither spoke a word. The door remained open. One by one, heads were raised around the room. The singer's song petered out. Gradually, for it was hardly conceivable, the travellers grasped that the miracle was happening. Here, before the very eyes through which they were condemned to look out at the world, a Perfect Union was taking place.

The acts for the celebration of Perfect Union were laid down by ancient law, rehearsed in a thousand sacred texts. All knew them by heart, though few had dared hope that

....

they might actually witness them. The two bodies were anointed, the two spirits fed with sacred songs. They were brought together in the minutely choreographed sacred embrace, and left in that position, to unite, for nine days and nights. Meanwhile, news of the Perfect Union spread along the forest tracks like the waters of a flood.

The two bodies lay locked in their embrace on a long trestle table. Every now and then they shifted slightly on their bed of ivy. At the first moment of Perfect Union, the man with the limp had felt a pang of loss. All his life he had desired this, and now with its fulfilment he had lost that sense of desire. Then the barriers dividing his consciousness broke down, and everything became one infinite and ecstatic ocean. In this state he lay clasped in the sacred embrace for three days. But on the fourth, something began to happen. A tiny speck appeared in the vast, pure ocean of his being. ('Where had it come from?' he would ask himself later.) He had no name for that speck, no language with which to describe it. For no one in that land had experienced anxiety before. That tiny speck in his consciousness told him that the Perfect Union was *too* wonderful. It told him to draw back. And just as the smallest impurity in a liquid can cause precipitation, so the man's anxiety grew and crystallized into revulsion. At the end of the fourth day, he suddenly broke the embrace and leapt from the table. He staggered crying and screaming out into the forest.

He ran and ran until he was deep among the trees. There, utterly alone, he sat down on a log and rested. His first feeling was of relief, as though he had escaped something dreadful. Then another feeling came upon him. It spread like a cloudy, oily liquid, covering his consciousness. Again he had no name for it, because no one in that land had experienced it before. It was guilt. He had committed an undreamt-of sacrilege. He had destroyed all he had lived for. He had nothing to live for now.

The man lived alone in the depths of the forest for months. Gradually, his guilt faded. New feelings sprang up to replace

....

it. Gone were the melancholy, the yearning he had felt in former times. Now he tingled with a new energy, an excitement and anticipation. Ideas that had never been thought by anybody in that land came to him, jostling in his head, creating sparks that took the form of even newer ideas. He longed to share all this commotion in his head with others. Eventually he could bear it no longer, and made his way out of the depths of the forest. He did not stop to consider what the reaction of others might be to one who had rejected and insulted their most sacred institution.

The people had no reaction. They did not know what to think. That someone should break the sacred embrace, should reject that Perfect Union that is given only to the luckiest individuals in countless thousands of unhappy generations, was beyond their comprehension. They could not even be angry. So when the man returned, and was seen on the forest tracks and in the inns, he drew only wide-eyed stares. Indeed, ever since he had broken the sacred embrace, a kind of dumbfounded silence had fallen on the whole of that forest-covered land.

The man started travelling with even greater restlessness than in the days of his quest for the Perfect Union. But now he was preaching to the people. He told the weary travellers in the inns – who attended him with slack-jawed amazement – that they did not need the Perfect Union. They could live without their sense of separation – their 'obsession', he called it. They could stop their wanderings and settle down to found villages and towns. They could clear the forest – whose dank darkness reflected as in a pool the dank darkness of their minds – and let in the sunlight. They could grow crops instead of chasing animals through the trees.

They listened to him. They began to obey. It was as though a new sun had risen on that unhappy land. The people began to clear the forests, to lay out fields, to build villages and towns. Their sense of separation evaporated, and a new looking-forward and confidence grew in them.

....

The life of that land was never to be the same again. It was never to return to the old ways.

But what of the other half of that broken Perfect Union? A tale is like a coin, and one side will always be turned away from the light. The unhappiness of the one who had been rejected in the midst of Perfect Union was boundless. It was dense, and as deep as could be. He knew that what had been broken could not be put together again. But even so, when he heard that the man with the limp had returned from the depths of the forest, he could not keep away. He trailed the man everywhere, looking at him longingly but without hope. So that everywhere the man went, talking to increasingly large and admiring crowds, there went behind him this dark and haunting figure.

In the midst of change and hope, the rejected one – that hapless sacrifice on the altar of the old ways – could bear it no longer. Like those in the songs, he took himself up to the heights at Puncak and threw himself off into the abyss. Someone saw him do it, and came down to what is now the main city of that land with the news. As a mark of respect, a vigil was held for the three days and nights that the unfortunate one would spend falling into the deep abyss. But when the vigil was done, the business was forgotten and the people returned to the exciting tasks that lay before them. Only legend has it, even to this day, that whenever the air rumbles with thunder or the explosion of a distant bomb – for they fight wars in that land now – they are hearing the far-off echoes of that moment when the last and most unfortunate representative of the old ways met his rest at the foot of Puncak.

....

Tarantula

ELISA SEGRAVE

Daniel's first obsession was with balloons. Laura didn't pay much attention at first. Then suddenly, after his second birthday party, her son wanted balloons all the time. She thought of the most obvious explanation and immediately felt guilty. When he was a baby she had often left him with the baby-sitter while she went out with her two-year-old daughter. On those occasions she had expressed her milk and left it in a bottle for him. Perhaps his mania for balloons meant that he was still yearning for the breast he had not had enough of.

Laura had a photo of Daniel on his second birthday, surrounded with balloons, looking very serious, as he often did.

When her friends realized he adored balloons they brought them to the house as presents. However the balloons appeared to cause Daniel intense frustration as well as pleasure. He went into a rage when a balloon popped, or when he was told he couldn't have one when he saw one in a shop, or when an adult blew one up and didn't tie the end quickly enough.

'Tie! Tie!' he would scream.

Soon Laura and her husband decided he should only have balloons on special occasions, as they seemed to cause him so much pain. However he wouldn't play with anything else. He simply wasn't interested. For this reason Laura sometimes gave in when her husband wasn't there and bought him balloons anyway.

Daniel called his balloons odd names, to differentiate

between them. The long striped party ones, which, when blown up and let go, made a snorting noise and whizzed everywhere, he called 'All March Down the Room Balloons'. When, occasionally, he was given a 'Fish Balloon', filled with helium, he was overjoyed but then often let the string go by mistake so that it sailed into the sky. Once, after a party, one reached the roof of South Kensington Underground Station and an official tried to get it down with a broom, unsuccessfully.

Over the next few years, Daniel developed several other crazes. Generally, each one lasted about eight months, except for the balloons, which went on and on.

Between the ages of three and nine these obsessions were: *The Snowman*, the Test Card, the cartoon of Robin Hood, Little Peg (a deceased Russian Blue cat) and tarantulas.

Laura could relate best to the film of *The Snowman*. She liked to watch this with her son. They both loved the part where the boy and the Snowman flew high over Brighton Pier, then up towards the North Pole. The boy looked so happy with the Snowman.

'Can the Snowman fly higher than the Sun?' Daniel asked. He was interested in God.

'I don't want to be an angel for too many days,' he told his mother. 'When I'm an angel, will God take the key and let me out?'

Because of the Snowman flying towards the North Pole, Daniel often pretended to strangers that he came from countries near the Arctic Circle.

'I hear you come from Iceland,' said an American lady to Laura. (Her husband was teaching Daniel to fish, on holiday in Florida.)

The next day Laura overheard Daniel, then aged six, telling some older boys in the hotel swimming-pool: 'I come from Finland.'

'But you speak English,' one of the boys said.

'I've learned to speak English very well,' said Laura's son seriously.

....

He made his own little books of the Snowman story again and again, folding up sheets of paper into four and drawing the whole cartoon with tremendous concentration.

At school however, he wouldn't concentrate.

At the end of Daniel's first term, the teacher had summoned Laura and her husband for a meeting.

There was something wrong with their son, said Miss Browning. He was too withdrawn. He did odd things. He bit his hand a great deal so that there was a permanent scar. In the classroom he put his hands over his ears and screwed up his eyes, then screamed very loudly. He did not always make sense when he talked, and did not want to do the tasks that the other children did, such as filling in circles and trying to form letters. He did not like the other children. If he pulled a child's hair he was put in the corridor; however he seemed to enjoy this solitary state more than being in the classroom.

When Laura asked him about this he said: 'I like being on my own. I don't like being in public.'

When she asked why he pulled the children's hair he said: 'I don't like them. They're silly. They speak like this:' and then he imitated a high squeaky voice.

It was arranged that he should do speech therapy so that he would make himself understood better.

On the first meeting with the speech therapist Daniel asked her: 'Would you like to live in a fish balloon? I'd like to live in a fish balloon.'

The speech therapist said that it was important to make him do what was 'appropriate'. She sat with him making him do simple puzzles, build bricks in a sequence, and concentrate on what was being shown in a picture, so that he would keep to the point and not get side-tracked by one of his 'obsessions.'

However, Daniel did not seem to improve. His new teacher thought he should see a child analyst as he seemed tense and unhappy and still couldn't relate to his own peer group. He asked adults repetitive odd questions such as:

....

'How many times have you had a nose-bleed?' and 'Which is worse, a penis or a snake?'

Daniel's next obsession was with the Test Card. This went on television late at night, then again in the early morning, before the programmes started. The BBC Test Card was a still image of a little girl with long mousey hair. A toy clown was propped beside her.

Laura found his preoccupation with it infuriating. What possible interest could this boring image have for him?

She tried to work out the significance of the Test Card for her son. Daniel had always had difficulty sleeping; not only did he have nightmares but he also woke very early. Presumably switching on the television, even watching a static image such as the Test Card girl, was a comfort to him. Laura gathered that, while everyone else was asleep, her son sat watching the girl and the clown for long periods. He admitted that he sometimes found the clown frightening.

Sometimes Laura thought that her son was like a disembodied voice, a soul floating in the universe. He would speak about himself in the third person as though seeing himself, and the people and events in his life, from a great distance.

Once, describing his sister, he said: 'That girl, Mary, my sister, my friend.'

That Christmas, when he was five, he said he wanted to be a reindeer and a few moments later added: 'The child said he wants to be a reindeer.'

Anything that seemed to start normally, out of everyday life, could quickly turn into an obsession. Mrs Penny, a lady in her seventies of whom Daniel was very fond, had had a Russian Blue cat called Little Peg which had been killed by a car. Daniel, who had never met Little Peg, became fascinated by the idea of a Russian Blue and kept repeating how rare the breed was. He recounted the story of Little Peg's death again and again to anybody who would listen.

....

Sometimes he changed the story, once saying that Little Peg was a foundling and another time that Mrs Penny had bought him in a pet shop in Australia.

Daniel was also fascinated by dreams, his own and other people's. He wheedled adults to tell him their dreams and built up a collection. A terrifying dream that Laura had had as a teenager, about a wailing silver-haired child in a wheelchair, was part of this collection, he told her. He was also interested in different categories of dreams.

'I just had rather a dull dream in pink and white colours. Do some people get those dreams when they're ill? . . . Could a dream go on for ever? Could a dream go on for a whole day? . . . I had a little dream inside another dream.'

Trying to get Laura to recount another of her dreams, he asked: 'Was it an adventure dream or was it a one-stand nightmare?'

He begged his mother to repeat her dreams to him over and over again. This appeared to give him comfort.

The analyst, at one of her regular meetings with Laura and her husband, said that Daniel was too interested in the dreams of other people. He wanted to enter their dreams, and wasn't sure where their life ended and his began.

He must be 'grounded' and try to concentrate more on real life, she repeated. When he talked about his obsessions, he must be discouraged. He must certainly not be given balloons as he was only using them as an escape. When Laura told her that she had read in a newspaper that there was a club of adults who met regularly to discuss the Test Card, in fact they had met a few weekends ago in a hotel in Ledbury, the therapist raised her eyes.

Then Laura fell in love.

Looking back, she saw that her obsession with this man was like a talisman. She didn't want to put it to the test in case it

. . . .

disappointed her. She wasn't sure when her feeling changed from genuine love into an unhealthy fixation. Was it when she realized subconsciously that he could never provide what she needed? When did her spontaneous feeling of love for him become stuck and turn into an amulet or a magic cloak, which, as her son did with balloons, she used to shield herself from everyday life?

She had fallen in love with him on their second meeting. Perhaps it was the way he had spoken to her children in the village shop. He had asked them if they had won prizes in the local fête the day before and spoken gently, bending his head down to their level, instead of speaking patronizingly from a great height as he, a very tall man, could have done. The four of them had all walked back towards her house, he pushing a bicycle. She remembered a sensation of happiness and freedom that she had not felt for several years, not perhaps since she had had her first baby.

The next evening he came to supper. He was spending that summer in a cottage in a nearby village. Laura couldn't take her eyes off him. He was so handsome. She felt she would do anything to be close to him.

In those first stages of love, she often pored over the postcards he sent then, in the first weeks of their friendship. There were two beautiful ones of orchids, painted in black, reminding her of the soft dark hidden parts of a woman. Another card was of Sir Galahad on his knees praying. Was it possible that he had chosen these images unconsciously? Maybe he had never felt anything for her.

All her meetings with him took on a sense of transience, of desperation. Ordinarily life was not like this; one was not aware of time passing so acutely.

Although she often imagined that she would have some future, or an affair with him, deep down perhaps she feared that it would never come to anything. It was like a balloon that she pushed all the time ahead of her, with its promise of

....

happiness. If she put it to the test, it would burst, leaving nothing to hope for.

One day when they met he had just returned from five weeks abroad. He had a new very short haircut and there were a few freckles over the bridge of his nose from the sun. She was so crazily in love with him that when he started picking his nose with his napkin she found it adorable. He had been making a documentary film on the Amazon. When she asked him about it, he did not seem to want to recount his experiences.

Laura had just seen a Polish film based on a story by Charles Bukowski, depicting three stages out of a man's life. She described a scene in which the man carried a dead woman into the sea. Her companion seemed moved by this, or was he moved by her? She couldn't tell. When she got home after the lunch, she started to cry. Her son found her.

'What are tears?' he asked.

Then he quoted from *Little Black Mingo*.

'"Tears ran down his cheeks and pattered on the sand like rain."'

'You're the best mother in the world,' he told her.

He ran into the garden and picked her some daisies.

Soon after this the man went away again, this time to the Far East. He sent a postcard to her and her husband, saying 'Look after yourselves and the children.' She thought she would die of loneliness.

She read 'The Little Mermaid' to her son in his bedroom at night. He was fascinated by the palace under the sea. The story was beautiful and sad. The Little Mermaid fell in love with a Prince whose life she had saved after a shipwreck. But the only way she could win him was to gain a human soul, and she would only be able to attain this if a man loved her more than anyone else in the world. To make the Prince fall in love with her she would also have to change her tail for legs and feet and have her tongue cut off. She would be

....

in terrible pain and she would be dumb for ever. The Little Mermaid agreed to make these sacrifices.

Laura was struck that in this story it was the woman who yearned for the man and did everything to win him, and also by the inevitable sadness of love.

Suddenly he was back. He telephoned and asked cautiously if he could leave several crates of books at her cottage in the country. He said he was moving around all the time and had nowhere to store them since his marriage had broken up. Stifling an instinct of self-preservation, she agreed. One June afternoon she left her children with a baby-sitter and they drove to the country in his dilapidated car.

She showed him a short cut, through lanes of cow parsley and green trees.

'This is a pretty road,' he said.

She pointed out a pond where she had skated as a child and a field where she had ridden a pony alone on summer evenings.

When they had unloaded the books they went back to London together by train. He had left his car at the cottage for the summer.

The whole way up in the train he hardly spoke to her. He was reading his newspaper. There were troubles in China.

She moved her seat once to sit opposite him. Some of the time she stared out of the window; the rest of the time she looked at him. She took in the whole of his body – his large feet in light brown shoes, his ankles showing beneath his trousers, his wrists covered with black hair, his dark eyes with their long dark lashes. She wanted him.

Once she looked out of the window and there was a hot air balloon floating over the downs, dark grey. As she watched, a violent flame glowed underneath and there was a roaring sound. Every few moments there was this vivid orange flame . . .

....

She jumped up to close the window. He looked at her at last.

'Cold?' he asked.

After that he did not get in touch with her. She did not know where he was. She became fascinated by the house where he used to live. His ex-wife was there, with their four children. Laura sensed that she was the stronger of the two.

For Laura this four-storeyed cream-coloured house was both a fortress and a palace. It was a fortress because Laura felt she couldn't go in and find out where he was, and it was a palace because, although he had left to go abroad, she imagined a stable family life going on in there, something she would never be able to provide for this man, or even for her son.

She sensed that what attracted her to him, besides his beauty, was some shared unhappiness in each of their childhoods, which they had never articulated to each other. He reminded her of her younger brother, who had died. Often when she saw this man, or yearned for him, she would begin to remember the first years of her life when she had lived with her parents and brother in a rented house on a common. She even smelt the smell of the new carrots which her parents had grown in the vegetable garden of that enchanted place. Once, just before he telephoned her, a vision of huge polyanthus, all different colours, their texture like silk, and smelling extraordinarily sweet, came before her, and she remembered them in the flower-beds of that house in spring, the place where she had been so happy.

Sometimes now she walked past the ex-wife's house, hoping she wouldn't be seen, or maybe she hoped she would be seen and invited in. The shutters were closed promptly every evening at twilight. She yearned to be a child in the wife's house, as she was sure this man still did. He was Peter Pan who had flown out of the window, behaved irresponsibly, and now would never be allowed back. When Laura

....

was a child, Peter Pan had been her hero. She had admired him and she also had wanted to be him.

One afternoon she met the man's ex-wife in the market. She was buying strawberries and when she saw Laura, whom she hardly knew, she held out her arms. Laura was touched by this. The wife said she had eight people coming to supper and was going to make a strawberry tart. Then, as though she knew Laura wanted to hear news of him, she explained that her husband was away in Spain making another film. He had been lent a house and preferred living there to living in London.

'He knows too many people here. If someone asks him out to lunch he'll leave his work and go. He's easily distracted,' she explained.

Laura thought she knew about their meetings and felt humiliated.

Her son, now aged nine, had a new obsession – tarantulas. Laura bought him a book about them and on holiday in Devon that summer she read out loud to him from the book every evening. She read about the Chilean Red-Leg, hairy and black with bands of orange across its back and legs, sometimes so big it could eat mice and birds. There was the Black Widow spider and the False Black Widow, which couldn't kill you as its namesake could. There was the Australian Funnel-Web, and the tarantula from Italy. (This was the origin of the dance called the tarantella. People thought they could cure the spider's bite by frantic dancing.)

At least tarantulas was a subject in which other people could be interested, about which her son could learn something, unlike the Test Card or balloons. Laura enjoyed learning about the different types of tarantulas herself. She imagined that one day she would travel with her son to Venezuela and they would go into the jungle and look for tarantulas.

That July in Devon there were beautiful sunsets. As Laura

....

and the children ate supper they watched the sun setting over the sea. They went for long walks on the cliffs and once in an empty cove Laura took off her clothes and plunged into the waves. She told her son about Roland, a boy she had fallen in love with in that village when she was nine. She had loved his blond curls and pink cheeks. She had waited for Roland every afternoon by the sea-wall but had never spoken to him.

'Maybe I could find him again on the beach tomorrow. Maybe he's here as a blond middle-aged man with his own children,' said Laura.

Her son listened carefully then said: 'I'll help you find him.'

The next morning however Daniel seemed annoyed with the idea of Roland.

His obsession with the tarantulas continued all that summer. Back in London he asked Laura to take him to the Zoo. They hung around the 'Invertebrates' section for two hours, Laura getting rather bored. A young zoo assistant was feeding one in a small tank. The cover was off. She answered all Daniel's questions and said that if he wanted one as a pet it was best to approach the British Tarantula Society, not just get one in a pet shop. They could be lethal and if you were bitten by a rare species you might not be able to get the right antidote.

Daniel talked to everyone he met about tarantulas even if they weren't interested. Then one local mother told him that there was one belonging to a teenage boy in a house up the road. This turned out to be the son of the man Laura had been in love with.

Daniel begged Laura to take him there but she hesitated, because of her past connection with the house and the woman who lived in it. At the same time, she was tempted to see inside the place she had always longed to enter.

One evening in August there was a party. The man whom Laura had been in love with, whom she hadn't seen for

....

almost a year, was there. He had avoided her ever since he had left the books in her house. He had sent a van to remove them, instead of coming himself, and he had sent a message asking her to drive his car back to London.

She marched up to him and said, 'You left your books with me for eight months and now you're damn well going to talk to me,' adding: 'I'm no longer in love with you so you needn't worry.'

As she said it, she realized it was true. He was ordinary, extremely handsome, and rather weak.

She felt crazily exhilarated. She drank some champagne and began a conversation with his wife about children's schools. She said 'I hear you have a tarantula,' and asked if she could bring Daniel over one afternoon to look at it.

A week later, she and Daniel entered the house for the first time.

The tarantula was alone in a small room at the top of the house. Laura and her son stared at it in its glass cage. It was surprisingly motionless and a dull brown colour, not like the exotic striped ones in the book. The teenage son, who had escorted them upstairs, explained that it only moved if it felt a vibration like a small wind. This reminded it of a cricket's wings. It lived on live crickets.

'Don't touch it. It can bite,' he warned Daniel.

When they arrived home, Laura felt calm. She had seen the inside of the house. She thought of the peaceful domestic scene in the kitchen. At the big wooden table the wife and her eldest daughter had been making pastry.

She promised to buy her son a tarantula when he was ten years old. Surely if he owned one he wouldn't be preoccupied with them in the same unhealthy way?

That evening however, she experienced the same sensation that she had felt before in connection with the man she had been in love with. Early memories, of a time when she had been happy and safe, flooded over her like a tidal wave.

....

She remembered a village street when, aged two or three, she had been given her first balloon. She and her friends, Lucia and Victoria, had been given one each. Perhaps it was one of their birthdays. Her balloon was red, Lucia's was white, and Victoria's was yellow.

By evening all the balloons had gone. Victoria's had burst in the car, Lucia's had blown away up the road, and hers had simply disappeared.

She realized that all her life she had remembered the magic of those first balloons, and she called her son into her bedroom to tell him.

Spruce Him Up

MICHAEL CARSON

The doctor said Len might soldier on for years or go just like that.

'What caused it, doctor?' I asked.

He ran his fingers across a great big lump of coal sitting there on his desk like the most natural thing in the world. He'd put it on a really pretty doiley. It's not every man who'd think of that. The doiley gave me confidence that Len was in good hands. 'Well, the cigarettes can't have helped,' he said. 'What was your husband's daily consumption?'

'You mean, how many did he smoke? About forty, give or take a few. I nicked the odd one, I have to be honest. Even after I gave up.'

'Did you try the patches?'

'I didn't get on with them,' I said, a bit tart in my tone. 'Anyway, I don't think it was the fags. Len's not been the same since the Falklands.'

'Yes, well . . .' he said.

I knew he didn't believe me for a moment. Doctors have got this bee in their bonnets about fags. But what about car-exhausts I'd like to know? You hardly ever hear them blaming car-exhausts. And Hollywood's the same. You know who the baddy is because he's the one who lights up. He's never the one in the fast car. Well, he might be but it isn't a surefire sign of badness, is it? It's funny how we get all moral about some things and ignore the other things. Now I'm the last person to get up on a soap box. I'd probably go straight through it. But I know it's not

....

right. 'Doctor,' I said, 'Doctor, I hope you don't mind me asking you this but why do you have a piece of coal on your desk?'

'It's a long story, Mrs Cotter,' he said, looking at his watch.

'You don't need to tell me,' I said.

The next day a nurse called me from Len's bedside, saying that there was a call for me from California.

'That'll be Sharon,' I said. I patted Len's hand. 'It's Sharon. Shan't be a tick, Len. I'll give her your love, shall I?'

Len just lay there. Didn't move a muscle. I combed his hair with my hand. Then, looking at him there, I put my hand to my mouth and the tears were coming. I felt like one of those mothers on *News At Ten* and didn't like it one little bit.

On the way to the phone, I said to the nurse, 'He's got a good colour, hasn't he?'

'A lovely colour,' she said.

'Do you think he knows me?'

'It's hard to know what's going on.' She looked at her fob-watch.

'That's a nice watch,' I said, for something to say. 'It's not often you see a digital fob-watch. I expect they're more exact than the others.'

'The telephone's here, Mrs Cotter.'

Sharon was in a state. I knew she would be and that always puts me in a state as well. She was tired of Norman and of being a Saxon Barmaid, she said. The braids she has to wear in her hair are, or so she reckoned, strangling the free passage of amino-acids from the follicle to the tip of each strand. They've split something horrible, she said.

'It's a job,' I said. 'If I was you I'd use the braids to cover the splits. You should be grateful.'

'Well, I'm not. I'm Sharon.'

....

In my book Len has it over split-ends, but it'd be a hiding
to nothing pointing this out to Sharon.

'How's Dad?' At last!

'He's as well as can be expected,' I said, trying not to
sound like a preachy Mum. It's much too late now.

'My life,' she said, 'is worthless. Sometimes I can't believe
my own worthlessness.'

'Come on, Shar!' I said. 'That's no way to talk.'

'I'm a worthless human being, Mum. I am! I am!'

I told her to calm down. I told her she had her health and
that if you have that it's greater than wealth.

Sharon didn't take that to heart, though. She's never been
what you might call a good listener. She bent my ear for half
an hour, going on and on about her worthlessness. I kept
interrupting to tell her that it must be costing her a bomb,
but she just kept on. She said that it was cheap rate there.
Five in the morning. And I told her I'd never got the hang
of time, and anyway cheap rate can't be *that* cheap. But she
wasn't listening, just rabbited on about her worthlessness. I
don't know why she goes to that therapy group if that's all
they can tell her. Mind you, they do have a point. After
listening to her whining on for half an hour I was getting to
be as certain of her worthlessness as she was.

'Any chance of you coming over? Your dad would love to
see you,' I said, as I couldn't think of anything else to say.

'It's a bit difficult, Mum. I can't afford to jeopardize my
Green Card. It's in the works.'

'Well, keep in touch,' I said. 'And don't you listen to
those silly Americans. You're not worthless. Do you hear
me, Sharon?'

Nothing much happened for the next week. I did a lot of
talking to Len because a nurse – not the one with the digital
fob-watch – said he might be able to hear me. I soon ran out
of subjects. We haven't been great talkers in recent years.
Well, after thirty years of married bliss, you've said most of
it, haven't you? So I looked for a magazine in the Paki

....

newsagent outside the hospital. They sell flowers too. Don't miss a trick. Anyway, I bought a magazine called *Arms and the Man* and read bits to him from that for a day or two. He's always had a soft spot for AK 47s and there was a story told by a soldier of fortune whose AK 47, he reckoned, was wife, child and mistress to him. The story was sad in a way because it had been found among his papers when he was killed in Bosnia fighting for Muslims against the Croats or for Croats against the Muslims. I forget now, and I'm not sure he knew himself. The poor little bleeder only lasted a week. That's how ideals end up, I suppose.

Anyway, that story really brought a tear to my eye. 'That's sad, isn't it?' I said to Len, but Len didn't show the least sign. And if that story couldn't rouse him, then I reckon nothing would. I gave up hope a bit then.

And I went on the fags again. Back to the Paki for a *TV Quick* and twenty Capstan Full Strength. Well, if you're going to do it, do it like you mean it, I say.

I was having one in the cubby-hole set aside for smokers between the interdenominational chapel and the Gents. Some jokers had put a sign on the door: DANGER: LEPERS AND SMOKERS. DO NOT ENTER! Well, I don't call that funny, even if they do. Some people have a rum sense of humour if you want my opinion.

There was only one chap in there and he didn't look like he was going home any time soon. We shrugged at one another for a while like smokers do, then he came out and said straight off: 'The name's Harry. Lung cancer.'

He was pulling on a Marlboro 100. Real Arab underpants. 'You shouldn't be smoking,' I said.

He looked at his fag. 'It wasn't these. I worked for London Transport. It was the asbestos brake-linings.'

I nodded, not knowing anything much about asbestos except we used to have a garage made of it until we had it taken away so that the Happy Wanderer Motor Home could fit on the spot. 'That's an interesting lighter you've got

....

there,' I said to the poor chap, more for something to say than to say something.

His grey face lit up. 'Well, it's actually only a lighter-cover. If you get my meaning.' He tried to pull the lighter out of the silvery cover but couldn't. I told him to give it over to me and, after I'd chipped a nail, out popped this purple Bic disposable.

'Fancy!' I said. 'That's clever. It really improves the lighter no end like.'

He nodded. Then his face sort of went out. He looked sad again. Then he started coughing into his hankie.

I pretended not to notice. 'I mean,' I said, 'while a Bic is very reliable and everything, it's no oil-painting, is it? But that cover – silver is it? – that perks it up. It's classy, that's what it is. I suppose the idea is that when the lighter runs out of fuel you discard it then put another into the cover. That's really lovely. A conversation-piece you might say. Where did you get it?'

'It was made by the Hopi Indians of Arizona,' Harry said.

'Was it, indeed?'

'I went to the Grand Canyon with Thomson's.'

'If Thomson's do it, do it!' I said.

'Well, I could have done without the South Rim,' Harry said. 'Like a bloody holiday camp. But the North Rim? Now that's a different story.'

Harry started coughing again. 'And now you've got this lovely lighter-cover as a souvenir,' I said. 'You'll never forget that holiday ever, will you? Not with that lovely souvenir to remind you.'

'You can watch them being made,' Harry said. 'Now I'd always prided myself on being a bit of a craftsman in my own way. Keeping those old double-deckers on the road takes a bit of craft, I'm telling you. You see, the public prefer the old ones that have the open deck at the back with a bus conductor and that.'

'There's no such thing as progress,' I said.

He reached for his purple Bic and looked at it and the

lighter-cover for a long time. He was panting like Juno does after her walk.

'Put it back in the cover. You mustn't let your standards slip,' I said.

He struggled for a while, but had to hand the lighter to me to push all the way in. It was a bit hard even for me.

'Bics were hard to find for a while in the UK. They're back now, thank God.'

'Flick my Bic!' I said.

'See the design?' he said, pointing to the black shapes carved into the silver. 'That's a whole story in itself. That figure is Salavi. He was an important holy man of the Bear Clan. He's lying down because he's dead. His legs are open because he has nothing to hide.'

'I've known quite a few like that,' I said. Harry looked at me and I felt myself going red.

'That jagged line represents water. It flows into that spring there. Out of the spring grows a spruce tree. You see, Salavi was transformed into a spruce tree after his death. The Hopi believe that the spruce tree is holy, the most magnetic of all trees. Its branches form a throne for the clouds to rest on. Then Salavi's spirit can rise up the spruce tree and leap straight into paradise.'

'Every picture tells a story,' I said.

'That's why I bought it,' he said. 'The man who made it told me all about it. He was what I'd call a real craftsman.'

'Well, there aren't many of them about,' I said and, believe me, I have reason to know.

'I liked the Hopi Indians a lot. They were really different from the Yanks.'

'My daughter's over there,' I said.

'They were quiet, the Hopis. Dirt poor, I suppose, but money isn't everything.'

'It certainly isn't,' I said. 'I think I'd better . . .'

'What are you here for?'

'My hubbie's had a stroke. It doesn't look too good, tell you the truth. He doesn't know me.'

. . . .

'I've only got a few weeks at most.'

I didn't know what to say. It struck me then and there that it's funny not to be able to say something useful to somebody who's going to shuffle off. I mean, we all do it, don't we? Sooner or later we're all for it. You'd think we'd have something helpful to contribute. You'd think they'd have put it in the National Curriculum by now. 'You shouldn't be doing that!' I said, pointing to his Marlboro.

'The doctor says it doesn't make any difference.'

'No, but still . . .'

'How old is your husband? What's his name by the way?'

'Len. He's fifty-six.'

'That's no age,' he said.

'No. He was never the same after the Falklands. I waved him goodbye on the *Canberra* but the man I waved back wasn't my Len at all.'

'I said at the time, "That bloody Margaret Thatcher." It's a wonder to me how she can live with herself,' he said.

'Steady on,' I said. 'Look, I must get back. Len'll be wondering. Well, I live in hope he will. Anyway, I always spruce him up in the afternoon. Give him a wash, comb his hair. That sort of thing.'

'Best of luck,' he said.

'Best of luck to you, too,' I said.

Harry nodded, picked up the lighter and turned it over and over in his grey hand.

Later that day I was telling Len about Harry's lighter when it hit me. Len should have his things about him. He's got such a lot of little trophies at home. Nothing that's very valuable, I suppose, but I remembered how Harry had got quite chirpy while going on about his lighter-cover, and I thought the same thing might happen to Len.

That night I set to work. In the end I had to get my old wheely out, give it a good rub down with the leather and load up with Len's bits-and-bobs. You see, I had known

....

where to start but not where to stop. I'm a bit like that. Bull in a china shop type.

I have a rather comprehensive collection of Hummel figures in the Gaybox, even if I do say so myself, and I wondered about taking 'Two Children at a Wayside Shrine' in. But I decided not to. For though we've had the Hummels for years – ever since Len and me were stationed with the forces in Germany – they aren't things that Len picked out for himself. They're sort of shared if you know what I mean. Like the Franklin Mint thimbles in their own thimblerama. I wanted to take him things which were *his*. In his own way he was as bad as me in the knick-knack department. The same but different. If I get one thing, I have to go on. I'm like a drunk after his first drink. I buy one snowman, I've got to have the whole set. I buy a pig, I won't rest until the table is covered in them. And then, when they're all out on display, I have a good sigh and I'm content. At least I think I am. Sometimes I wonder why I bothered. Sharon's got that in her too. With her it's everything George Michael ever recorded, everything bloody Barbie ever wore. Now Len wasn't like that. There's no rhyme nor reason to his stuff. Every single bit's in a class of its own and makes you sort of wonder.

There were lots of things like that, to tell you the truth. And I began to assemble everything I've polished and dusted over the years wondering why he kept them. Now would be my chance to ask. Of course, I might not get an answer. Len might not know himself. But there was no harm, I reckoned, in trying.

The nurse with the digital fob-watch was talking to the doctor with the lump of coal on his desk. She gave me a look from behind her desk as I pulled my wheely in. I was all ready to argue the toss with her, but she didn't say anything.

'Any change?' I asked her.

'He's stable,' she said, not even bothering to give me a

....

173

straight look. The doctor didn't even look round. A hello doesn't cost anything in my book.

'I've brought some things in from home, Len,' I said to him by way of greeting.

I sat down beside him, arranged the wheely at my knee, cradled his big hand in my small one and, looking at our hands mixed together, suddenly shivered. A real woman's shiver it was. I saw myself on my back with my legs round Len's waist and him sweating above me, St Christopher dancing on his hairy chest and that soldier's face looking down at me as if he hated me, and those big hands crushing mine. And the shiver was followed by the first real tears I've wept since he jerked forward in Tesco's and started writhing on the floor, upsetting the Andrex display. And I was thinking, *I may never be there again. I may never have Len pulling me this way and that, jerking and falling apart, killing me as he dies, falling like a soldier in Flanders, and making me cry out with pity as he lies there crushed, crushing my breasts.*

Anyway, I pulled myself together and reached into the wheely for the first of his souvenirs.

'And the first object is . . .' I said to him and got out the hairy thing like a troll with a squashed-up face that he brought back from Borneo after that Confrontation thing. I held it out above his face so that, if there was any life behind those eyes, he couldn't miss it. 'Remember this?' I asked him. 'You wouldn't let me put it out for the bin-men. Tell me what it's for? Why do you like it so much, Len?'

I thought for a minute that he blinked but, though I moved the horrible thing about, he didn't do it again and I wondered if he had done it at all.

I laid it aside. 'And the next object is . . .' I continued, reaching into the wheely, 'a shell-case lovingly Brassoed by yours truly over many a long year. I can't remember where you brought it from. Was it Aden, Len? Oman?'

No reaction. Pass. Still, I'd started so I'd finish. I tried him with the rubber bullet that we kept on the right-hand

. . . .

step of the lounge fireplace mantelpiece. It was a bit of an embarrassment – I always thought people might get the wrong idea – but Len wouldn't be told.

Not a flicker from Len. And nothing either for a signed copy of *Who Dares Wins* which Len had had sunk in perspex, open at the title page. Nor for the novelty donkey cigarette box from Malta. It's clever all right. You press the donkey's ears back. The donkey raises his tail and pushes out a cigarette from his b-t-m. It's disgusting in a way but you have to laugh.

Len didn't laugh. Still, it's early days, I thought. If these don't get a reaction before the day's out I'll bring some more in tomorrow. I put the things I'd shown him on the table that straddles the bed, thinking that if his eyes were working they would be in range still.

I had another delve. 'You must remember this!' I said, producing his monk in a brown gown. You tug his beard hard and out pops his big stiff willy through a slit in the gown. 'Where did you get this, Len?' No answer. 'It's disgusting! Was it Aldershot? Colchester? I can't remember, Len. Tell me, Len! Please, Len!'

Nothing. Not a flicker. An Omani dagger. I know it's Omani because I saw it presented to Len after his two-year stint training the National Guard out there. Lovely workmanship. I should show it to Harry. It knocks his Indian lighter-cover into a cocked hat.

Nothing.

A big piece of agate that's the spitting image of a frozen gammon joint. One surface is polished and if you look carefully you can see water trapped inside. The man who sold it to Len in Cyprus said that the water has been stuck there for 500 million years. Or was it 50 million years? Anyway one hell of a bloody long time to be stuck. And the man said that the water inside was deadly poison because of all the heat and chemical reactions and everything. We keep it in the hall. Len puts his car-keys on it religiously.

Anyway, I waved the piece of agate in front of him. 'Can

....

175

you see the water, Len? Can you see it? 500 million odd years . . . that's how long the water's been trapped inside the stone. Makes you think, doesn't it, Len?'

But if it did, Len wasn't letting on.

The wheely was empty and the table full with Len's clutter. I stood at the end of the bed and said, 'They're your souvenirs, Len. They speak of a life full of travel and interesting things. Your life's there, Len. Come on, love, snap out of it!'

Nothing for a long moment. I was having those feelings again. I was empty, hollow, and I didn't like it one little bit.

'I think I'll go and get myself a cup of tea, love. Back in a tick.'

I heard the crash when I was walking down the corridor. The nurse with the digital fob-watch ran ahead of me into Len's room. I ran after and there was Len slumped sideways. His arm still waving. He had knocked everything I had brought him off the table, made a clean sweep. Everything that could break had broken. The nurse with the digital fob-watch stood on the monk's willy. It'll never be the same. The agate was split wide open and the 5000-million-years-old water was spreading across the floor like Juno's wee when she gets carried away.

The nurse was feeling Len's pulse but I knew that was that. She let go of his wrist, arranged him neatly on the bed and looked at me.

'He's gone, isn't he?'

'Yes,' she said. 'I'm sorry.'

I nodded but I didn't cry or anything. I didn't want to look like someone on the news again. I just said, 'When the porter clears up the mess make sure he watches out for that water. It's deadly poison.' And I walked off to the little cubbyhole for lepers and smokers between the interdenominational chapel and the Gents.

Anyway, Sharon flew home with Norman for the funeral. Len got what you might call a good send-off, though I'm not

....

sure I'd agree with you. I don't get on with floral tributes. Never have. A dartboard done in carnations, which is what he got from his mates at The Short Sharp Shock, stared at me during the internment. And the smell coming off Sharon's bouquet of orchids from California made me – I'm sorry – want to puke. I kept thinking. *Not like this. It oughtn't to end like this. I know we weren't perfect but we were better than this! Sweet Jesus, we don't deserve all this CRAP!*

I was dry as a bone all the way through it. The vicar – whoever he was – said that I'd probably gone through the grieving process at Len's bedside. Florrie from the florists said that I'd know when to let it out . . . Cow.

It came this morning. A brown envelope with the name of the hospital on the outside. I thought it must be one of Len's knick-knacks but when I opened it it was a letter from the nurse with the digital fob-watch. She said that Harry had died. Just before his peaceful end, he had asked for his lighter-cover to be sent to me, as I had admired it and been kind to him. I unwrapped the bubble-wrap around it and there it was, rolling in my palm, still with the purple Bic inside.

Well, Harry's gift did it. I started blubbering and have been blubbering on and off ever since. Florrie from the florists would say I'd started my grieving in earnest now. And she knows. That business of hers would have gone to the wall ages ago if it wasn't for the funeral trade. It's odd, though. I can think of Len and nothing happens but if I just say 'Harry' or look at the lighter-cover, I'm off like bleeding Niagara.

Anyway, I've put Harry's lighter in the centre of the coffee-table, where Len kept his silver tank. Daft in a way, I'll never stop smoking now. A fag won't be a coffin-nail any more. More of a candle lit for Len . . . for Harry . . . for worthless Sharon . . .

For Harry.

. . . .

Rat Mother

URSULE MOLINARO

Twice a year, at the time of the equinox, in March & in September, raw eggs can stand by themselves. You place the egg, plumper side down, on a level surface   like a dining-room table or a dormitory dresser   hold it gingerly between your hands until you feel the yolk settle, you withdraw your hands, & the egg stands. You feel a strange primal thrill, like seeing a bird put its head under a wing during a solar eclipse. The egg stands by itself for the duration of the equinox, unless a truck rattles past, or someone deliberately upsets the level surface.

Ramona Bear & I used to perform elaborate egg-standing rituals twice a year, during the 4 years we were college room-mates. The believers would tiptoe in, & crane their necks from the door, awed by the miracle of a balanced universe in miniature, in the basic pre-commitment shape that had most likely preceded the hen. The heretics would make a rowdy entry, hoping to upset the righteous equilibrium & keep the high priestess from repeating the feat.

They all came to the standing of the eggs, because Ramona Bear was the most beautiful woman they'd seen off screen or off stage or outside glossy fashion magazines, & they came to prove their equality, if not their superiority, to the flawless face & flawless figure they couldn't dismiss as a hollow surface. The arrogance of a beautiful woman, proclaiming that she was in love with surfaces. With proportion. Which was why she was studying to be an architect.

It thrilled her to feel an egg get ready to stand while the sun crossed the equator: she'd say to us while she performed the ritual: The ubiquitous oval of the egg, which had inspired the Arabs to invent zero. The pre-choice position between positive & negative, in which the light enfolds the dark, & no judgement is passed on either.

After college we both returned to New York City. The aspiring architect became the fashion model her fellow-students always thought she ought to be. & my studies of languages, with an emphasis on etymology, qualified me for translating technical manuals.

Ramona Bear lived in stony respectability on the Upper West Side. I found a former butcher store in Greenwich Village, which a painter had converted into a studio. He had covered the walls of the toilet in black lamb fur, & gold-leafed the lion-footed bathtub in the kitchen, but had left a little yard in the back littered with rusting skeletons of bicycles, tricycles, & inner springs. Eventually, my son made it into a rock garden with small lakes full of waterlilies & salamanders.

Once a month Ramona Bear & I met halfway for lunch in a mid-town restaurant, & compared lives. Which began to show similarities we thought were beyond the promptings of biology: We married within a month of each other, produced one child the following summer – her daughter was born on July 31, my son on August 4 – & divorced 11 years later, both in November.

We were friends, but not close friends. Our lunches were a non-commital constant from which we returned with regained perspective & cheerful. She always said I made her laugh. & I enjoyed looking at her. Aging became her. At 40 she was modeling expensive coats & suits for the executive woman. A few times she sold me a piece she'd worn during a show, at a price I could afford. Beautiful clothes which I'd model for my son when I got home. My son had shown interest in what people wore since babyhood. He drew well, & at 13 he wanted to be a fashion designer. He asked me to ask Ramona Bear if she'd smuggle him into a show sometime.

....

I didn't want to ask her. We'd never intruded our lives on our luncheons, except as subjects of comparison & subsequent amusement. But my son insisted, & so his mother gave in. Ramona Bear thought that might be arranged. No problem. & added: That I was lucky to have a son. A daughter was her mother's nemesis. At least her daughter was.

& then she broke the tacit luncheon rule, & told me that: Since the divorce her daughter rarely spoke to her. When she did, it was with sarcastic disdain. Her daughter was deliberately destroying her body, as a judgement on her mother's superficiality.

I asked: If her daughter was on drugs.

In a way. Except that her daughter's drugs were legal. Her daughter was eating herself to death. The father was bribing the girl's affection with lavish gifts of money; as was the paternal grandmother. Her daughter was buying food with the money. Food of the most fattening kind: candy
pastries   cakes   pizzas, which she ate behind the locked door of her room. At dinner time she'd glare at her mother across the table, & hold forth about health fanatics with atrophied tastebuds.

There were moments when Ramona Bear was sure she saw her daughter grow fatter before her very eyes. She found it painful to see a girl of 13, who measured 5 foot 3, weigh over 200 pounds. For months now she'd been dragging the protesting blimp from diet doctors to therapists. To no avail. Nothing & no one seemed able to distract her daughter from the all-consuming thought of: FOOD.

Ever since her daughter was old enough to sit on a chair, they'd done the egg-standing ritual together twice a year. The last time they'd done it, her daughter had accused her of sadism, making her play with food. & although she'd smiled when her egg stood up, she said: She'd be a lot more thrilled to see it sunny side up, or in an omelette.

& then she'd crushed her egg between her sausage fingers, & slurped down the slimy mess. Telling her mother between

....

slurps how her father had told her that he'd just had to get out, to save his life. How her mother claimed all the space in a room, with her perfect face & perfect figure, until everyone else started to choke. That was why her daughter was making herself huge, to preserve her breathing space.

At that point Ramona Bear had suggested that they should perhaps not live together for a while. That her daughter should perhaps go to a boarding school, or else stay with her father. But her daughter had started screaming that: Her mother wasn't going to get rid of her that easily. She was going to stick around & embarrass her mother, until her mother understood the meaning of embarrassment.

It was true: Her daughter had become an embarrassment to her. It was almost impossible to have friends over just friends, not even lovers   with an ever-vigilant sentinel in the house. Who'd act pointedly left-out. Or else came on to the friend until he ran out of the house. Her daughter had alienated all her own playmates as well.

I offered my son as a possible companion, worrying how he would react to my fixing him up with a fat girl, even if the fat girl was maybe an entrance to the fashion world. Ramona Bear sensed my hesitation. She thanked me, but thought we'd be inviting trouble. It might even be the end of our lunches. Which were her oases of sanity in this nuthouse that was her life. & the last thing she wished to give up. Her daughter was a master manipulator.

She rummaged in her handbag, & handed me 3 sheets of paper, covered with minuscule handwriting   in brown ink   which her daughter had left lying on the dining-room table, for her mother to read & get upset about.

The first one was a poem, retelling the fairytale of Hansel & Gretel. A stylish witch in a forest-green pants suit sticks only Gretel into the rabbit cage. She seduces Hansel who falls completely under her spell, & stuffs his captive sister the way Alsatian peasants stuff geese for gooseliver

....

pâté. When Gretel weighs 200 pounds, they smother her with kindness & make an exquisite pâté of her liver, which they serve at their wedding reception.   – Ramona Bear was wearing a forest-green pants suit to our lunch that day.

The second poem was entitled: THE RAT. An enormous pink rat in a forest-green bathing suit is sitting on a beach under a forest-green beach umbrella, surrounded by roasts cheeses   breads   cakes & a long list of desserts & sweets as far as the eye can see. Its fat aquiver with anticipation, the rat devours everything. Breathlessly with frenzied jaws . . . / Then eats itself . . . / Beginning with its paws.

The third piece was called: JUDGE YOUR HONOR, an imaginary dialogue with a tone-deaf mother.

You ask: If I have no self-respect. I don't need to ask: If you have no vanity.

You say that: Shame begins where beauty stops. Let me be your shame then, as I burst into a fashion show with cries of: Mommy . . . Mommy . . .

You say that our body is our temple. I say: It's an instrument of perception. If we spend our life adoring the instrument we sure don't perceive very much.

Her daughter must be extremely intelligent: I said in response to Ramona Bear's questioning eyebrows.

She sighed & shook her head: 200 pounds for a 5 foot 3 body wasn't her idea of intelligence, at age 13. Or any age.

That was the last of our lunches. She canceled the next one. & the one after that. Then called to tell me that she was going away for a time, & would let me know as soon as she came back. During the almost 15 years of silence that followed, my son often asked about Ramona Bear. & when I had nothing to tell him, he decided that a prince or a millionaire had carried her off to a castle in Spain.

Suddenly, one evening in March   on March 19, to be exact   Ramona Bear is on the phone, sounding urgent.

....

Can I come to her house right away, to stand up some eggs & have dinner with her afterwards. She's still at the same stony Upper West Side address. When I hesitate she remembers that I don't like to eat in people's houses, & argues eloquently that: I will have a tremendous variety of food to choose from, all of gourmet quality, catered by La Goulue, where her daughter is the chef. When I accept, she asks that: I wear my black glasses, in a voice that sounds breathless & over-precise with anguish.

I don't know the person who's letting me in. Who vaguely resembles Ramona Bear. A blow-up of the Ramona Bear I remember, hiding under a forest-green tent. I briefly wonder if she may be the overweight daughter, but the huge face looks too old for a woman of 28.

A woman who speaks with the voice of Ramona Bear, as she sways down the hall ahead of me with the rolling buttocks of a farm horse, & ushers me into a dimly lit dining-room, dominated by a long table covered with food. Toward one end, a narrow space has been cleared for 2 raw eggs on a plate. It is only after the enormous creature settles into the chair across from me that I can no longer doubt that this is what has become of the once glorious, perfectly proportioned Ramona Bear. I don't know what to say, & she says nothing either. We stare at our eggs between our hands. They stand very quickly.

Well, that's that: she says, laying her egg back down on the plate: Now we can eat.

I find it hard to swallow, trying not to stare at the feverishly chewing mouth across from me. Into which fat fingers clenched around a fork   a knife   a spoon rapidly shove chunks of bread topped with all kinds of pâté devilled eggs   snails   prosciutto on melon   fish in aspic   marinated mushrooms   chicken legs duck breast   asparagus   arugola   endives rolled roast beef   roast potatoes   ham   string beans   strawberry shortcake   raspberry sherbet rhubarb soufflé   flan   cherries flambées. Of course

....

Ramona Bear is aware of my staring at her from behind my black glasses, but she chews away unconcerned.

How's my son? she finally asks during a brief pause. She sounds defiant.

I tell her: My son's fine. He's living on his own now, doing what he always wanted to do: designing clothes. He made the jacket I'm wearing.

Very nice.

I feel her voice hating me. Despising my normal middle-aged silhouette in well-cut clothes.

Her daughter moved out, too. & is very happy working at La Goulue. She'll drop by later. Maybe I can stay & meet her. She makes wonderful food, don't I agree?

The way she says 'food', with her lips pursing for suction, turns my stomach. I don't know what to say. I feel that she is trying to provoke me into verbalizing the shock I'm trying to hide. My disgust   mixed with anger & contempt at the destruction of what used to be exceptional enviable   beauty.

After another long silence, punctured by resumed chewing, she says that: It took her years to work up the courage or the indifference   to let me see her again. In case I'd wondered what had become of her. Well, now I knew. But what I didn't know was that she achieved what no overpaid professional   doctor   therapist   psychiatrist specialist in any field achieved: She cured her daughter. & her daughter is grateful for it. They're getting along beautifully now.

She had an insight, the day of that last luncheon of ours, almost 15 years ago. Do I remember how she was telling me about her daughter's addiction to food . . . complaining about her daughter? On her way home she had a realization: Addiction   to anything   makes you independent from anything but itself. It's like solitary confinement, supplying the company inside your solitary confinement. It's your prison & your refuge. So she thought if she could gain access to her daughter's prison & keep her company, if only

....

for a short while every day, the addiction would lose its autonomy. Perhaps with patience she'd be able to wean her daughter back to a normal shape.

While they're eating their hostile, calorie-conscious dinner that evening, she asks: If her daughter would perhaps like to share the strawberry shortcake she knows her daughter is going to eat in her room by herself after dinner. That way, the strawberry shortcake might provide the social pleasure of shared enjoyment, instead of a shameful private act, committed in hurried secrecy.

Her daughter looks surprised. She thought her mother hated sweets. Desserts.

Yes, well . . . Maybe the strawberry shortcake will change her mind.

She almost chokes on the huge piece of cake her daughter piles onto the plate before her. But she forces herself to eat it. Her daughter rapidly eats the rest. Then thanks her mother with a kiss on the cheek.

The next evening they share an apple strudel.

That's how it began. Ramona Bear started to gain weight, & her daughter started to get thinner.

There was a stage, about 9 months into the shared desserts, when her daughter had lost enough to look normal for a 14-year-old. When Ramona Bear still looked plausible. When they were both . . . pleasantly plump. But when Ramona Bear stopped sharing the desserts, her daughter's weight instantly shot up again. & so Ramona Bear kept eating. The way I'd seen her eat tonight. Now she's no longer able to stop.

She starts to cry then. & I start feeling sorry for her. & afraid for myself, that I, too, might catch the disease of obesity out of compassion for a fat friend. As I stand up, ready to run from the temptation of compassion, her daughter walks in. She's very thin, almost emaciated, with a saintly radiance & a wonderful smile. She's carrying 2 shopping bags which Ramona Bear snatches from her hands. She's no longer crying. She's refilling the platters on the table with

. . . .

pâtés   devilled eggs   marinated mushrooms
fish in aspic   prosciutto on melon.

I ask the radiant daughter: If she drops by like this every night?

Oh yes! she smiles: She couldn't disappoint her mommy. Her mommy is particularly fond of her midnight snack. Why don't I sit down again & help her eat it.

Findings

CHERRY WILDER

At the corner of Willy-Brandt-Strasse and the Southern Ringroad there was another large green sheet of cardboard fastened to a high wooden garden fence; it carried a protest in black letters about noise. Clare wondered if the number of decibels produced anywhere in the town of Breitbach warranted a protest in this day and age.

In the side street it was very quiet; Michael had sent a polaroid of the house, with a small ornamental plum tree and ragged fields stretching downhill. The photo had not revealed that the house was semi-detached, at the end of a row of doll houses, brown and white, very well kept, the small front gardens filled with bright flower-beds. The row of houses was isolated: when their stretch of paved sidewalk ran out Willy-Brandt-Strasse meandered on like a country road: a group of newer and larger houses was going up further on.

'Dividing their trash,' said Bernard. 'Would you look at those damn containers!'

Each front garden had a small rustic enclosure, built with dressed, darkly impregnated logs, holding two tall plastic containers, one black, one blue. Sometimes these were down by the front gate, sometimes up by the porch or on one of the side fences or under a shrub. Clare had parked the rented Golf now, opposite number 24, and was able to observe the houses on this side of the street. They were old and more relaxed, with nice trees and the pairs of plastic trash containers hidden away round the back.

'They have no room over there,' she said, 'nothing but those dinky little front gardens.'

Clare saw that two of the houses had automobiles parked in the street.

'Did Mike say where he parks?' she asked.

Bernard, who had been very good all the way from the airport, begn to polish his sun-glasses with a tissue and speak in rapid bursts.

'*You* were carrying the letters! Where he parks? How can I tell where he parks? You spoke with the girl, with Erika, you had her on the end of the line, why not ask her then where you were going to goddamn *park* . . .'

'Come on,' said Clare. 'We'll just go inside.'

'You going to park over here?' continued Bernard. 'What if the weather breaks? I haven't driven for two years, now I have to solve your parking problems.'

They had taken the three pieces of baggage from the trunk and the in-flight bits and pieces from the back seat. Clare led the way across the quiet street; she opened the gate of wooden lattice and walked up the pathway of number 24. The weeping plum tree was in full bloom, scattering pink and white blossom.

As Bernard came to the narrow sidewalk a woman, about their age, walked past in the direction of the ringroad wheeling a plaid shopping trolley. He set down a suitcase, smiled, raised his panama hat, wished the woman a cheery good-day to which she responded, blank-faced. Two houses down she came to a halt, turned and stared at the pair of them with the inexorable, shameless stare of the housewife that Clare remembered from their previous visits to Germany.

Clare opened the door of her son's house, saw the airways bag and the green parka on the hall-stand, heard some sound of movement – upstairs? in the kitchen? She was thrilled and relieved: Mike and Erika had waited after all. None of this cheerless business of coming to an empty house . . . of coming to an empty house with Bernard. She edited out this thought and called: 'Hello there!'

'Are you crazy?' said Bernard. 'They've gone long ago.'

. . . .

There was no reply to her hail; the house *was* empty.

'I thought they might have waited,' said Clare.

'Did you hear something?' asked Bernard in a hoarse whisper.

'No,' lied Clare.

She checked the airways bag, found it empty, and hung up the parka on the empty coat-rack.

'I'll rustle up some coffee,' she said cheerily. 'You want to take the blue bag upstairs?'

Bernard stood alone in the narrow hallway and knew that something was wrong. Spotted it the moment they came in: that stuff on the hall stand and the noises upstairs. He mustn't alarm Clare of course, Mike was *her* boy, after all, though he had always got along pretty well with his Stepdad, old Bernie. Working quickly before Clare noticed that he was not on his way upstairs Bernard Meyer examined the airways bag. Nice-looking red bag with a bird logo. Cathay Pacific? He went through the central compartment and the two pockets. Nothing. Not a scrap of paper or a small coin. He turned to the parka that Clare had hung up then thought better of it and went up the stairs too fast, lugging the blue softside bag.

He stood gasping on the landing and the noise came again. Yeah, just as he thought, it was a window left open. This proved it, something was wrong, wrong, wrong, something funny was going on. Who went on a trip and left open an upstairs window? Or maybe it was a sign, call for help, last desperate act before . . . Bernard heaved the blue bag the rest of the way, set it down in the larger bedroom. Nope, no luck here, window-wise. He went searching: second bedroom, bathroom, aha! got lucky. Tiny little utility room next to the bathroom, not much bigger than a closet. The small window, which had a net curtain attached to its frame, had been swinging open and shut at about four-minute intervals.

Bernard waited patiently, running his eyes over the contents of the storeroom, sewing machine, ski-boots, shelves of linen, until the window obliged with its routine one more time. He stood on a stack of old catalogues and peered out

. . . .

of the window. He looked down between the white walls of the house and its neighbour at a patch of lush green grass. Something lying there, piece of cloth, garment of some sort, yeah sure, it could still be a message. He must check it out. Clare was already calling from downstairs.

'Oh Bernie . . .'

'Be right down!'

He went back to the master bedroom, if you could call it that, and found some things that frightened him badly. A set of muddy footprints on the carpet and the very shoes that made them. Pair of new track shoes, caked with mud. Puma brand, in black and green, size 43, say about 10½, must belong to Mike. They were just sitting there, all anyhow, with the socks inside, dirty white socks. Mike had been sitting on the bed – Bernie sat beside his place – probably changing his shoes. But what's the hurry? Why not take your muddy shoes away, leave them in the bathroom even – were they running so late? Wouldn't his girl, his German girl, have had something to say about that, about leaving mud on the carpet for visiting in-laws to find?

Bernie saw that one of the drawers of the night table was open a little. He stood up to pull it further open, so as not to disturb the place where Mike had been sitting. The drawer was empty except for a piece of loosely knitted cream cotton cloth, stained with dark oil, and the oilcan itself, labelled *Jägerstolz*: hunter's pride. He slammed the drawer shut and went down the stairs so fast that the small house seemed to shake.

Clare saw that he was in a state but took it for his on-going angry mood, his state of cerebral irritation, which she had to work around. It was not time for his next medication. She served the decaffeinated coffee which she had found in the cupboard and praised the kitchen. She was surprised when he came out with the beginnings of a delusion.

'Now I don't want you to worry,' he said, 'but there is something I must say . . .'

'Are you sick? Bernie?'

. . . .

190

'No!' he snapped. 'I'm telling you something has happened in this house. They didn't go away according to plan. Upstairs . . .'

He told her what he had found upstairs. Clare tried to hide her unbelief.

'I'm sure it's nothing,' she said. 'A little odd with the shoes, maybe. But a gun?'

'The place where a gun *was kept*!' he insisted. 'In the drawer.'

'Well okay, maybe there was a gun and Mike took it along – didn't want to leave it in the empty house.'

'Without its cloth?' cried Bernard. 'Clare, what was the arrangement? Do you have a number to call?'

'Mike is supposed to phone today,' she said warily. 'He didn't know where they might be.'

The young couple were driving to Salzburg for a music festival. Clare, who believed she had a sixth sense where members of the family were concerned, sat in the kitchen after they had finished their coffee and tried to locate Mike and Erika. Bernie had gone out through the back door. She clenched her hands and squeezed her eyes shut, imagining Mike's new burgundy Passat whizzing over the long straight-aways and sweeping curves of the autobahn.

She relaxed, fell into a dreamy state, found herself wandering through to the living-room and sinking into the puffy grey leather sofa. Of course they were all right . . . *Mike, you're all right aren't you?* Through the window she could see the front garden, the young tree shedding its blossoms. Bernard hurried past on the street, hatless of course, heading purposefully, madly, along the row of houses in the direction of the ringroad.

As she sprang up with a cry of exasperation Clare saw the envelope lying on top of the television. It was a card with a picture of a comical dog, a kind of Snoopy clone, flinging open a pink house door: the caption said *Herzlichen Glück-wunsch!* Inside the dog was drinking champagne; the written message read: *Best wishes from Mike & Erika.*

....

There now. Of course nothing was wrong and her family sense *was* working, she had been led in here to find the card. Oh surely, surely this would convince Bernie. Please dear God let him not give trouble. Let him understand, let him not fuss. The impossibility of getting Bernard to do any of these things under certain circumstances was something she found harder and harder to face. She took the card with her and went out on to the front doorstep. Bernard was talking to the woman from next door, number 22, over her garden gate. Clare retreated at once, before they spotted her.

Bernard had gone out into the green corner behind the house in search of whatever had fallen from the open window upstairs – disappointing, only a hand towel. Then he pressed on round the front and checked Mike's black trash can, which was empty, then the blue one, which was half full of newspapers and cardboard. The woman next door came out to put cardboard in her blue bin and he pounced.

He wished that he had been wearing his hat so that he could doff it to her . . . touch of gallantry. The woman was dressed from head to foot in black. Bernard judged that she was about sixty years old, the same age as his pretty Clare. He got her name from the letterbox.

'*Frau König?*'

He had an American accent by now but German had been the speech of his family for two centuries of the diaspora. Frau König was polite; they shook hands, as temporary neighbours. Frau König was cool but interested; something was bothering her, beyond her natural reserve and her widowed state. Herr König had passed on five months ago aged sixty-five, a year older than Bernie himself.

He went on to explain that Michael Rose, the young Herr Rose, was his stepson, his wife's son. He passed a remark about young people nowadays, shaking his head.

'Did they get away all right?' he asked. 'On their trip?'

Frau König's blue eyes glinted behind her glasses.

'I haven't seen the car lately,' she said. 'Perhaps the girl took it to the workshop.'

'Where did Michael park, by the way?'

'When he had the car?' said Frau König. 'He rented a garage from the people in number 18.'

'Perhaps I might enquire.'

Frau König's round pale face twisted into something like a smile.

'We have all sorts of funny people in this row of houses,' she said.

Bernard took his leave, wondered whether he should go back indoors and process this new material, but was driven onwards. He must go on, look at the rest of the houses, see if he could raise anyone at number 18. There were a number of notices and brass plates indicating who the people were or what they did. Sometimes they did it on the premises like the lady who offered foot-care approved by health insurance or the couple with a double name who made and repaired dolls. There was a lawyer who gave the address of his chambers down in Brcitbach. Number 18, the house which had prompted Frau König's remark, was the home of a Turkish family who were all out, probably at work.

The street numbering was a little strange; the last of the semi-detached houses was number 8, then there were two older places, number 6 and number 4, followed by an apartment house numbered on the Southern Ringroad. He walked back to number 8, which had a provocative notice in the garden. It stood on its own sign post to the right of the garden path and was professionally painted in blue on white: *Anton Selig, Dipl. Psychologe, Lebenshilfe, Vermißte, Fundbüro*. This was repeated in English: Counselling, Missing Persons, Lost Property.

Now *this* guy did qualify as a little funny, thought Bernie. He looked back down Willy-Brandt-Strasse and saw Clare standing outside the gate at number 24. He was suddenly angry at her fussing, damn near rushed in to consult that freaky psychologist, but he put it off and went back.

'They left us a card,' said Clare. 'There is absolutely nothing wrong. Why on earth are you carrying that towel?'

....

'Because I'm a crazy freak!' he snapped. 'Come in the house!'

Every time he went in that front door he was convinced all over again that something was wrong. Clare sat him down in the living-room and went to fetch the lunch; Bernie was uncomfortable among all the heavy mail-order furniture. Why would young people, not even married yet, want this kind of leather couch, this massive mahogany combo with two different kinds of shelves, three kinds of cupboard?

He was unconvinced by the card. Congratulations? Best wishes? This wasn't anything for Mom and Dad, it was meant to go with a present Mike and Erika had given to one of their pals. Perhaps the present was unwrapped here in the house and the card was forgotten. He chewed over the implications of his little talk with Frau König, wondering how much he should tell Clare. She had rustled up some goulash soup and the fresh rolls from the airport shop.

'When did you call and speak to Erika?' he asked. 'How many days ago? How long since you spoke to Mike?'

'What is it?' countered Clare. 'What did that woman next door say?'

'Look, I asked you how many days . . .'

'You're starting again!' said Clare. 'Bernie *please!*'

She ate her soup, then she said carefully, 'I spoke to Erika sixteen days ago. Two days after that I had the letter from Mike with all the arrangements.'

'Posted *before* the conversation?'

'I guess so.'

'How was she?'

'Far away,' said Clare, sadly. 'You know what she's like, Bernie. Shy, stand-offish, very sweet really. Good English but I'm never sure that she gets what I say.'

'What did she say about Mike?'

'That he was out at a management seminar – this was about eight o'clock in the evening, here in Breitbach.'

'Nothing there,' sighed Bernie. 'Mind you, sixteen days is a long time. Maybe we should have called again.'

. . . .

'You mean *I* should have called again!' snapped Clare. 'You and Mike both complain about the cost whenever I call and whoever is paying for the call. Anyway I *did* call three days ago . . . I tried to catch them in the early morning, it was six o'clock. No one was home. I thought they left early for their trip, or maybe they were jogging or something.'

Bernard sighed.

'Honey, that woman, Frau König, made out there was something with the car. That Mike had been without the car for a while. That Erika might have put the car in a workshop. Maybe, I thought maybe she drove away and – and left him.'

'No! It's not true! Mike would have *called*,' insisted Clare. 'Oh God, how do I know what that Frau König said? You could be making something out of nothing! You don't believe that card, you took away my belief in that card.'

'I know what the card *says*!' Bernie boiled over. 'You're clutching at straws. The card wasn't for us. Something could have come up in the last two weeks.'

He felt his face flush, his heart pound; they were both worried and he took his medication twenty minutes early. They were too upset to go walking although it didn't get dark until nearly ten o'clock. They sat before the open window and watched the strolling couples, many of them in their own age group, passing by on the road. Then they drew the curtains, brought the phone into the living-room, and watched television, even picked up NBC news on the Superchannel.

The phone rang twice over the weekend. On Saturday morning it was a wrong number, a man who sounded outraged because he wasn't connected with a flower shop. On Sunday afternoon it rang just as they were setting out for their walk. Clare raced back, unlocked the door, but missed the call. She shed tears of frustration. They went back indoors in case the caller, in case Mike or Erika tried again.

At six o'clock Bernard pottered out again and tried the Ozcan family at number 18. Herr Ozcan took the chain off the door and spoke to him on the doorstep. Yes, sure, Herr

. . . .

Rose, the American, had rented his brother's garage round the corner in Konrad-Adenauer-Strasse until a couple of months ago. His brother had sold the house and the garage was no longer available. They exchanged some civil remarks; Bernard was moved to explain that he was Jewish, not German. They shook hands and parted, smiling.

Clare and Bernard had both begun to check out number 24 more carefully. When Clare went up to the attic the emptiness nearly set her off again, crying. The kids had nothing to store away, no old toys, no old furniture, they hadn't started their lives. There was a stack of out-dated software, an old monitor, a trunk of winter clothes, a carton of books. She thought of all the attics she could remember, each one fuller, more rich with memories than the last. She went down and announced that she had been right up so that Bernard wouldn't try the attic stairs.

Bernard went down to the cellar after tea on Sunday night and stayed so long that Clare became worried. It was a spacious four-roomed cellar; the central heating hadn't been switched over for the warmer weather although it was already May. The garden tools were not well kept, look at that shovel now, caked with red earth.

Mike didn't have anything like a proper workshop, fine cellar like this was wasted on him. In the laundry there was a full basket of dirty clothes, a bunch of dish towels on the line. When Clare came to fetch him she straightaway put on a load of laundry; she made a small sound when she emptied out the big cane basket.

'What is it?' asked Bernie in alarm.

'Nothing,' she said. 'It's only . . . these are all Mike's things. Nothing at all from Erika.'

They had already checked out the wardrobes upstairs in the bedroom and the spare room: both the closets had been full of clothes, hanging or neatly folded, sometimes freshly dry-cleaned, swathed in plastic. Clare had moved armfuls of clothes to the spare room bed so that she and Bernie would have a little closet space themselves. While she was there

. . . .

she noticed Mike's desk, with his computer and printer. She sat down at once and went in; no messages, nothing like a diary, it was all taxes, bills, business correspondence, a lot of it in German. Clare could speak German a little and read it a little better. She scored a point – name of a hotel in Salzburg.

When they went back upstairs from the cellar she decided to settle things, to try for some peace on their holiday. She told Bernie about the Hotel Kaiserhof and he put through a call. There was a little cross-talk number with a certain Herr Rosen but he got back to the switchboard. No, a young American called Michael Rose was not a guest.

'Well,' said Clare. 'It was just a letter of enquiry. So they went to another hotel.'

Bernard was feeling strangely peaceful, as if they were in the eye of a hurricane. Something *had* happened, it was just a matter of time before they found out for themselves or before the world turned up on their doorstep. Clare cooked filet steaks from the freezer, with boiled potatoes and broccoli and they shared a bottle of Sekt, German champagne. Before they went to sleep Bernie said with a chuckle:

'I'll call that New Age guy, the god-damned psychologist. Want to bet he knows everything that goes on in the street?'

Clare slept heavily and towards morning she dreamed that she was walking along the beach at Cape Cod with little Mike. They saw Bernard running towards them waving his arms; as he came nearer he began to utter a strange cry which went on and on and dwindled to the sound of the chimes at the front door. She sprang up and went down, pulling on her robe. The postwoman had an envelope from a stamp firm for Mike, it was a COD for fifty marks. By the time Clare had run upstairs for her purse Bernie was on deck in his track suit; he took the purse, went down to the door and chatted to the postwoman for a good five minutes. When he came into the kitchen and announced that he had refused the COD Clare was put out.

....

'It's too darn much,' said Bernie. 'Might be some pro forma thing for all we know.'

She began to defrost a loaf of toast bread.

'Mike stopped the post ten days ago,' he said.

'Then why did she come today with the stamps?'

'She brought it along on spec and saw that a window was open upstairs.'

It was nine o'clock when they finished breakfast; Bernie waited until Clare went up to take her shower then he rang Anton Selig, the finder at number 8. A cultivated female voice told him discreetly that he could drop by at nine forty-five. He had wondered about jogging along in a track suit but now he decided to dress the part: an American on holiday. He chose a cream leisure shirt and carried his seersucker jacket. He gave Clare a kiss and said that he might buy some bread rolls.

He felt his compulsive anxiety, the unrest in his head building as he walked along the street. The sameness of the gardens bothered him; he searched for differences. The grass at the Selig place was close-cropped with a round bed of pansies. A woman with a little boy in tow had just been shown out of the house. Bernard watched them critically, thinking of his own daughter, Esther, and his grandson, Josh, who was going on ten, about five years older than this kid. He felt guilt because he didn't get along with them, with his own flesh and blood. Mike was a whole lot kinder to him, more of a pal.

The woman wore smart beige bermudas, sheer panty-hose and pumps, with a long red blazer. The kid wore jeans and a blue T-shirt with a pink brontosaurus and the caption DINO LOVE. They both had a look of care and misery that belonged on two starving refugees. Selig didn't leave 'em laughing, thought Bernie. He was irritated by their affluence, the nice shiny red coupe that the woman drove, by the way the kid baulked, dragged, hindered, complained.

'*Ich will kein' Uhr!*' said the boy with increasing violence.

He jumped up and down beside the car and shouted, inexplicably.

....

'Ich will kein' Uhr!'

What was he on about? *I don't want a clock? A watch?* As he hurried up the path Bernie felt a fierce double reaction: poor little devil/make that damned spoiled brat shut up.

The door was flung open before he could ring by a man taller than himself.

'Mister Meyer?'

They shook hands. Selig was good-looking with strongly marked features and a heavy, cultivated German tan. He was in his fifties, a little vague, touch of the absent-minded professor. His charisma was very strong. He was decked out in jeans and a white T-shirt; his brown arms were firmly muscled.

'Come in, come in,' he said, keeping on with his English, which was pretty good. 'My wife's putting on fresh coffee. Or would you prefer tea?'

'Coffee is fine.'

Frau Selig came bustling in from the kitchen; she matched her voice, faintly aristocratic in the continental manner; she wore a billowing cotton dress and strap sandals. She shook hands with Bernie and he noticed that she was wearing contact lenses which made her green eyes large and lustrous.

'We have friends in Florida,' she said, 'in Melbourne, Florida.'

'We've driven through,' said Bernard. 'My daughter lives in Fort Lauderdale with her family.'

'My husband has a following there,' she said proudly. 'He visits every year.'

'Bring down the coffee, Ursula,' said Selig. 'We'll go down to the workrooms, Mr Meyer.'

Bernie followed him down the same narrow plastered staircase that he had experienced in Mike's house but after that there was no likeness. The basement had been thoroughly 'done up', with expensive wallpaper, an impressive computer spread, Scandinavian furniture, modern lithographs on the walls.

....

Selig went to work efficiently, taking down Bernard's particulars.

'I guess you're in retirement now, sir,' he said, 'but what business were you in?'

'A family business,' said Bernie. 'We have three clothing outlets, two in Jersey, one in Connecticut – wholesale and retail.'

'So what is the nature of the problem?'

He tried to explain. Fairly. Rationally. From the beginning. Selig did not sit behind his desk but sprawled comfortably in a large armchair of pale wood with dark turquoise cushions. Bernie sat on a matching couch. Selig, who had been making casual notes on a lap-top, became excited.

'Yes!' he exclaimed. 'Yes! I know him. The young American who lived at the end of the row. Missing? What has happened? Tell me!'

Bernie made an honest effort to tell him everything. He felt himself staring into Selig's eyes, trying to set forth all his findings, to explain his fears. He saw that Selig was processing all that he said and that he did not *doubt*. There was no trace of the kind of doubt that he had been subjected to by his wife. Selig was eager to grasp the nettle, to speculate about the extreme, about death and destruction. When Bernie finally came out with something the psychologist's pale eyes flashed.

'I did think,' admitted Bernie, 'of a young guy I knew at college who shot himself. Everything became too much – he lost his girl, had bad grades, his father was a god-damned slave driver.'

'You thought of suicide,' said Selig, making a note.

Bernie found that he was teetering on the edge of an abyss: Selig wanted to believe that something had happened and he wanted Bernard to put a name to it.

'I never mentioned it to my wife,' he said. 'It certainly doesn't fit with anything I know of Michael.'

'Financial problems?' asked Selig.

'No, no, I really doubt that.'

....

Frau Selig called out as she came down the stairs with the tall thermo jug of coffee; she drifted about discreetly fixing a tray in the kitchen alcove of the treatment room. Selig said to her in German: *'Uschi dear, wasn't there something about the little Adler at the end of the street?'*

'Living with the young American?' asked Ursula Selig. She flicked a glance at Bernie, as if she understood the connection. *'I believe she went away. Perhaps it was just on holiday.'*

'You knew Erika?' said Bernard hoarsely.

He saw that they were surprised when he slipped into German. It had not occurred to him to deceive but now he remembered making his appointment in English.

'Michael is my stepson,' he explained to Frau Selig. 'We wondered if there might have been a quarrel.'

He saw the gleam in Herr Selig's eye again: this time he would say, in German, 'You thought of – murder?'

'We wondered if Erika might have taken the car, left him,' he added hastily.

Frau Selig glanced at her husband; Bernard realized that he had not behaved as a patient or consulter should, he had drawn the counsellor's wife into the consultation.

'Fetch yourself a cup, Uschi,' said Selig tolerantly.

'I *am* acquainted with Frau Adler,' she said at length. 'Such a sweet girl, what one would really call "a young girl from a good family". The family is from Hamburg, of course; they have a big house in the Blankenese . . .'

'Yes,' nodded Bernard.

He was being spared nothing. Of course he knew where Erika came from. That high-toned suburb of Hamburg was a place he had never revisited and did not care to think about.

'She drove away in the car, the Passat,' Frau Selig came out with it. 'About ten days ago. I personally wouldn't have thought anything of it, but poor Frau König, the neighbour, said it was unplanned. Middle of the day while the young man was away at work . . . he took the bus.'

. . . .

'But there was no quarrel?' put in Selig.

'It could have been a family emergency,' said Bernard. 'She might have had a call from Hamburg.'

Frau Selig coughed.

'Herr Rose came and asked in the evening,' she said. 'Asked Frau König if she had seen his wife. He only asked once.'

There was a silence. Frau Selig gathered the coffee things on to the tray.

'He asked the postwoman to hold his delivery at about this time,' said Bernard.

'A search begins,' said Selig gently, 'with certain simple and rational actions. The hospitals, the police . . .'

Ursula Selig reached out and touched her husband's hand.

'Anton, dear,' she said, 'let me show Herr Meyer the archive. It shows how much can be achieved!'

The psychologist gave an indulgent smile. Frau Selig flung open a door and Bernard followed her into a spacious display room. The walls were covered with photographs and maps, some of them very elaborate, with flashing lights which Frau Selig activated. Bernard was struck first of all by the figure of a small child, a little girl about five years old, which stood just inside the door. It was a cardboard cutout, made from a life-size colour photograph and mounted on a wooden stand. There were three taller examples of these figures gathered eerily in a corner: a teenaged girl, a young man, a middle-aged woman. He remembered an expression '*Papp-Kamerad*', cardboard comrade, used for the photo-replicas of policemen, sometimes used as keep-out signs or in traffic control. Further down the room was a store dummy: a small boy dressed in jeans and a sweater. He began to notice articles of clothing, often children's clothing, pinned up in the displays.

He concentrated on the case of the little girl, which Frau Selig was explaining: it had happened ten years ago, right here in the neighbourhood. It had been an intensive search.

. . . .

Little Anna had disappeared in summer on the way to school, through the fields beyond the cemetery. For the next two summers, during daylight hours, one of her life-sized replicas, in full colour, had been placed at the spot where she was last seen.

'The figures were often defaced,' said Selig, who had joined them.

He made Bernard jump.

'The police caught a fellow defacing a figure of Anna,' he went on.

'And he knew something?' said Bernard eagerly. 'He took the child?'

'No,' said Selig, 'but they gave him a good going-over.'

He indicated the adjoining map.

'It was an indication of just how much one could discover about a certain place on a certain day,' he continued. 'Hundreds of automobile numbers – of locals and of people passing through.'

'But the child was never found?'

Selig shook his head.

'Under ten there is usually a sad result anyway,' he said. 'We search for a certainty, to prevent false hope. Of course the child is usually alive when it has been kidnapped by a parent.'

'It is all so terrible!' said Bernard feebly. 'Why do you . . . What makes you . . .'

'I must. I have the keenest interest in such things.'

Bernard gazed into Selig's striking blue eyes and saw a cold and obsessive passion that would not let the man rest. Frau Selig went on, with a touch of reproach for Bernard's question, about the amount of good that was done, by the searches, by the counselling. There were a number of successful findings on the walls, marked with a gold star, but Selig was modest about them.

'It can all be codified,' he said, 'the likelihood of a finding . . . age of subject, state of physical and mental health. A healthy teenager is more likely to turn up, safe and sound,

. . . .

than an old woman in poor health. Of course we have to take care in assessing the searchers, even if they are close relatives . . .'

'You mean,' said Bernard, controlling his distress, 'the parents who may have caused the death of a child . . .'

'I must admit to a good nose for *those* cases,' smiled Selig. 'But I was thinking of the teenagers or wives who get attacked again after they are found. There's a time lapse, usually, a tearful reunion and then a burst of rage some days later, a reaction to the anguish caused by the runaway. Of course some searchers cannot control themselves. There have been cases where the parents of returned teenagers started beating them in front of the television cameras.'

Frau Selig was particularly proud of a line of milk cartons from Florida with photographs of missing children from Selig's own files.

'In a mild climate,' explained Selig, 'little children who run away can sometimes survive out of doors. On the other hand these are often the ones who should not be returned to the home situation.'

There was a display stand with a number of cases from North Africa. Young Germans were apt to set off into the desert ill-equipped, without enough water, petrol or maps. They lost their way and died of thirst. On rare occasions they were kidnapped, robbed or murdered.

'Affluence makes it harder to leave home,' said Selig. 'The lure of freedom battles with fine clothes, electronic equipment, autos, a live-in girlfriend, a separate flat in the parents' house. I think these exotic disappearances are sometimes a bid for freedom.'

'Now we have a flood of enquiries from the former DDR,' said Frau Selig.

'Plenty of historical disappearances from that area too,' said Selig, 'but we don't touch them. So many of these people are not to be trusted.'

Bernard found himself thinking, 'And they have no money.' He changed the subject.

. . . .

'What do you think about these psychics?' he demanded. 'The ones who try to find . . .'

Selig smiled generously; he reached out and laid one of his large well-kept hands upon the face of a smiling young girl, missing for five years from her home in the nearby city of Frankfurt-am-Main.

'Some of them are gifted,' he said, 'but never very practical.'

'Anton is highly sensitive,' said Frau Selig, 'but he does not depend on psychic methods.'

They had come right round the room, past the polaroids of lost and found pets – including parrots, monkeys, and a cheetah – jewellery, cars, luggage, and an article from a glossy news magazine on Herr Selig, using a *nom-de-guerre*. Now they stood before a wall of photographs with names and dates, the sort of posters that Bernard remembered meeting in post offices and elsewhere during his previous visits to the old country. These persons were no longer lost and they were not terrorists. They were young adults who had become separated from their families as children in the aftermath of the Second World War. The Red Cross, for instance, never slept, and brought families together after twenty, thirty years.

'It is really too long ago to go on looking,' said Anton Selig.

Bernard, who had never rated his own psychic powers very highly, had a flash of insight. His gaze was drawn to a line of three photographs in the centre of the display. He bent forward and read a faded handbill with the photograph of a small blond boy. *'Found unaccompanied during the flight from Königsberg 1945, a small German boy, at that time about two years old, blond, blue eyes. Recalls the names "Toni", "Minna". Now in care of the Seamen's Mission and Orphanage "Stella Maris", Bremen, British Zone.'*

In the next photograph the teenage boy, still unclaimed, had been given a name; in the third photograph of a young man in his twenties he was recognizable as Anton Selig.

. . . .

'Saint Anthony,' said Frau Selig, 'has a special affinity for lost things.'

'As I was saying,' said Selig more mildly than ever, 'it is really too long to go on looking for a lost family.'

Bernard was gripped with conflicting thoughts so powerful, so inadmissible that he could scarcely control himself. It was a blast of the ambivalence which had troubled him with the unfortunate child/spoiled brat at the front gate.

'As you say,' he said. 'It all happened a long time ago. Whole families were lost, were most deliberately put to death. The witnesses are dying out. Scores of the old murderers live out their lives in peace.'

He strode blindly out of the archive into the treatment room with the Seligs after him. As he fumbled in his wallet Frau Selig said: 'I don't know why you bring this up, Herr Meyer. Is it because of the new trouble we've had with foreigners, with the hatred of foreigners?'

'*You said it the first time!*' said Bernard in English. '*Always a bit of trouble with foreigners!*'

Selig was quietly presenting a bill and signing a receipt at his desk. Now he made a sound of distress; he burst out: 'Mr Meyer, you are surely not linking your stepson's disappearance with . . .'

Bernard gave the man top marks for gruesome thoughts but he said firmly: 'With neo-nazis? Anti-semitism? No of course not. I'm not sure we can even say that Mike *has* disappeared. He could be calling his mother on the phone right now. This . . . this was all some kind of obsession of mine. You understand?'

Selig bowed his head in assent. Of course he understood.

'Related to circulatory problems,' finished Bernard, 'and to childhood experiences . . .'

He did not have the nerve, the bad taste to make a typical gesture, showing them his forearm with that small dead-white scar. The tattoo that he had received when he was nine years old had been removed when he was fourteen, far away in America.

....

He ran upstairs and went out into the sunshine. The beauty of the month of May gathered him in; he stood and took deep breaths at the garden gate. He looked up and down Willy-Brandt-Strasse and said a prayer for everyone he loved. He walked slowly back to number 24 and when he let himself into the hall he found the atmosphere completely changed. He heard Clare speaking fondly, joyously on the telephone.

'Here comes Bernie!' she cried.

He raced into the room and caught his wife round the waist as he seized the receiver. Their faces were close together as he spoke to Mike.

'. . . all going crazy up there, Dad? Yeah, sure I'm in Salzburg. It is Monday and I was supposed to call Friday – why is Mom so upset for heaven's sake?'

Bernard heard his own happy voice trying to explain: he guessed that *he* was to blame, old Bernie was turning into a real worry-wart these days. And what was that with Erika driving away in the car?

'It's a bummer,' said Mike. 'Her mother had a stroke. Erika drove up to Hamburg . . . I really couldn't go with her, so close to the vacation. I finished up and then drove to Salzburg to keep our booking. Yes of course, a rented car.'

So Erika's mother was okay? Bernard hugged his wife and Clare kissed his cheek. She felt the tension slowly go out of them both. Bernie really seemed better; something had happened, the man who looked for missing persons had found the way to help him. Yes, sure, Frau Adler had made a great recovery, Mike assured his stepfather. Erika was driving all the way down to Austria, bringing her young brother and his girl for company.

'Michael,' said Bernard seriously. 'Do you own a hand gun?'

This was a sensible question but he felt foolish about the way he had over-reacted.

'Yes, sure, I have it with me, sir,' said Mike. 'I wouldn't be without it, in this day and age. The way things are. In this part of the world.'

. . . .

Biographical Notes

THE EDITORS

Stephen Hayward was born in England in 1954. Since the early Thatcher years he has been obsessed by the extraordinary variety of recipes for cooking offal, *A Dance to the Music of Time* and the papacy's capacity for inhumanity and corruption. He lives in London, where he works as a publisher, and is the co-editor, with Sarah LeFanu, of *Colours of a New Day: Writing for South Africa* and *God: An Anthology of Fiction*.

Sarah LeFanu lives near Bristol. She is obsessed by a determination to read *A La Recherche du Temps Perdu* and puts down her failure so far, depending on her mood, to too much work, too many children, too much to drink and spending too many hours reading long articles in the *London Review of Books*, especially the ones about *A La Recherche du Temps Perdu*, and worrying about whether 'For a long time' is more appropriate than 'Time was'. Meanwhile she reads a great many short stories.

THE CONTRIBUTORS

Michael Carson was born in Wallasey, Merseyside in 1946. He taught English as a Foreign Language for fifteen years in Sumatra, Borneo, Oman, Iran, Saudi Arabia, Nigeria and Texas. Returning to Britain in 1986, he started writing stories for the BBC Radio Four short story slot – he has had forty-five stories broadcast – and through this managed to attract the attention of a publisher. He has published seven novels and a collection of short stories. He is single, lives with friends in Wales and is obsessed with the history of the Congo 1880—1910.

Mary Flanagan was born in New England. Her short story collection, *Bad Girls*, was published in 1984, and she is the author of two novels, *Trust* and *Rose Reason*. Her latest story collection, *The Blue Woman*, appeared in 1994.

Kirsty Gunn would love to be able to write short stories in proper notebooks and yellow lined pads, but she is obsessed by the need to recycle paper by writing new stories on the backs of old ones. She has lost many drafts this way and her desk is now piled high with stacks of paper, yet the obsession continues. Recently she has also become obsessed with spirulina, an alga. Her first novel, *Rain*, was published in 1994.

Allan Gurganus is the author of *Oldest Living Confederate Widow Tells All* and *White People*. His forthcoming book is *Recent American Saints*. His own obsessions include food, leather easy chairs accompanied by very good reading lamps, the collecting of American folk art, the avoidance of television (rays very harmful), and a continual re-reading of Henry James. But his greatest obsession and favourite subject is: Obsession itself. How it organizes one's vices, one's time!

James Hamilton-Paterson lives in Italy and the Far East. He has written extensively about the sea, in *Seven-Tenths*, in *Playing with Water*, which describes his life on an uninhabited island in the Philippines, and also in his novel *Gerontius*, winner of the Whitbread First Novel Award in 1989. His other novels include *Griefwork*, which is set in a palm house in the botanical gardens of a northern European city, and *Ghosts of Manila*.

Adam Lively was born in 1961. He has published four novels, *Blue Fruit*, *The Burnt House*, *The Snail* and *Sing the Body*

....

Electric, and in 1993 was named one of the Twenty Best of Young British Novelists by *Granta*. With his father, Jack Lively, he has co-edited an anthology on *Democracy in Britain*, and he is currently working on a study of race and the imagination. He lives in London and has two children and several obsessions, including jazz and Indian cooking.

Ursule Molinaro is the author of 11 novels, including *Fat Skeletons*, *The New Moon with the Old Moon in Her Arms*, *Positions with White Roses & The Autobiography of Cassandra, Princess and Prophetess of Troy* & 4 collections of short stories. Her most recent novel, *Power Dreamers*, retells the story of Oedipus   mainly in the voice of Jocasta obsessively see-sawing between knowing/suspecting/& again doubting that she is marrying her son. A painter & translator   she lives in New York City with OWLBEAR a black Manx obsessed with a dust-coated catnip mouse.

Joyce Carol Oates is the author of twenty-three novels, the most recent being *Foxfire: Confessions of a Girl Gang* and *Black Water*, seventeen collections of short stories, not to mention poetry collections, plays and essays. She is a three-time winner of the Continuing Achievement Award in the O Henry Award Prize Stories series. She has been obsessed, since childhood, with the mystery of human personality; the uniqueness within species-hood, and what possible interpretation to make of it.

Michèle Roberts has for long been obsessed by mothers and daughters. Her sixth novel *Daughters of the House* was shortlisted for the 1992 Booker Prize and won the 1993 WH Smith Literature Award. Her collection of stories, *During Mother's Absence*, was published in 1993. Other short stories have appeared in *Tales I Tell My Mother* and *More Tales I Tell My Mother*. Her poetry includes *The Mirror of the Mother* and *Psyche and the Hurricane*. Her latest novel is *Flesh and Blood* (1994).

....

Jane Rogers' novels are *Separate Tracks*, *Her Living Image* (winner of a Somerset Maugham Award), *The Ice is Singing* and *Mr Wroe's Virgins*, which she adapted as a four-part drama for the BBC. Her TV play *Dawn and the Candidate* won a Samuel Beckett Award. Her fifth novel, *Promised Lands*, will be published in 1995. She has a number of obsessions, but cooking and cleaning the house are not among them. She lives in squalor in Lancashire with her husband and two children.

Elisa Segrave's articles and short stories have appeared in other Serpent's Tail anthologies, the *London Review of Books*, the *London Magazine*, the *Independent* and the *Observer*. She is currently obsessed with her own writing. Her book, *Diary of a Breast*, was published in 1995.

Adam Thorpe was born in Paris in 1956, and brought up in India, Cameroon and England. He has published two collections of poetry: *Mornings in the Baltic* (shortlisted for the 1988 Whitbread Prize for Poetry) and *Meeting Montaigne*. His first novel, *Ulverton*, was a best-seller and won the Winifred Holtby Prize for best regional novel. He lives in France with his wife and three children.

Jeff Torrington was born in the Gorbals district of Glasgow around the time, as he puts it, Hitler and his henchmen were drawing on their jackboots. His diverse occupations have included: locomotive fireman, fruitmarket porter, postman, telegraphist and car worker. Married, with three grown-up children, he has published short stories and articles. His first novel, *Swing hammer swing!*, won the 1992 Whitbread Book of the Year award. He claims to be obsessionless although he owns up to 'compulsive re-writing'. His wife confirms this: 'He is the only person I know who can get writer's cramp when asked to leave a simple note for the milkman!'

Lisa Tuttle was born in Houston, Texas. After selling her first novel she quit her job to write full time, and moved to England to make getting a new job practically impossible.

....

For ten years she had all the time in the world to write and produced *An Encyclopedia of Feminism*, three volumes of collected short stories, three more novels and various other odds and ends. Then she married, moved to Scotland and had a child. Since then she has been able to write when her daughter is asleep and she is not, which is not very often. So now she thinks obsessively about writing, which has become her grand obsession.

Ivan Vladislavić was born in Pretoria in 1957. He is the author of *Missing Persons*, a collection of short stories which won the 1991 Olive Schreiner Prize and *The Folly*, a novel, which won the 1993 CNA Prize, South Africa's major literary award. He lives in Johannesburg where he has the largest privately owned authentic pencil stub collection in Southern Africa, almost one thousand, all of which started out life as full-length HBs and which he single-handedly wrote into submission. The collection is housed in a pickle-jar, along with dozens of blunt sharpeners and erasers no bigger than peas.

Cherry Wilder is a New Zealander who has lived in Australia and is currently resident in Germany; she is a keen observer of obsessive behaviour. Her novels include *Second Nature*, *Cruel Designs* and the fantasy trilogy, *The Rulers of Hylor*. Her stories have appeared in *PRISM International*, *Meanjin*, *Interzone*, *OMNI* and *Isaac Asimov's Science Fiction Magazine*. Looking back on years of Biographical Notes she finds that she has been falsely accused of being an Australian, a Taoist and a writer of children's books.

....